POWDERHOLE

POWDERHOLE

Blaine C. Readler

POWDERHOLE

This is a work of fiction. Names, characters, places and incidents are either the product of the author's wild imagination or are used fictitiously. Any resemblance to actual events, locales, organizations, or persons, living, dead, or one foot in the grave, although inevitable and in a weird way complimentary to the author, since it shows he is not so insulated from reality that the products of his imagination are totally alien to the average mind, is nevertheless entirely coincidental and beyond the intent of either the author or the publisher.

Visit us at: http://www.readler.com

E-mail: blaine@readler.com

ISBN: 978-0-9834973-7-0

Printed in the United States of America

To Aunt Ada, for showing me that family extended far beyond the walls of our house, where vigilance is required against the tripwires of prejudice.

ACKNOWLEDGEMENTS

This story was a herd of overfed words roaming an unmanaged literary countryside until my editor, Jennifer Silva Redmond, jumped on her horse and coaxed the feral prose into a rational corral (and, if she'd edited this acknowledgement, it would have read "Thanks to my editor").

www.jennyredbug.com

A hearty thanks to Jackson Finley for the cover concept and design:

www.jwfinley.com

"The greatest danger to our democracy could be the secrets the government keeps under the excuse of national security. We don't know, and that's the problem -- we don't know."

-- Steve Byars, 1984, two years before the Iran Contra Scandal broke and ten years before the revelation that the US government secretly exposed US citizens to lethal forms of radiation after WWII to see what would happen.

Chapter 1

A fat drop of late summer rain smacked Bruce squarely in his ear, and he shook his head as the water tickled its way down, searching out his ear canal. Thousands of little wet bombshells found targets among the crowd, hastening them to their cars.

Bruce was the only mourner not dressed in his Sunday best. He'd explained a dozen times in the last half hour that he'd arrived directly from the airport. It was his own father's funeral, and though nobody had questioned his jeans and polo shirt, these were people he'd grown up with, and he knew that they were just too polite to voice their critical assessment. In a small coal town with German and Polish origins, congeniality ruled, but judgment whispered through the back chambers of the court.

The isolated splats thickened, threatening a sudden deluge as thunder rumbled among the foothills of the Pocono Mountains. The people of Powderhole scurried into their cars, leaving Bruce to rue the fact that he hadn't taken the time to rent a car, opting for an expedient, if expensive, fifteen-mile taxi ride from Wilkes-Barre.

"It's called rain!"

It was Larry waving from his '98 Toyota Tercel. "It rains in San Jose," Bruce said as he tossed his travel bag into the back seat and slid in the front just as a gust delivered the first real blast of the storm. "We know it ahead of time, though."

Seeing his old friend was the final step in the journey from California for Bruce. Larry had been his friend since first grade, and they'd managed to stay connected even as one of them took a two-year degree at Luzerne County Community College, then a Bachelor's from Wilkes University and moved to the west coast, while the other was content to rent a studio apartment above Hellman's barber shop, work part time at Wayne's Garage and Tire Depot, work another part of the time for the Powderhole Municipal road crew, and smoke a lot of pot. Larry worked only enough to pay his rent, buy ganja, and purchase food, in that order.

His hair had started to recede when he was a junior in high school, and now, twelve years later, while the rest of the balding world chose to fashionably shave their depleting domes, Larry let what was left grow unhindered on the theory that the substantial mane would balance his shiny pate. That his hair was unusually curly for his Pennsylvania Dutch heritage, resulting in a head that was uncannily, painfully, similar to that more celebrated Larry from The Three Stooges, never occurred to him.

"Sorry I didn't pick you up at the airport," Larry said as they waited in the downpour for their turn to pull out of the cemetery. "I didn't get your message until, like, just an hour ago."

"I left it yesterday," Bruce said, though he wasn't surprised or angry. Larry was completely reliable when he understood what he needed to do. It was the understanding that was often the problem.

"I'm not one of those slaves to their phones, you know."

"Meaning that you got really stoned last night, and didn't think to check."

"Since slaves don't smoke pot, then I agree."

This was what Bruce considered Larry-logic. It made knowing whether his friend was currently stoned difficult.

"Why did you wait until the last minute, anyway?" Larry countered. "Your dad died, like, four days ago. Heck, if you'd waited just an extra hour, you could have missed the whole grave part, and made it just in time for the condolence lunch in the church basement." Larry grinned, but then frowned. "Sorry. That wasn't very sensitive."

Bruce shook his head. "Nah. It's okay. He was overdue. He's been running on borrowed time ever since . . ."

"Your mom died?"

"I guess."

"Yeah, your dad became a real soak the last coupla years," Larry agreed as he finally pulled onto the road, leaning forward to peer through the momentary gaps between wiper-swipes.

Bruce smiled and shook his head. Larry's simple honesty could be endearing if you were up for the knocks. It was the big reason they had remained friends.

It was true, too—his dad had checked out three years before when Bruce's mom had died. After that it was as though the man was making up for a lifetime of deprivation. The alcohol had slowly morphed his dad into something despicable in Bruce's eyes. This was the man who had taught him how to fly-cast, who had encouraged and praised him when he'd joined the Little League team, and then hid any disappointment when Bruce decided to quit. He wasn't a mean drunk, or even a grumpy one. Most of Powderhole sympathized and considered the near-constant inebriation an inevitable and acceptable salve, a temporary tranquilizer that he'd eventually be weaned from.

For Bruce, though, the sloppy, weepy old man had become a travesty of the father he'd known. The importance of fathers as role models had become a cliché, but Bruce knew that didn't make it less true.

"He was probably drunk when he took out Alfred's front porch," Larry said.

Bruce sighed. "The police report said that his blood alcohol level was 0.15, but he probably just fell asleep. He didn't fasten his seatbelt, and his head hit the door post. The blow caused an epidural hemorrhage."

"No kidding?" Larry said. "I thought for sure he was crushed."

Bruce's dad had lost control of his old Buick Regal at 10:30 in the morning, sailing across the lawn of Alfred Bauer. The cross-country excursion was cut short by the retired welder's front porch, demolishing it with 3,600 pounds of Buick momentum traveling at twenty miles an hour. The porch roof had collapsed onto the car, but the old rusting mass of metal stood up to the assault.

"Dad hadn't talked to Alfred," Bruce commented, "ever since he asked him to weld a broken joint on the patio table and the old German charged him ten dollars for the repair."

"Yeah, Trish mentioned that. Your dad told her that Alfred shouldn't have said he was retired if he was still in business."

Bruce nodded. That sounded like his father. "Well, Dad got his revenge—who's Trish?"

"She wasn't here the last time you were? She's Alfred's stepdaughter—you knew he re-married after June left him."

"Yeah. A woman from Baltimore."

" 'The witch,' as Donald calls her," Larry added.

"She's mean?" Bruce asked.

"Probably not, just astute enough to know what Donald's after."

"And that would be Trish."

"Of course. She's a girl and available."

"They're dating?"

"According to Donald."

Bruce didn't care for Donald. He was a year older than Bruce and Larry, and the social advantage this had provided in high school seemed to have stuck. Donald was confident, and just smart enough to understand that his confidence could carry him where his intelligence might lag. It was the kind of bravado that needed others to brace against, so Donald ended up dominating any group, not that there were many possibilities available within the four thousand souls of Powderhole.

"Trish is just here for the summer break," Larry added.

"College?"

"Johns Hopkins—that's in Maryland, right?"

"I think so. Donald'll go after anything female, no matter how young."

Larry glanced at him. "She's, like, our age. Or close, anyway. She's working on her doctorate degree. Anthropology."

Bruce's eyebrow's shot up. "And she's dating Donald? I don't think he even owns a book!"

His friend shrugged. "It takes all kinds. She has all the brains she needs—maybe she wants some brawn to go with it."

"Huh," Bruce grunted. People were unpredictable. "So she needed a free place to stay for the summer," he said. It was a good segue. He had to get around to it eventually.

"I guess. Hell, why not?"

Why not, indeed. "It looks like we're in the same boat."

"You and me?"

"No! Me and Trish. I'm, uh, moving back home. That's why I was late getting here. I finished packing up my apartment just yesterday."

"What!" Larry sat up straight and his head ratcheted around, a joyful smile on his face.

"Watch the road!" Bruce admonished. "Yeah, I, uh, sort of quit my job."

"You loved that job! It was your career! You got to live in California! It never snows there!"

"Yeah, yeah. Can it. Don't I know all that?"

"So, why'd you quit, for God's sake?"

"I said that I sort of quit. They were going to lay me off, and they offered a position in the test group, but I didn't take it."

"Why not? A job's a job."

Maybe for you, Bruce thought. Changing tires in one garage is as good as any other. "Test engineering's a dead-end. It's a tar-baby—once you're tagged, it's impossible to get back into development. Besides, they offered me that position just so they wouldn't have to pay me severance."

"You couldn't find another job? You were in Silicon Valley!"

Bruce sighed. "It was a catch twenty-two. If I'd taken the test position, I could've stayed in my apartment. If I didn't take the position . . . well, no income, no rent money. I'll keep looking from here."

"You had no savings? You were making boatloads of money!"

Bruce stared out the window at the lush, solid wall of green flying by through the sheets of rain, so different from the pleasant, but sparsely treed bay area. "No, I didn't have any savings. You're not supposed to worry about that at twenty-nine."

It sounded lame even as he said it.

"Let me guess—you had to sell the Boxster."

"Oh yeah. The monthly payments were almost as much as my rent."

"No more vacations in Martinique."

Bruce didn't say anything. He was really going to miss the Club Med excursions. It all seemed so frivolous now, but the work-hard/play-hard lifestyle was the norm for career singles living and working—mostly working—in the tech companies of San Jose. Driving sports cars and jetting off on exotic singles-oriented vacations were the reward for the long hours and high-pressure.

"Well, now you have the whole house to yourself," Larry observed, then glanced at Bruce with a pained look. "Sorry. That probably wasn't appropriate."

"It's okay. It actually works out, since otherwise I'd have to arrange for someone to look after the place."

Larry glanced at him again, this time expectantly.

Bruce groaned. "We tried that. It was a disaster. We have different lifestyles. I'm normal, and you're a pig."

"Come on! We were nineteen, and you didn't wash the dishes either."

"That's because I gave up in protest!"

It was an epic legend among their friends. He and Larry had taken a two-room, dirt-cheap apartment together in Wilkes-Barre, throwing themselves into the glamorous metropolitan life. It was the first time either of them had been away from home, and the first time Bruce truly understood that a clean and tidy home was not the natural order of things, that the hours his mom spent on household chores were not some superfluous obsessive-compulsive routine. Unfortunately for Bruce, his tolerance for crud was a lot lower than Larry's, and every few days the stench of fermenting rice and putrid remnant Dinty Moore's beef stew got the best of him. He'd then invest ten uncomfortable minutes washing away the worst of the wreckage, often clogging the sink drain in the process.

He realized that they'd crossed a threshold one evening when he followed his nose to discover that the swarms of flies that shared their apartment had procreated in a glob of hamburger, which had mysteriously found its way under the sink, where it was kept moist and fertile by the sweating drain.

Bruce flinched. Larry had repeated something at a raised volume. "Huh?" Bruce said, looking at his annoyed friend.

"I said, we could use paper plates if you still don't trust me."

"Sure," Bruce agreed without enthusiasm. He was suddenly fatigued, ready for a beer. He could argue with Larry later. A curtain of hopeless defeat descended now that he'd revealed his fall from affluence. What a disaster. Two months ago he had been snorkeling among gorgeous Caribbean reefs, and now here he was retreating home jobless, facing a life of Dinty Moore stew on paper plates.

On the bright side, he told himself, his dad had finally solved his drinking problem.

He closed his eyes. What the hell kind of thought was that? Emotional bottom, that's what.

Chapter 2

Larry dropped Bruce in front of the house that had been his home for the first two decades of his life, and would be again for an indeterminate amount of time. His boyhood home—three bedrooms, one bath, and an expansive front porch— sat among a crowd of other similarly clean and humble houses, wood frame structures with green and white aluminum awnings over the windows. Sidewalks, worn smooth by thousands of passing feet, were nearly submerged in grass planted by Bruce's grandfather.

This residential enclave, five blocks wide and eight blocks long, was built during the coal boom of the twenties when Powderhole was birthed overnight. From its seed as a village consisting of a post office and tiny grocery store, the Pennsylvania borough blossomed into a bustling little commerce town, complete with three churches, a fire station, and a small county library, all indirect benefits of the Hanover Coal Company's grab for a piece of anthracite coal fortunes.

When the anthracite industry collapsed in the fifties, Powderhole was left with an infrastructure, but no significant source of revenue. The town didn't collapse—it slowly drained, all its entrepreneurial vitality leaching away year by year. The salaried firemen were replaced with local volunteers, and the Powderhole police disbanded, leaving the jurisdiction to revert back to the county sheriff's office. The town was left with a future of inexorable decline. That reality permeated the fabric of the place.

Bruce, already feeling caught up in the decline, stood at the porch steps trying to remember where he'd stashed the house keys. He finally found them and was about to enter when he noticed a yellow post-it note lying on the porch by the door. He picked it up and read: Sorry! I didn't realize your father was gravely injured. Please call!

Bruce stared at the note. He was tired enough that this minor mystery clogged up his brain, and he read the words a second and third time, hoping to understand why someone would leave a message for him without indicating who they were. And why apologize?

Bruce jammed it in his pocket, relegating the problem to another time.

Inside, the tidy small rooms were arranged exactly as they'd been for as long as he could remember. The interior arrangements—the furniture placement, choice of throw pillows, and knickknacks—had been his mother's domain, and his dad had kept it all as it had been when she diede.

Bruce picked the mail up off the floor, and noticed one envelope had "settlements" written by hand. There was no return address, and no stamp. Apprehensive, he opened it to find a single sheet addressed to him, with two typed paragraphs of dense information. He glanced through it enough to gather that the person was providing suggestions about damage reparations. At the bottom, he saw that the letter was signed by Trish Adeline. It must be about the damaged porch.

He sighed, and set it on the table with the rest of the letters, deciding he'd rest easier if he dealt with it right away. He called the number at the bottom, and Trish answered immediately. "Bruce?" she said.

"Er, yeah. How did you know?"

"Your California area code."

The woman sounded assured but friendly.

"Oh, right. I uh, got your letter."

"Thanks for calling—I'm so sorry. I didn't know the situation when I wrote that. The EMT told me that your father was fine, but the guy obviously didn't know his head from his butt-hole."

The gears in Bruce's exhausted brain rotated a quarter turn. She had obviously posted the note on the door after finding out his dad's terminal condition. The meaning would have been obvious once he opened the letter inside. At least, it would have been obvious if he wasn't so tired. Or maybe if he was as intelligent as she assumed.

"It's okay," he said. "My dad's probably better off now."

His brain wasn't properly filtering the thoughts emanating from the bottom of the emotional well. It was too late to correct the callous words, though.

"Perhaps," Trish replied, hesitantly. She obviously wasn't sure how to take this. "Maybe we should sit down and talk about the . . . uh, damages."

"To your porch," Bruce clarified.

"Right, but it's Alfred's porch, not mine."

"Of course. Alfred's porch. The porch that my father obliterated in a drunken stupor."

Bruce would have smacked himself if he'd had a third hand. He'd thought he could support and justify his original insensitive remark, but he realized he probably shouldn't be trying to talk at all.

"Would you like me to come there?" she asked.

Her tone begged him to interpret her offer as a polite gesture only.

Bruce at least had the presence of mind to recognize her reluctance. "Maybe I should come there to see the damages."

"Great!" she replied, a little too enthusiastically. "How about six? Alfred will be home then."

So you won't have to be alone with me, he thought. "Sounds good. If I can't get to the front door, I'll stand on the street and shout."

There was silence at the other end.

"Because of the wrecked porch," he explained.

"I know," she said.

"It was a joke."

"I guessed."

He sighed. "See you at six."

Bruce went upstairs to what had been his bedroom. He opened the door to a cluttered space that his parents had begun using for overflow storage once he moved out. The Christmas decorations, off-season clothes, and a plethora of shoes were all in cardboard boxes that could be hauled off to his sister's old bedroom when he came to visit. Underneath it all, like ancient ruins buried beneath subsequent epochs of discarded trash, was his original bedroom, complete with his Transformers action figures.

He lifted the boxes off his single bed and flopped down to rest a bit. It was great to close his eyes and not think of anything, just float in the peace and quiet of this little room, his lifelong safe haven. The drone of a distant lawn mower was comforting, the anthem of lazy summer vacations. Of course, this haven was just a bedroom inside a house, now. No Mom, no Dad to watch over him. He was an orphan.

But in a way, Powderhole was like his extended family. The little town might be dumpy and plebian—a word he'd picked up in college—but at least it was safe. And quiet. And warm. And cozy.

ж ж ж

Bruce opened his eyes and didn't know where he was. He was looking at a ceiling of white, finely textured tiles. The fog cleared, and he remembered that he was lying in his childhood bed.

He sat up and steadied himself a bit against the sudden transition. He blinked the film from his eyes and looked at the alarm clock. It was six-fifty. He blinked again. That was bad. Why? He remembered. He was supposed to have been at Alfred's house to talk to Trish at six.

Frantic oh-crap mode. It was just an ad hoc arrangement, and it shouldn't have been a big deal, but years of procrastination and arriving at college classes and work meetings five minutes late had worn the oh-shit-I'm-screwed-again groove in his psyche. He'd left his phone downstairs, and he found that there were messages waiting. He didn't even check them, avoiding what he knew they contained. Instead, he grabbed his wallet and stood trying to remember where he'd left the car keys. His brain was still only firing on three cylinders. He didn't have a rental car this time. He was carless. He didn't know where his dad's car was—probably at the garage. Or maybe impounded.

Uttering a curse that he wouldn't have gotten away with if either his mom or dad had been there, he ran out the door and down the sidewalk. It was five blocks to Alfred's house. The air was late-August muggy, and five blocks was plenty far enough to work up a good sweat. He turned the last corner damp and sticky, feeling grungy and unsuitable company.

The sight of Alfred's porch brought him up short. It was one porch in the sea of neighborhood porches that had collectively comprised the permanent landscape his whole life. Seeing it crushed in on itself was disturbing beyond the practical consequences of the accident.

Alfred had placed a two-by-eight plank across the splintered jumble, and Bruce teetered up to the front door, holding his arms out for balance. He knocked on the screen door. "Hello!" he called. "It's Bruce!" There was probably a doorbell, but using it when you could call out a greeting was considered unnecessarily formal.

"Hello!" came Alfred's voice from inside. "Come in, boy! I think Trish was expecting you."

He stepped inside and a woman's voice called down from upstairs. "Is that him?" The voice came clearer as she moved to the top of the stairs. "I thought we said six o'clock. I've been calling and leaving messages."

She started down the stairs, and Bruce saw that she was indeed a prize catch that Donald would want to net. It wasn't that she was a knock-out babe, or even Barbie doll pretty. But she was slim—obviously athletically maintained—with regular features. This was important, because it allowed the sparkling animation that enlivened her face to be appreciated without distraction. Bruce wondered what the hell she was doing with Donald. Larry had already voiced the answer. As much as they denied it, women couldn't resist the prime-beef hunk factor.

"I . . ." he started in answer. Oh hell, he wasn't going to lie. "I fell asleep. It was a long flight."

She watched him as she descended the stairs.

"I normally rent a car in Philly . . . but when I found out about my dad, I had to, um, you know, I had to get here—"

"I got it," she said, interrupting him. "I guess you saw the damage to the porch."

"Uh, yeah. It's really trashed . . ." An imagined lawyer threw him a cautionary look. "It, uh, needs to be fixed."

She threw him a look that wondered if he was perhaps daft. She flipped her wrist to look at her watch and pursed her lips. "Sorry. Out of time. I have to go."

She looked at him. Bruce felt like a contestant on a talent show, waiting for the judges' results. She glanced at her stepfather. The old welder had settled himself into an easy chair. "Alfred, I'd like to be here when we talk. We'll have to re-schedule. Do you mind?"

"Nah," he replied, waving off the concern. "It was an accident, anyway. Not really anybody's fault. I can fix it, you know, if I had some lumber—"

"That's exactly why I have to be here," she cut him off. Her voice was playfully stern, and the twinkle in her eyes said that she cared for him, and was watching out for his welfare.

She turned back to Bruce and it seemed like she was sizing him up for the team. "Maybe you'd like to come along. We can talk about it along the way."

"Where?"

"You don't know about the meeting tonight?"

"I just got here a few hours ago."

One eyebrow went up in curiosity. "You haven't heard about the bank vault?"

"The United Penn?" It was the only bank left in town.

She nodded. "They want to break into the vault."

He stared at her. He sensed that his mouth was open.

A grin spread across her face. She waved for him to follow. "Come on. Let's break into a bank."

Chapter 3

The United Penn was *not* the last bank left in town—it had closed, leaving Powderhole bereft of yet another key institution. Trish explained why they wanted to break into the vault. The Bloss boy had been accidentally killed while playing with his father's loaded pistol. Bruce had known Henry Bloss all his life, but only had a vague recollection of his son, since he was just a toddler when Bruce headed for the sunshine coast.

But he'd apparently been a darling specimen and a favorite son of the whole town, for after the accident Angie Pylund was able to convince Cab Tibulski, the town constable, to oversee a voluntary firearm repository. Angie mobilized her handful of followers to canvas the town and cajole, or failing that, intimidate, virtually everyone to check their guns. Pastor Himmel even weighed in the following Sunday with a sermon reminding the parishioners that guns were the product of man's ingenuity, not God's, and that a repository didn't mean relinquishing ownership, just keeping the firearms safe.

"Let me guess," Bruce offered, "the repository is the bank's vault. But why would they need to break in?"

"Angie had the combination changed," Trish explained.

"So? Did she forget to write it down?"

Trish glanced at him, her auburn, shoulder-length hair flashing gold as the lowering June sun peeked through the maples along

Main Street. She stopped, and Bruce turned to face her. She looked concerned. "Do you know about Angie?"

"I don't really know her. I know of her."

She was Powderhole's liberal troublemaker, according to the conservative faction. According to her small group of friends, she was a progressive leader with the insight and courage to champion the poor and underrepresented. She had appeared out of nowhere some years before, a friend of a friend from Boston, and had decided the town could use her activist skills.

Trish studied him. "Bruce, Angie is dead," she said levelly.

Bruce's world spun five degrees. He really didn't know Angie; in fact he'd talked to her exactly two times. But it was a shock to find out that someone he knew, no matter how slightly, had died.

"How?" he asked.

"She fell. From the railway bridge over the falls."

"No."

"Yes."

The bridge consisted of two giant rusting iron I-beams spanning massive rock shoulders that framed the top of the falls. This was all that remained of the cogwheel railway that had once eased hundreds of tons of anthracite coal each day down to waiting rail cars along the Susquehanna.

"What was she doing up there?"

It was kind of a dumb question, since anybody would have to cross the bridge if they were following the path from above down to the river. A better question might have been, why she was coming down the path.

"According to Donald, she was snooping on SPF."

"She wanted to catch someone applying an inappropriate amount of sunscreen?"

Trish looked at him with surprise. Then she rolled her eyes and groaned. "I get it. 'Sun protection factor.' Ha, ha. You don't even know about them?"

"Who them? If Donald's part of it, there's probably football or guns involved."

She threw him a quick, disapproving glance. Bruce guessed it was because he was poking fun at her boyfriend. "Not this time. SPF stands for 'Save the Powderhole Foundation.' "

"Ah, ha! I have heard about that, but I didn't know they'd promoted themselves to official acronym status. Apparently a company wants to lease the falls to experiment with a new kind of portable power generator, and some stick-in-the-muds in town don't like the idea."

"It's Penn State University that wants the lease, not a private company, and if you think that being stuck in the mud equates to wanting to preserve the last natural environment within a hundred miles, then it's probably good that you live in Silicon Valley. Also, it's not an acronym since it can't be pronounced as a word."

They had continued walking along the sidewalk, but Trish was staring straight ahead. "I think I touched a sore spot," he offered.

She shrugged, still not looking at him.

"I don't live in California anymore," he added.

She finally glanced at him, curious.

"I'm moving back to Powderhole," he explained.

Now she looked at him full on. "Because of your father?" she asked.

"I was already coming back. No, I lost my job."

She nodded thoughtfully. "I'm sorry," she said. Thankfully, she didn't press him about the details.

He hesitated, reluctant to probe her sore spot, but his curiosity refused to be denied. "What were the Powderhole saviors doing below the falls in the first place that Angie had to spy on them?"

She threw him a quick Watch it, Bub look, and took a few seconds to reply. "They were scouting for native artifacts," she finally said.

"You're kidding."

"Why on Earth would that be a joke?" she asked, her voice edging back towards the anger.

"Hey, sorry! I'm not trying to ruffle your feathers. Native artifacts, as in Indian stuff?"

"If you mean Native American cultural remnants, then yes, they were looking for 'Indian stuff.' "

"Yo! Chill, already! Sheesh." He could see that she was blushing. It seemed crazy, though. "You know where the town got its name, right?" he asked.

"Of course. During the Civil War they built waterwheels in the falls to make gunpowder."

"Right. So that means that the falls have been trampled by white men for, like, over a hundred and fifty years. Don't you think any broken pottery would have been either found already or crushed?"

Her blush deepened. Bruce remembered Larry saying she was majoring in anthropology.

"And, besides," he pressed, "why would Angie care if they were looking for Indian—excuse me, Native American—artifacts? From what I heard, she would have been out front spear-heading the preservation."

"She thought we were trying to find a place to hide firearms," Trish replied, giving in, exasperated.

"'We'?"

She looked like she was going to retort, but just shook her head in frustration.

Her explanation registered in his frontal cortex. "Wait a second, I thought the SPF crowd was fighting to protect the falls from the clutches of evil Penn State. Was Angie confused? Did she think that SPF stood for 'Save our Precious Firearms'?"

But he already knew the answer to that. When Larry had told him about the whole save-the-falls thing, the people he'd mentioned was like a rundown of the conservative faction of the town, those with Rush Limbaugh's artfully impassioned voice drifting from their open windows. Despite his youth, Donald was a hardcore Republican. His prominent leadership role in football seemed to have set the mold for his political bent. Bruce had been joking, but with this crowd, the "F" could, indeed, have stood for firearms.

"Angie wasn't exactly the epitome of logical reasoning," Trish said.

Bruce shook his head. He was moving back to a town that was collectively losing its marbles. "So, she died trying to get a peek at people who were looking for non-existent Indian pottery so that they could keep the town from earning much-needed revenue. That's why they were looking for non-existent pottery, right? To build a case to preserve the falls."

She stopped and stood facing him with her fists jammed into her sides. "Will you shut up about the non-existent pottery already? That's not the only kind of artifacts."

Bruce lifted his shoulders. "What else? Arrowheads?"

He'd said this to be sarcastic, but her face said he'd hit the bullseye. "You were looking for arrowheads!" he said as an accusation.

"We weren't just looking," she snapped. "We found three. It proves that the falls were once populated by Shawnee Indians."

"Three arrowheads. What does that prove? My grandfather had a cigar box full of them that he found plowing his fields."

"I doubt they were all—or any, even—actual arrowheads, and besides, if we dug in the ground, who knows how many we might have found."

"But, of course, that would be counter to preserving the area," Bruce stated flatly, watching her carefully.

She knew he was poking at her. "You don't expect me to answer that, do you?"

The cigar box was still in the attic somewhere. He remembered picking up the heavy flint artifacts and turning them over in his hands. If the cupped chip marks, and the distinct Christmas-tree shapes weren't made by American Indians, then God was a real kidder.

But Bruce didn't push it. He was sorry that they'd stumbled into discord. "Well, I hope your arrowheads represent three dead deer, and not three dead Indians," he said reaching for common ground.

She smiled, happy to be leaving troubled waters. "Probably neither. An arrow that found its target, whether food or enemy, would have been retrieved. They were valuable items that took time and craft to make. The ones we found would have been misses that were lost."

He nodded. That made sense. "Are they your doctoral subject—Indians?"

Her smile widened into a grin. "It's a small town, all right."

"What do you mean?"

"You're here a few hours, and you already know my dissertation subject. Unless you have the means to travel to remote places on the planet, American natives are about the only choice for anthropology study in the aboriginal field. But that's perfectly fine, since so much about their cultures has been lost."

"I guess the European settlers didn't much care to study them before they drove them away."

"Actually, there were a fair number of historians at the time who did try to capture the traditions and mores, but so much had been lost before they even arrived."

Bruce puzzled a moment. "Ah—smallpox."

"And measles and typhoid and a dozen others. Without firing a shot, the Spanish conquistadors decimated the American native population. And the irony is, they never even knew they did. By the time the Dutch, French, and British settlers arrived, the invisible massacre was already a hundred years in progress."

"Yeah, the Spanish suck."

Her eyes went wide in disbelief.

"Kidding! Just kidding. So what makes arrowheads around the falls so valuable? I could show you my grandfather's cigar box. There might be one, even two, that are real."

He was immediately sorry that he'd made that last poke, but Trish didn't seem to even catch it. "The terrain around the falls is difficult for hunting," she explained.

"How so?"

"An arrow almost certainly wouldn't bring a deer down right away—remember, these were chiseled stones, not razor-sharp metal tips. A hunter would expect to track the prey for hours—a whole day—before the wound slowed it down enough to allow a final kill."

"I see. The Indian hunter would need to be able to follow the wounded deer. And it's nearly impossible to navigate the cliffs and rocks around the falls."

"Exactly. Also, back then, Pennsylvania was one big, continuous old-growth forest. Very little under-growth, and easy for tracking. The bluffs around the falls, though, would have been, like now, covered in thick brambles and brush—perfect escape opportunity for a wounded animal."

"Okay . . . so if the arrowheads you found weren't from hunting, then—"

"Exactly."

"Exactly what? They were shooting at each other?"

"Of course. These are war artifacts."

"You sound so confident."

"It's just logic. I don't think they were having target practice."

"Fine. So they were playing Indians and Indians. A few spent arrows doesn't a doctorate degree make. Or so it would seem."

"Of course not. It's just a piece in the bigger picture. I'm guessing that these arrowheads are either Shawnee or Iroquois. The Shawnee moved into the Wyoming Valley from the Carolinas about the time the Pilgrims arrived. A hundred years later, they were driven west by the Iroquois from the north who had created a widespread confederation—known as the Six Nations—and were subjugating surrounding tribes with the help of the white settlers. But the Shawnee refused to be enslaved."

"You think that the falls was the scene of a battle?"

"The same characteristics that make it poor hunting ground provide excellent cover for fighting. It's defensible, with plenty of high ground to source fire. The Iroquois raiding party would naturally have come down the Susquehanna River in canoes—rivers were their highways. The Shawnee women and children would have been above, where the town sits, safe from the marauding Iroquois warriors."

She looked at him sideways, as though checking to see if he'd lost interest. He took the cue. "Unless the Shawnee lost the battle," he suggested.

"Yes," she agreed enthusiastically. "But there's no record of Shawnees taken as slaves from the Wyoming Valley."

Her passion spoke of a long evolving study. "It sounds like maybe we're getting to the meat of your doctoral thesis."

She grinned and blushed. "It's a dissertation, not a thesis," she corrected, then launched happily into an explanation. "The Shawnee were unusual in that their governing councils included women. My theory is that this affected their strategies, including warfare."

"What, like they would avoid fights?"

"Because women are afraid of fighting?"

Bruce suspected that he'd wandered onto thin ice. He gave it a little tap. "Not afraid, exactly. Maybe apprehensive."

"You're kidding, right?"

Oops. The ice was cracking. "Of course," he fibbed.

"It's probably more accurate to say that women's influence would moderate the council decisions. Less testosterone in the mix would allow more rational analysis, and less die-for-honor bravado. Maybe the Shawnee council women would have recognized the inevitable, that with the white settlers' support, the Iroquois couldn't be defeated, and this battle may have been part of a retreat strategy."

"Sounds like a lot of conjecture."

"It is. That's why it's a theory. If there were already proof, then the subject wouldn't be suitable for a dissertation."

"Is that why you're here, in Powderhole?"

"Not specifically. My mom and Alfred are nice enough to give me a free place to hang my hat for the summer. Access to Shawnee archeology is a bonus. My main studies have been of the Delaware group of tribes—the Lenape—that inhabited the northern Chesapeake basin—"

"Not far from Johns Hopkins," he said, just guessing.

"Close enough. The historic Delaware sites are maybe an hour from Baltimore. The Delaware were—are—a matriarchal society. But more importantly, at least for me, they had indirect control of the tribal leadership. They could remove any male leaders they didn't like."

"Sort of like veto power."

"In a way."

Bruce was happy talking with her about a subject with substance and not just small talk. It was obvious that she was intelligent and connected, the way she watched you when you spoke, searching behind the words to find the motivations and desires driving them; the way her eyes glittered, and indeed her whole face lifted in celebration, when she found something funny.

They were a block from the small town hall where the meeting was being held, and Bruce saw people filing in. He knew enough about Powderhole to recognize that this was a crowd that shared the patriotism gene, the type who attach a US flag to anything that will hold it.

"I understand why you were at the falls when Angie fell," he said, "but the rest of the SPF group—I doubt that they were all there just because they wanted to help you with your college work."

She was silent a moment as they walked the last block. "No. You're right. They'd love to have the place designated as some sort of historical site. It's silly, of course, unless significant archeological finds turn up, which is almost impossible, since the Shawnee didn't live around the falls."

"But you didn't tell them that," he ventured.

She grinned and sighed. "I didn't want to burst Donald's bubble . . . and, okay, I was hoping they'd help me find arrowheads."

"Is the SPF thing Donald's baby?"

It was odd; he found that he was resentful that the town's shining star had elbowed his way into the conversation.

"He didn't start it," she said, "but he's more or less taken the copilot's seat."

"He tends to do that," Bruce offered, stealing a glance at her.

She just shrugged.

Bruce chuckled. "Maybe you could borrow a lesson from the Shawnee female elders and convince the town to leave all the guns locked away in the bank vault."

They'd arrived at the town hall, and his attention was taken up by everyone wanting to say a word of welcome and shake his hand. They also expressed gratitude that he was coming along to lend support.

"Great!" he whispered sideways to Trish between well wishes as they walked up the front stairs. "Now everybody thinks I'm some kind of pro-gun advocate."

Trish had stopped, and he turned to face her. She was looking at him with skeptical disapproval. "Why do you think I've come to the meeting?" she asked.

"Um, because you're a spy, reconnoitering the enemy?" he suggested without conviction.

She shook her head in disgust and continued past him up the stairs.

He caught up with her. "You want the guns liberated?" he whispered into her ear.

She stopped a step above him and glared at him, inches from his nose. "The constitutional right to bear arms was created before guarantees of trial by jury and prohibition of unreasonable search-and-seizures and cruel and unusual punishment. You're damn right I want those guns back in responsible citizens' hands."

Bruce watched as she stomped away from him up the stairs. The disapproving look she'd given him earlier when he'd commented that Donald's involvement must be football or guns wasn't because he took a poke at her boyfriend, but because he'd taken a poke at guns.

Trish wouldn't have been one of the Shawnee women sitting on the council, she would have been running headlong at Iroquois warriors screaming a war cry.

Chapter 4

Bruce caught up with Trish inside the hall. She seemed to have cooled off, but offered no olive branch.

Donald, the self-appointed copilot, sat with two other SPF officers at a folding table set up on a low dais at the front of the room. Bruce saw Donald wink at him, and forced a smile and waved, then realized the handsome hunk was not winking at him, but at Trish. From across the room, Larry called them over, pointing to two empty chairs beside him. Bruce was totally baffled—Larry was the last person he'd expected to see here.

"Oh, great!" Trish muttered with disgust.

"What?"

She indicated Larry. "The troublemaker."

"Actually, he's, like, my best friend."

She nodded glumly, as though she should have expected this.

"Yo! Trish!" somebody called out.

It was Leslie Mudnick, standing up in the very front row. Leslie was only four years older, but Bruce thought of him as part of his parent's generation. The opinionated man was thin as a rail and the closest thing to a redneck the town had ever spawned. If Larry was the last person to advocate the dispersal of guns, Leslie was the first to declare you a communist if you so much as hinted at gun control. In fact, Bruce wasn't sure Leslie understood that the Soviet Union no longer threatened America's security.

"Oh, lord," Trish whispered. "That guy give me the willies."

Leslie was waving for her to come forward, gesturing frantically for his brother Mort to make room. Mort, two years younger, was the opposite of Leslie, being obese where Leslie was emaciated, although the two did share the same straight and narrow-minded might-makes-right philosophy.

Trish lifted her shoulders and hands in apology and pointed across the room. "Come on," she said quietly. "Let's sit with Larry. Maybe we can keep him quiet."

As they made their way over to Larry, Donald came down from the dais and met them. "Hey, Bruce," he greeted, shaking his hand, then put his arm around Trish's shoulder and leaned down to give her a kiss. She coyly turned her head so that his lips landed on her cheek, then turned to adjust one of the chairs, dislodging his arm, but catching it with her hand and guiding it gently off, so that the separation wasn't an obvious rejection. The result was that he was no longer advertising his claim on her. Bruce found this vaguely encouraging.

Donald pointed his finger at Larry, the tip of his fingernail hovering just an inch from the seated man's nose. "No wisecracks tonight, right?" he warned.

"No cracks for the wise," Larry assured.

Donald stared at him. Bruce could almost see the gears working back and forth in his head, trying to decide if that itself was maybe a wisecrack. "Just watch it," he finally warned, then to Bruce and Trish, he said, "I'll catch up with you guys later," and trotted back to the table.

Bruce glanced around the room. Somebody had set out all the chairs, a hundred at least, and this had been a mistake, since the majority of people—perhaps two dozen—all clustered at the back, giving the impression of feeble interest. Dick Armstrong, who owned a car dealership forty-five minutes away in Berwick, was the obvious leader of the group, and he encouraged everybody to move down front. Bruce noticed one lone young woman he didn't recognize bringing up the rear. She stood out by being the only one not engaged in conversation, and also because she was strikingly pretty. She wore a blouse and skirt, and this set her apart from the other women as well. She caught his eye, and he glanced away,

Blaine C. Readler

embarrassed at getting caught gawking. The impression her bright eyes conveyed was curious interest, though, not defensive warning.

"He sounds like he's talking to a bunch of children," Bruce muttered, as the three of them complied with Dick's request.

Larry snorted. "But we go along anyway. B-a-a-a," he bleated as they took their new seats.

"We evolved to work in groups," Trish observed. "And groups need leaders."

"Great," Larry grumbled. "Evolution has turned me into a herd animal."

"Natural selection operates on the individual, not the group," Bruce said, "so you—or your ancestors—must have benefited from the arrangement somehow."

Trish looked at him with a raised eyebrow.

"Don't get him started," Larry warned. "He'll dive right into Darwin's life story. And Darwin lived a long life."

"Darwin happens to be one of my heroes," Trish commented. She turned to Bruce, placing her hand lightly on his knee for emphasis. "I have a Darwin fish on my bumper."

They were interrupted, though, as Dick Armstrong brought the meeting to order, and she removed her hand to turn and face forward.

Bruce's knee tingled where her hand had been. He was amazed and puzzled by her seemingly incongruous right-wing gun stance and ardent defense of evolution.

Dick opened the meeting by introducing Donald and Tom Chancy as the SPF treasurer and secretary, and Larry immediately raised his hand. Dick sighed. "Yes, Larry, what is it?"

Larry stood up. "I'm confused. I thought that this was a meeting about breaking into the bank vault."

"I told you," Trish hissed to Bruce. Larry didn't look at them, but simply extended his middle finger downward so that only they could see it.

Dick eyed him with a long-suffering glare. "The foundation has volunteered to steer the project along. And nobody's talking about breaking into the vault."

"I am!" Leslie called out, but nobody acknowledged him.

"I'm still confused," Larry said. "See, I was curious, and looked into what a charitable foundation is all about. The important point is that it has a tax exempt status. The IRS website says that a charitable foundation can't be an action organization. Now, even though it might be argued that—"

"Larry," Dick interrupted impatiently, "what's your point?"

"I thought I was in the middle of it. But let me make it real small. It seems to me that SPF can't run this meeting because breaking into the bank vault would be, like, a political action."

Dick stared at Larry like a grizzly might a cougar that had flopped down twenty feet from the bear's fresh kill. "Larry," he finally replied, "try to listen to my words. We. Are not. Breaking. Into. The vault. We simply want to find the combination. That's all."

"But you want to get the guns out."

"Of course. Everybody knows that."

"Then I'm confused, because that's a political action."

Donald could contain himself no longer. "You're confused all right," he growled, getting up, "and I'm gonna set you straight."

Leslie also stood up, shaking his fist and spitting nasty curses. Mort shouted from his seat, not willing to heave his mighty mass upward.

Dick put his arm out and eased Donald back into his chair, and motioned for Leslie to sit down. He then took a deep breath, and shrugged a demonstration of his infinite Christian patience. "Larry, you have exactly one minute to explain how getting our rightfully owned firearms back is a political action, and then we're getting on with the meeting."

"Well, I'm glad we're limiting comments to one minute, that should keep the meeting short." Dick narrowed his gaze, but Larry pressed on before the car dealer could interrupt. "But stupid me, I'm wasting my remaining fifty seconds. Here's the thing: trying to take the guns is a political action because retrieving any guns requires checking an ID."

Dick snorted. His Christian patience was about used up. "Larry, you're an imbecile. Checking identification is not a political action."

"It is if you do it."

"What the hell . . ." Dick glanced around. "What the heck are you raving about?"

"The repository charter that Angie drew up, and the majority of the town voted for, says that checking an ID to release a gun is the responsibility of three people—any of those three can release a gun. In order to get the charter up and running, the selection of the ID people was postponed. For the time being, the charter included just one person."

Dick was watching Larry carefully now. He turned and addressed Cab Browning. The town constable was leaning against the doorframe at the back of the hall—present, but demonstrably not part of the group. "How about it, Cab?" Dick asked.

The retired truck driver nodded. "I think you can guess who that one person is."

Dick slumped and put his head in his hands. "Angie," he said to the floor.

"Right as rain," Cab confirmed.

Larry had told Bruce that Cab was pleased with the gun repository. He'd said that doing his job right meant having nothing to do, and having all the guns locked away went a long way towards making that happen.

"Of course," Larry interjected, "selecting an ID committee is just procedural. Somebody just needs to draw up nominations and call for a town vote."

Dick's head popped back up, and he was glaring again at Larry. "Then why the hell—" he gave a quick glance around but didn't rephrase this time "—are you holding up the meeting?"

"I'm just trying to keep you out of trouble with the IRS," Larry insisted, his voice dripping sarcasm. "Breaking the guns out of jail requires political action, and the SPF can't do that. You introduced the meeting as an SPF event. You can't do that."

Dick's eyes bulged. He turned back to the constable. "Cab, will you please toss this troublemaker out?"

Cab shook his head sadly. "Ah, Dick. You know I can't do that. It's not my place to judge who's right or wrong here, but what I've heard is valid debate so far." He looked at Larry. "Kinda stupid debate, but valid nonetheless."

Dick looked around the room as though searching for an answer. His gaze landed back on Larry. "Fine. You win, you little whiner. This is not an SPF meeting. This is now simply a gathering of concerned citizens."

"Well," Larry said with feigned reluctance, "I think the hall was reserved by the SPF. And from what I gather, that meeting is still in progress."

"Okay," Cab declared, walking towards the front of the room. "I think that's enough. Dick, why don't you call for a motion to end the SPF meeting, and then all you concerned citizens can get on with your concern." He walked over and stood at the end of the row where Larry sat with Bruce and Trish. "And, Larry, you're going to sit quietly and listen for a while, right?"

"Oh, yeah," Larry agreed. "I'm just as concerned as the next citizen."

Larry was indeed quiet as the Meeting of Concerned Citizens proceeded. He'd made his point, which had nothing to do with the IRS or political actions, but simply that he thought all the people in the room were themselves imbeciles for loving guns.

After an hour, the concerned citizens were no closer to their guns, but they'd had a satisfying time accusing everyone from the governor to the president of being too liberal. When they pulled the liberal bashing home to Powderhole, though, Dick brought down the curtain on the bile fest. He seemed almost as frustrated with their single-track, non-productive ranting as he'd been with Larry's veiled heckling.

Bruce wasn't sure what Dick had hoped to achieve until the man picked up some papers and stood up to address the small gathering. He explained that he'd tried to contact the company who had built the vault, only to discover that they'd out-sourced the service contracts. That offshore company had no record of Angie's combination change, but would be happy to open the vault for twelve hundred dollars plus change. "We will either have to come up with the money, or hope I can get the records straightened out, which frankly could be forever."

The hall erupted into a storm of angry shouting, and it took Dick some minutes to regain order. Calling on frantically waving arms in turn, he took suggestions that ranged from suing the vault company to breaking into the vault—or at least trying to. Leslie claimed he had dynamite. Finally, the inevitable point was raised: SPF had sufficient funds to cover the service call—why not use that, and pay it back later?

Dick seemed to grind his teeth before replying, "Chuck, you know that's not an option. That point has already been jammed down our throats." He refused to look at Larry, who sat watching with a smug smile.

The meeting broke up soon after that with no conclusion beyond the general agreement, muttered loudly, that the liberals were somehow to blame.

Trish hung back, waiting for Donald, who was talking with Dick. Bruce hung back because he wasn't sure if Trish was done talking about the porch problem, but also because he was reluctant to walk away from her. Larry hung back because hanging back was essentially hanging around, and that's what he did whenever the opportunity allowed.

Leslie stopped and said hi to Trish, all smiles and yellow teeth.

"Don't you have a gun to clean?" Larry eventually asked. "Oh, that's right!" he exclaimed with mock sympathy. "They're all locked up!"

The skinny man's eyes narrowed. "Bite me," he hissed.

"Communication, Leslie," Larry urged, "communication. When you grunt things like that, I get a general idea that you don't like me, but your limited vocabulary is failing you."

Leslie leaned in, nose to nose. "What if I actually still had a gun?"

Larry leaned forward so that their noses touched, forcing Leslie to pull back. "If you had a gun? Gosh, you'd be breaking the new town ordinance and maybe we should talk to Cab?"

The weasely little man uttered the same crude epithet and stalked away.

"Now there goes the best reason for repealing the second amendment," Larry observed. He glanced at Trish. "Oops. Tell you what—let's pretend that you didn't hear me bashing the second amendment and save the debate."

"A debate requires two parties with informed positions," she countered, then grinned, showing she wasn't at all upset.

"You're just glad I got lizard-man out of your face," he accused.

"And I thank you," she replied.

Donald finally came over and suggested they grab some pizza. "You too, Rabbit," he said to Larry. This had been Donald's nickname for Larry ever since high school track—it had been derogatory at the time, but nobody remembered any longer exactly how. Donald seemed to have completely forgotten his angry promise to set Larry straight about his confusion. This didn't surprise Bruce. He wasn't sure if quickly letting go of animosity was due to a commendable decision, or simply Donald's inability to carry an involved thought for very long.

Walking the three blocks to Desiderio's Pizza, Trish said to Larry, "That extended finger in the meeting was pretty rude."

"Not as rude as what I wanted to say," Larry replied.

"But maybe more effective," Bruce added. "The use of sign language is carved into our genes. Our homo erectus ancestors used it before developing speech."

"Actually," Trish observed, "that's something of a myth."

"Oh, really? A myth? Like the story of Adam and Eve, or like George Washington chopping down the cherry tree?"

"Okay, maybe myth is kind of strong. In 1930, Sir Richard Paget introduced a theory that humans formed the earliest words by moving their tongue to mimic their gestures. But by the sixties anthropologists had abandoned the idea."

"Fine," he countered. "But just because language didn't evolve directly from gestures doesn't mean that we weren't already communicating using gestures."

"You're right. But no reputable anthropologist believes that we had any kind of cohesive sign language before speech developed. If anything, they would have evolved simultaneously. Look at chimpanzees. They use both gestures and unique sounds to communicate basic information."

Donald was blowing impatient little snorts. "What're we, back in school?" he interjected. "Geez! You two are really going out of your way to act like geeks. And I don't appreciate you blasting the Bible."

Bruce had to think a moment about what he'd said. "Because I called the story of Adam and Eve a myth?"

"Ye-ah," Donald affirmed, as though it was obvious.

"Well, I'm sorry. I didn't mean to imply that the story was, er . . ."

He didn't mean to imply that it wasn't true? Bruce didn't believe it was verbatim true. Heck, he didn't think there ever was an Adam or an Eve, except in some allegorical way.

Trish rescued him. "Of course it's not true," she stated. "The story of Adam and Eve is a perfect example of a myth."

Donald seemed stymied by a parry from his own girlfriend. "The Bible is the word of God," he finally asserted.

"So God can't use metaphors? Donald, do you actually believe that God created Adam and Eve and in a few thousand years they spawned the seven billion humans on Earth?"

"It's possible. Evolution is just a theory," he reminded.

"So is Einstein's general relativity. Do you doubt that? What about cellular metabolism? Just because it's called a theory doesn't mean that it's waiting to be proven."

"The Bible doesn't need proof."

Trish looked at him a moment. "That's a truism, you know."

Donald glared at her defiantly. Bruce guessed he wasn't sure what a truism even was. "So you agree that it's true," Donald finally said.

Trish winced. "You can't agree or disagree with a truism. It just is. When you say that you believe without reservation that every word in the Bible is true, then it follows directly that you don't need proof."

"That's right," Donald concurred. "That's what I said—the Bible doesn't need proof."

Trish put her hand to her forehead a moment. "Donald, it doesn't need proof for you," she explained patiently, "because you come from a position of absolute belief. But I need evidence, I need that proof."

He smirked. "Then I guess you're just out of luck."

"No, no! You're not listening. The Bible is a book based on ancient writings. There's no attempt to present logical arguments in it because, well, it can't. That wasn't its purpose. But evolution has all the evidence in the world to back it up."

"Well, that's debatable."

"What do you mean?"

"The supposed evidence. It's all weak."

"What about the reams of genetic tracing that coincides closely with fossil dating and geological sequencing?"

"Not all scientists agree with that stuff."

Trish stopped walking. "What are you talking about? Of course they do."

He stopped and shook his head confidently. "Maybe the ones that are in bed with the liberal media."

She stared at him a moment, and then glanced around at Bruce and Larry as though confirming that she wasn't imagining it all. "Where did you hear this?"

Donald lifted his head in defiance. "I read it."

"Where?"

He didn't answer.

"You read it in your Christian magazines," she accused. Bruce saw that her hands were balled into fists. "Oh, boy," she said. "I've gotta tell you. This burns me up more than anything. People can believe whatever they want, but when they start commandeering science for their own agenda, that's when I draw the line. Science is about truth—about finding the truth, no matter where that leads, like it or not. When people try to use for any other purpose, they're . . . well, they should be ashamed. But when they try to use it for the opposite—to try to prove something that isn't true—well, that's a crime. Or at least it should be."

The four of them walked the last half block in silence. Larry stepped ahead and opened the door to the pizza restaurant. "Right now," he said, holding the door for them, "I'm glad all the guns are locked up."

Chapter 5

The uneasy silence lifted when they had to place their orders. Donald and Larry split a large pepperoni pizza, while Bruce and Trish each decided on a Cobb salad. Bruce knew from experience it was going to be a bowl of iceberg lettuce topped with cheap cold cuts, sliced Velveeta cheese, and stale croutons. But he still preferred it to the calorie and fat orgy of a Desiderio pizza.

Larry nudged Bruce and nodded towards the door. It was Betty Stickltow with her stuck-in-tow wisp of a husband, Ted. Betty had been the bane of every Powderhole fourth-grader for thirty-odd years. Her innovative teaching method consisted primarily of letting her students know how dumb they were if they couldn't answer a question, and whacking uncooperative shoulders with her worn and gouged ruler, at least until the PTA mustered the courage to remind her that this was technically illegal. She found that merely prodding their shoulder with the stick was almost as effective. Embarrassment and indignity were excellent tools of discipline, right along with pain.

Bruce and Larry ducked their heads into their menus, but it was too late. She hurried, or rather, waddled over, since she'd added at least fifty pounds since retiring. Ted followed along behind. "Well, well," she announced, standing over them with her arms crossed over the vast pillows of her bosom, "our expatriated technician has returned for a visit."

"Hello," Bruce replied, feeling intimidated, though it had been nearly twenty years since the last shoulder poke. "I would wish it were a happier visit," he added, trying to sound mature.

She nodded. "Your father," she said. A statement of fact, that she, the teacher, already knew.

She just stood there, watching him. Judging him.

"I'm actually an engineer," he finally said, wanting to end the silent inquisition, "not a technician."

Her mouth tightened in disappointment. *Wrong answer.* "You don't contribute salaried hours in a technical field?"

"Well, sure. But an engineer needs a four-year degree—"

"A technician is someone who contributes in a technical capacity," she affirmed simply. There was no debate. He was lucky she didn't puck a fork and poke him in the shoulder.

Bruce had felt defiant as a student, but helpless nevertheless. *I shouldn't feel helpless now, dammit.* "A technician is almost never a salaried position," he blurted. It was a technicality, but it was a fact, and she couldn't deny that.

He caught himself from visibly wincing, though, when she uncrossed her beefy arms. Instead of hitting him, she reached into the pocket of her dress for a handkerchief, into which she blew audible volumes of phlegm. She couldn't poke him or send him to the back of the room, so she chose instead to ignore him and turned her august attention to Donald. "I heard that Dick was unsuccessful in his bid to commandeer the SPF funds."

She hadn't been at the meeting, and Bruce was not surprised. She held no opinion about gun ownership, and her enlightened presence there—or so she would have assumed—would have lent unwarranted bias. On the other hand, she apparently knew beforehand that SPF funds were at stake. As far as Bruce could tell, the only enlightened contribution she could offer would be the result of snooping.

Donald smiled amiably. He tilted his thumb towards Larry. "Rabbit here made sure of that."

She smiled at Donald, and her eyes might have been communicating a come-hither invitation. He'd always been her darling; not too bright, but handsome and polite. Twenty years later, he was still her favorite. She didn't even look at Bruce's heckler friend. In Mrs. Stickltow's eyes Larry was the polar opposite of Donald: clever, maybe, but completely wasting his innate intelligence by refusing to align it with the flow of the world—her world, of course, the world of an enervating rural Pennsylvania town.

Mrs. Stickltow barked at Ted to "don't just stand there, find a table," and then eyed Donald with a conspiratorial smile. "I've discovered something that Mr. Seward failed to disclose."

Trish leaned across the booth table to Bruce and whispered that Seward was the Penn State doctoral student who had come to inquire about leasing the Powderhole falls.

"He told us," Betty Stickltow continued, "that he'd constructed the power-generator apparatus that he wants to test."

"I remember," Donald agreed.

"Well . . ." she paused for dramatic effect, and Bruce played a tight snare drum roll in his head. "General Aerospace is actually behind it."

Bruce knew the company well. He'd interviewed with the Allentown division, but their offer had come in way lower than the high-flying Silicon Valley firms.

"Seward isn't at Penn State?" Donald asked.

"Oh, he is a student there, all right. But he completely failed to disclose the connection with General Aerospace."

Donald gave a little shrug.

Had it been Bruce doing the shrugging, he would have been tensing for a poke. But since it was Donald, Mrs. Stickltow patiently persisted. "Donald, what does General Aerospace do?"

"Manufacture, uh . . ."

"'Aerospace?'" she hinted.

"Um, like, airplanes?" He decided to hedge his bet. "And rockets?"

"That may be true," she encouraged. "But who is the company's main customer?"

"Uh, airlines? Or, NASA?"

"Close," she agreed. "But who else uses jet planes?"

"The Air Force!" Donald exclaimed triumphantly.

"And the Air Force is part of . . .?"

"The military! General Aerospace is, like, a defense company!"

"Not *like* one," she gently corrected. "It is one."

Donald absorbed this revelation. "Why would the military want a portable electric generator?"

"Why wouldn't they?" she countered.

Trish broke in. "It's a hydro-electric generator, and from what I've heard, it's supposed to be small, but I doubt that it's very portable."

Stickltow gazed down on Trish, an unknown variable. The girl hadn't been pressed through the Powderhole fourth grade crucible, and Stickltow wasn't sure how to categorize her. "Portable would be in the eye of the beholder," she finally stated.

"True," Trish conceded, "but in this case, from what I've heard, Seward is interested in the Powderhole falls specifically because of the combination of it being somewhat accessible, but still undeveloped and pretty rough terrain."

"How does that render the device non-portable?"

"I just mean that his interest in the falls lines up perfectly with the stated purpose of the generator."

"And what's that?" Bruce asked. He'd been dying of curiosity, but wasn't about to interrupt Stickltow on his own.

"Penn State is developing a small-scale hydro-electric generator for third-world countries," she explained. "A full-scale generating plant costs billions of dollars—you have to start by building a dam! But what many developing countries need is a modest amount of electric power in remote areas. In the dry areas of the world—arid countries—solar power is great, but in a lot of tropical locations there's more clouds than sun."

"Voila!" Bruce concluded. "Clouds mean rain, and rain means running water."

He glanced up at Stickltow. She was watching them, as though they were detaining her. She turned slowly to address Donald. "We can talk more about it before the next SPF meeting—when there's less interruptions."

She started to waddle away to the table where Ted sat staring out the window, but stopped and added to Donald, "And I don't trust that insurance investigator. I'll bet he's connected somehow."

"What insurance investigator?" Bruce asked, once she was out of earshot.

"Another fur'ner poke'n around, up ta no good," Larry drawled, imitating a hillbilly accent.

"He came through a few days ago," Donald explained. "Said he was looking into a claim involving lost air baggage. He went and talked to old Dagger."

"Why Dagger?" Bruce asked.

"The old coot came in just the day before that and told Cab about a meteor that had put a hole in one of his sheds." Donald chuckled. "He wanted Cab to contact the government, thought he deserved compensation or something. Cab told him with a straight face that he'd look into it."

"But he didn't," Bruce guessed.

"Of course not."

Dagger's real name was Carl Dagmar, but his nickname had been bestowed after he'd returned from Vietnam missing a few screws after being drafted and dragged away from Powderhole. He had a habit of keeping a fearsome Army-issue knife at his side at all times, thus the moniker. He lived in a shack tucked away up in a hollow along the river, a local hermit legend of insanity and dark, frightening rumors. Bruce knew him as a wiry rag-tag man that he would gaze at out the window of his dad's car after they'd trundled the half-mile of rutted lane with trout his dad had caught. Bruce knew vaguely that his dad and Dagger had served together, but his father had always sidestepped the subject when asked, saying simply, "Carl's finding his peace."

ж ж ж

Trish woke Bruce the next morning by blowing her car horn out front. Sunshine streamed through the window. The storm front had passed, leaving behind unusually clear air for late summer.

When he came to the door bleary-eyed she was standing on the porch waiting. "Did you have to make such a racket?" he grumbled. "You'll wake the neighbors."

"I rang the doorbell," she replied, "but you didn't answer. And I doubt they're still sleeping at seven-thirty."

He looked at his watch. She was right, it was seven-thirty. He mumbled something about still being on west-coast time, and told her to come in. He saw Larry sitting in her car, and waved him in as well. Bruce went upstairs and got ready, and when he came back down, a box of cereal and carton of milk were on the table, and Larry was scooping spoonfuls from a bowl into his mouth.

"Don't be shy," Bruce said dryly. "Help yourself."

"Okay," Larry responded, reaching for the box to pour more.

Bruce grabbed it, poured himself a bowl, and then put the box back in the cupboard.

"Indian giver," Larry accused.

"You want an Indian? Talk to Trish."

"You know," she said, waiting for them to finish, "when I was little, I thought my friends used that phrase because the US government repeatedly gave land to Native Americans, and then took it back."

"Then they would have said, 'Native American giver,'" Larry quipped.

Trish rolled her eyes and told them they had three minutes before the bus left.

Bruce was pleased that Trish had invited him and Larry along today instead of the SPF crowd. She'd said that the group had spent more time gabbing than looking for arrowheads, and most of them really just got in the way. He wondered, though, whether the absence of Donald, who was making his wireless service sales calls in Berwick, had more to do with it. In any case, Bruce was looking forward to scrambling around the falls. He hadn't been there in years, and having the company of Trish—and Larry—was a bonus.

Fifteen minutes later, Trish parked her Subaru Forester next to a black new-model Ford sedan in the grass along the road. This was the de facto falls parking lot. Harry Bloss, who owned the land as part of his hundred-acre farm, didn't seem to mind. If he did, he never mentioned it. The morning was getting warm in the bright sunshine, and standing along the road, Bruce could almost see the cool air wafting out from the shadows of the nearby trees. Even more enticing was the distinct rushing roar of the first falls, invisible behind the dense grove of oaks and maples.

"Ready?" Trish asked, grabbing a handful of cloth bags from the backseat.

"Let's hunt some injun's!" Larry crowed, stepping onto the carpet of previous-season leaves covering the forest floor.

"Your disrespect is treading a fine line!" she called after him, but he just kept going.

Bruce gestured at her fistful of cloth. "Aren't you being a little optimistic? You've got enough bags for dozens of arrowheads."

She smiled and shook her head. "One per bag—otherwise, they scratch each other. I couldn't find anything smaller."

They made their way through the trees, following Larry. The forest sloped a little from the road, and at the bottom, the Nescopeck Creek meandered along as though it had all the time in the world to deliver its contents to the Susquehanna. He could see bright sunshine where the Powderhole canyon opened up, and the creek disappeared, dropping away. And beyond, the roar rose like the crackling bellow of fighter jets taking to the air. Even before they approached the edge, Bruce could feel the wonderfully cool mist thrown up by the churning avalanche. Although called a creek, in other parts of the world, the Nescopeck would have been a river.

Larry waited for them at the canyon's edge where the forest suddenly stopped and the land fell away in tiered layers of rock ledges and steep slopes of tumbled boulders. From here, the Nescopeck flowed down across four short plateaus, like a five-layered wedding cake. Below each waterfall, the roiling creek collected its wits, and then hurried along a hundred yards around smooth-worn boulders to the next drop. Along each flat stretch, the layer of the god-sized cake was wooded, and if you wandered a ways into each so that the sound of the falls below and above merged, it was like the whole world was being lifted up and away on huge booster rockets.

The three of them stood next to the first falls' edge looking out across the treetops of the next plateau. The thundering roar, the cool blowing mist, the opening vista to the sun shining across the surface of the distant Susquehanna—together it was mesmerizing. Bruce could have stood there all day basking in nature's best.

"The arrowheads aren't going to jump out of the ground and fly up here," Larry said, and started down the path. Trish followed him, and Bruce brought up the rear.

The path eased down in three switchbacks, the second leg taking them just below where they had stood. From here one could see that the edge had long ago been carved out underneath, making a long, open cave, so that when you stood above—like they just had—you were perched on a three-foot ledge of rock hanging over air. When Bruce was small, he'd crouched in the cave pretending that he was hidden from the world.

The first falls dropped thirty feet, and the second was more—nearly forty feet—but because it was not a vertical drop, but cascaded to the next plateau through fifty feet of churning, swirling chaos, the effect was not as dramatic. At least not in the same iconic Niagara-perfect way. Passage around this falls was the most difficult of the five, since the creek made a turn here, so that high-water floods dumped the felled trees they were carrying, forcing humans to navigate a maze of horizontal trunks and tangled branches.

The third falls was actually Bruce's favorite. It too was not vertical, and in fact offered even less slope, but unlike the battering jumble of the second drop, this one slid along a smooth span of bedrock—no boulders to crack your skull, just a mad rush of clear, wet exuberance ending in a giant swirl around a catch-pool at the bottom. This was nature's original waterslide, predating man's fun parks by a few hundred thousand years. As teenagers, Bruce, Larry, and their friends had come here to ride the mad surge of adrenalin. The activity was strictly forbidden, which meant only that they didn't tell their parents.

They were headed for the penultimate plateau above the final and highest falls—where Angie had fallen from the bridge—but stopped short when they came to the fourth, the wimpiest ones. A woman stood there, apparently unsure of how to proceed. She must have heard them, for she turned, and Bruce recognized her. She was the pretty woman who had caught his eye at the town hall meeting. She had traded the skirt and blouse for jeans, a T-shirt, and running shoes. Her eyes were a brilliant blue-green, and gazed out at the world with a sharp, perceptive assessment that one imagined was absorbing every detail and filing away the result for further analysis.

The lone woman waited until they'd come up to her, then extended her hand, "You must be Trish," she said.

Trish accepted the offered handshake and replied, "How did you know?"

The blue-green eyes twinkled as she glanced briefly but piercingly at Bruce and Larry before responding. "It's a small town, and you're still the new girl on the block."

"And you are . . .?" Trish inquired.

"Sorry. Of course. I'm Ariel—Ariel La Rochelle. I'm from Penn State," she informed, watching Trish's reaction.

Trish nodded slowly. "You're a colleague of Seward?"

"That's right. I'm here to follow up."

"Follow up?" Trish said, inviting more.

Without taking her eyes from Trish, Ariel La Rochelle replied, "With the project." When Trish didn't respond, she added, "The power generator."

Trish nodded, seemingly satisfied.

Ariel looked at Bruce and Larry a moment again, maybe wondering what their role was. "I'd like to talk to Mr. Dagmar," she explained. "I was told I could get to his place down this way, but I think somebody's played a joke on me."

Trish threw Bruce a surprised glance. "For thirty years the man lives the life of a hermit, and now suddenly everybody wants to talk to him."

Ariel flinched slightly then leaned in, as if to make sure she didn't miss the tiniest detail. "A man was here asking about him?" she said, as much a statement of fact as a question.

"That's right," Trish confirmed.

"Did you notice if he had red hair?"

Trish shook her head. "I didn't see him." She looked at Bruce, and seemed to speak to him instead of Ariel. "Donald said that he had red hair."

"Verdammlich bloede!" Ariel hissed with such vehemence that Bruce assumed it must be a German curse.

Everybody stood, silent, contemplating the utterance. Larry finally broke the spell. "For once it seems that Stickltow is right."

Chapter 6

Ariel recovered quickly, but her jaw was set a little firmer than before. "Can you please tell me how I can find Mr. Dagmar?" the young woman asked, amazingly calm now, almost as though the utterance had been imagined.

"How do you know the insurance agent?" Bruce pressed. It was hard being at all unpleasant to such a beautiful woman.

Ariel waved it off. "Oh, he's not an insurance agent. He just wants to beat me to the meteor."

Bruce and Larry exchanged glances. "Why would he lie about that?" Bruce asked.

She gazed at him a moment, and Bruce could almost feel himself melt. "Okay," she finally said. "I'm going to tell you, but you have to promise not to tell anyone else."

The three of them nodded solemnly.

"What Mr. Dagmar saw—it wasn't a meteor."

"It wasn't?" Bruce said.

"No. It was a satellite."

"A satellite?"

"That's right. It's a satellite that Bill Gates launched a couple of years ago."

"Bill Gates?" Bruce's voice was rising in pitch with each volley.

"That's right. Bill Gates. He launched something into orbit that's very important to him. But the satellite malfunctioned and fell."

Bruce glanced at Trish. She was looking at him with her brow scrunched. "What does this have to do with Penn State?" he asked. "And why is the red-haired man trying to get to it first?"

Ariel stared at him and blinked once, obviously deciding whether she could trust them.

"We promise not to tell anyone," Bruce reiterated.

She nodded. "Mr. Gates is willing to pay a lot of money to get . . . his thing back. It would go a long way towards funding our project."

"The power generator."

"That's right. The power generator."

"But why are you competing with this red-haired guy?"

She shook her head disgustedly. "That's Tom Walker. He wants the money for his own project."

"A Penn State project."

"Of course."

Bruce took a deep breath and sighed. Trish said, "Ariel, you have to admit, this sounds . . . a little bizarre."

She nodded in agreement. "It is. Really bizarre. But will you please tell me how I can find Mr. Dagmar?"

The three of them exchanged quick looks, a silent vote. "Bruce, Larry?" Trish finally solicited. To Ariel, she explained, "I have no idea how to get there."

Larry took his turn basking in the attention of this babe. "Whoever told you to come down here wasn't steering you wrong. You can get to Dagger's place from old Highway 339 that runs along the Susquehanna, but getting around to there from town is, like, six miles. It's only twenty minutes from here on foot."

Bruce let Larry lead the way. The path that ran along the canyon wall into the next hollow seemed ancient. The local story held that it was an old Indian trail, and now this didn't seem at all unreasonable. He noticed that Trish was falling back, and when Ariel wasn't looking, she gave him a little wave to join her. She leaning in and whispered, "Satellites don't fall out of orbit when they malfunction."

She was right. The thought had skimmed through his brain at the time, but hadn't stuck. Satellites by definition were in free-fall. The only thing keeping them up was their initial velocity. In low orbit, telltale wisps of atmosphere presented a tiny bit of drag that eventually brought them down, but it took years, and was predicted well in advance.

"What do you make of it?" he whispered back.

"I don't know. Why would she lie?"

He shrugged. "Maybe she didn't mean it that way."

"Why don't you ask her about it?"

He looked ahead to where her trim figure maneuvered the uneven ground in fluid movements, almost a sensual dance. He really hated the idea of irritating her. "Why don't you ask her?"

Trish was looking at him with impatience, almost disgust. "Fine, we'll let it go. We'll just assume that a post-graduate student working on an advanced power generator system has forgotten the basics of Newtonian motion."

Not long after, Larry had to stop to tie his shoe. Ariel looked out over the flood plain to the shallow waters of the Susquehanna. "I heard about a woman who fell at one of the waterfalls," she commented. She turned her gaze back to the river, as though she was just making casual conversation.

Trish, though, perked up. "That was Angie." She nodded forcefully. "The falls can be treacherous, more dangerous than you might think. Angie was obviously very familiar with the terrain, and yet she fell to her death. Horrible tragedy—"

"Trish!" Bruce reprimanded.

"What?" she responded with exaggerated innocence.

To Ariel, Bruce explained. "Trish is part of a movement in town to save the falls from you."

"From me?"

"From Penn State."

Her face lit up with understanding. "The power project. Of course."

"Anyway," Bruce went on, "Trish would love for you to find the place unappealing—wouldn't you, Trish?"

The anthropology student rolled her eyes. "Fine, fine. Guilty as charged."

"But if Angie was so familiar with the place," Ariel countered, "why did she fall?" She was watching them closely again.

Bruce shrugged, but Trish offered, "Donald—a friend of mine—actually saw her fall."

"He did?" Bruce exclaimed.

Trish looked puzzled a moment. "I didn't tell you that? Yeah. He happened to be looking at her from below as she fell. Actually, he was yelling at her to go away, but he doesn't like to dwell on that. He thinks that she just couldn't see where she was walking. She was always paranoid about getting too much sun, and was wearing a big, floppy hat; even had a silk scarf over her face. Plus, he thinks she was distracted by a bug."

At this, Ariel put her hand up to pause her.

"What?" Trish asked.

"A hat, and a scarf, and a bug?"

"Yeah. What a combination, eh?"

"Why does your friend think that she was distracted by a bug?"

"He said that she slapped the back of her neck. Although, that was maybe a minute before she fell, so I'm not so sure about that part."

Ariel took a deep breath and held it.

"What?" Trish asked. "Did you hear something different?"

Ariel seemed to look through her rather than at her a moment, then wagged her head. "No. It's just . . . like you said, a real tragedy. Tough luck for the poor woman."

Ariel was silent the rest of the way. Larry tried several times to start a conversation, but the enigmatic knockout parried each one with simple one-syllable responses.

Ж Ж Ж

Dagger's place looked long abandoned. They had stopped at the top of the last few switchbacks to catch their breath, and were looking down from midway up the wall of the hollow, carved by a long-defunct stream. Bruce knew that the chest-high untamed weeds, the missing planks in the side of the shed where barn swallows whipped in and out, and the torn-out screen door were all perfectly normal in Dagger's eyes.

"Is he . . . safe?" Trish asked, peering at the apparent ruins.

"Sure," Bruce assured. "Of course, it's been a while since I last saw him."

"How long is a while?"

Bruce counted. "About twelve years."

Trish looked at him. "Twelve years? World wars are fought, and the defeated countries made into allies in twelve years. Dogs live a long full life in twelve years."

Ariel apparently didn't share Trish's concern, since she had already started down the last hundred yards. Before the other three could catch up, two of Dagger's dogs saw them and leaped forward, howling murderous threats. A moment later, Dagger appeared on the porch holding a shotgun ready. The old man let the barrel fall at his side when he saw that half of the party were women. He wore blue jeans, a white T-shirt and running shoes, all in fairly good condition, all probably purchased at the Salvation Army store in Berwick. Only his canvas hat matched the decrepit style of the rest of his property; it sported numerous moth-eaten holes, and flopped limply on all sides except his face, where he'd pinned the rim up out of his eyes.

He called to his dogs, but they might as well have been deaf. Bruce held his arms out, halting Trish and Larry. He knew the best thing was to stand still until Dagger came to get them. Ariel, though, walked on down the path, even as the first mongrel reached her. Bruce called to her to stand still, but she had already delivered a sharp kick with the tip of her shoe to the under-jaw of the dog, who jumped back, his howl now one of surprise and pain. This time, the dog listened to Dagger and retreated.

"What the hell you doing to my dogs?" he called angrily.

"He bit me!" Ariel cried back, holding up her ankle as proof, although Bruce couldn't see anything wrong.

"Well, sure he did! You kicked him!"

"He bit me first—" She stopped herself, then held her arms out, palms down, soliciting for calm. "I'm sorry, Mr. Dagmar," she said, collected again. "I just want to talk to you for a minute."

"About what?"

The rest had caught up with Ariel. Bruce raised his hand in greeting. "Hi, Carl!"

"Who the hell are you?"

"Carl, it's me, Bruce. Bruce Weiss."

Dagger squinted at him. "Harry's boy?"

"That's me. Don't you remember? I used to come along with my dad when he brought you trout."

The old man leaned the gun against the side of the house. "You've grown, boy. How's your dad?"

"He . . . had an accident. He's dead, Carl."

It sounded like harsh, but it seemed appropriate when telling Dagger. It was honoring him by telling it straight, and not sugar-coating the news. At least, that's the sense Bruce had.

Dagger put his hands in his pants pockets and studied the dirt. After a few seconds he looked up. "I'm real sorry to hear that, Bruce. Your dad was about the best friend I ever had."

Bruce nodded, not sure what else to do, but the nod felt like a lie, since he had no idea what relationship the two had.

"What do you want, Bruce?" he asked.

Dagger hadn't invited them in, or even to come over to the porch, but Bruce walked forward and waved for the others to come along. No sense yelling across a field of weeds. "I'm actually here with a . . . friend," he explained as he approached the porch. "This is Ariel," he said gesturing.

"The dog kicker."

"Uh, yeah. And this is Trish, and you probably know Larry."

Dagger pointed a crooked old finger in Larry's face. "I'm surprised you're willing to show your face here. Burn down any barns lately?"

"That was, like, six years ago!" Larry cried. "And it was an accident!"

"Anyway, no need to dig up old skeletons. So, what is it, Bruce?"

"Carl, Ariel here's from Penn State—"

"The university?"

"That's right. She's interested in that meteor that you saw. She thinks that it might actually be a satellite that fell."

As Bruce spelled out the idea, it suddenly struck him as ridiculously coincidental that the satellite—or anything—would fall from the heavens at the very place that she'd happen to come on other business. What were the chances?

He realized that Dagger was giving Ariel a hard stare. Bruce turned and saw that she was staring back. She seemed to be blushing.

"I've already told Cal and that other busy-body," Dagger barked, "that there was no god-damn meteor or satellite or even bird shit." He looked at Bruce, and seemed to soften. "Sorry, son. I'm getting cranky in my old age."

"Getting?" Larry asked, but everybody ignored him.

"But, Mr. Dagmar," Ariel said, "surely you saw something, otherwise you wouldn't have reported it."

His eyes bore into her, but she returned his stare with equal resolve. The blush was gone. "I'm sorry, missy," he finally said, with a tone much gentler than the look that preceded it. "I was mistaken. It was probably just one of the old anthracite mines collapsing. That's the short and long of it, and there's just nothing more to add." He turned to Bruce. "They buried your dad?"

"Yesterday."

The old man nodded his farewell, picked up his gun, called to his dogs, and went inside, letting the screenless screen door slap closed behind him.

Bruce looked at the others, shrugged, and started to walk away. Trish and Larry followed, but Ariel stood for a moment, staring through the dark square framed by the empty screen door. Bruce called to her, and she strode over.

"He's lying," she declared quietly when she came up to them.

"Oh, yeah," Trish concurred.

Bruce shook his head slowly. "It does seem like he's hiding something. But—"

"But what?" Ariel asked.

"What would he hide? Why would he hide whatever it might be?" He looked at Ariel. He was completely dismissing the idea that a satellite had fallen with something valuable. It suddenly came to him that it was she, not Dagger, that seemed to be hiding something.

"Come on," he said feeling disgusted at having bothered his dad's old friend. "Let's get out of here."

ж ж ж

They heard the helicopter long before they arrived back at the Powderhole falls. The droning chud-chud-chud of passing copters, whether military or commercial, was occasionally heard over Powderhole, but always high in the sky; the town was just a population blip far below on the way from somewhere significant to somewhere else important. But what they heard through the trees and scrub as they retraced their steps along the ancient trail was a distant thrashing that grew louder and louder, until the machine was close enough to transform the droning whir into a powerful thump-thump-thump that Bruce could almost feel beating against his chest.

None of them could imagine why a helicopter would visit the falls, but Ariel grew taciturn. Where before she was out front, pressing forward towards answers, she now brought up the rear, and occasionally stopped to stand, staring at nothing.

They broke out into the open expanse of the falls just in time to see the medevac copter lift away from Bloss's field above, tilt to the right, and thunder off, presumably towards the hospital in Bloomsburg. They turned when someone called to them. It was Cab, huffing and puffing his way up from the lower falls. They waited while the constable continued on up. The roar of tumbling water suspended conversation until he reached them.

"What's going on?" Bruce asked while Cab took deep breaths, recovering from the unaccustomed exertion.

"It's Ted—Ted Stickltow," the constable breathed.

"What about him?"

Cab shook his head in dejection. "He's dead. At least, it's pretty certain he is. I guess a doctor will have to make the formal call on it."

"What happened?" Bruce asked, incredulous that someone else he knew—knew personally—was dead.

Instead of answering, Cab asked, "Where have you four been?"

"We went to see Dagger. We—Ariel—wanted to ask him about the meteor."

Ariel didn't seem to be listening. She was looking around, as though watching for something.

"You should leave Dagger alone," Cab scolded. "Give the guy some peace, already." Then he shrugged. "It don't matter, I guess. Lenny saw the whole thing."

Bruce blinked. Cab had been considering them as suspects in some way. "Dagger can vouch!" Bruce exclaimed. "We just came from there."

"Nah," Cab said, waving it off. "Like I said, Lenny saw what happened."

Lenny was the Stickltow's nephew, a tech-savvy teenager who Mrs. Stickltow tapped into when she needed online snooping done. "What did he see? How did he die?"

Cab lifted his shoulders and palms in a gesture of resignation. "Ted fell. It's as simple as that."

"From the bridge? From the trestle? Like . . ."

"No. Not like Angie at all. They were just below the fourth falls there, not even close to the top of the fifth. Lenny says that Ted was frustrated that he couldn't find you—"

"He couldn't find us?"

Cab sighed. "Betty sent them down to spy on you—so come to think of it, it was kind of like Angie, but sort of in reverse. Anyway, Ted got frustrated. He didn't want to go all the way down to the lower falls. Lenny thinks he was spooked about Angie. He let his anger out by throwing some stones down the creek. A bee stung him, and then he just slipped and fell—must've hit his head."

"Maybe he was allergic to bee stings," Trish suggested.

Cab shrugged again. "Could be, but I don't think so. It don't happen that quick, but that'll be for the coroner to figure out."

Bruce noticed that Ariel was watching Cab intently. "What direction was he throwing the stones?" Ariel asked.

"What direction? Down the creek, like I said."

She turned to gaze down where the water fell away over the fourth falls.

"Do you know something, missy?" Cab probed.

She looked back at him, distracted. "Why is everybody calling me 'missy'?"

"Okay, do you know something, ma'am?" he repeated, emphasizing the more formal title.

She hesitated just a moment. "No. Listen, is there another way back to the top? Besides the path that comes down along the creek?"

Cab glanced at Bruce and Larry for confirmation, then shook his head. "Nope."

"Okay," she continued, all business now. "We need to get to the top. Right away. Stay together and don't make any threatening gestures."

"At you?" Larry asked, joking.

"At all," was her curt reply.

Cab looked hard at her. "For somebody who doesn't know anything, you seem to have something specific on your mind. And it don't sound soft and fuzzy."

She looked him in the eye. "Try sharp and lethal." Before giving him a chance to challenge that, she exclaimed, "Now go! Get moving," waving her hands as though shooing cattle.

They started up the path and Bruce wondered aloud, "How do I know if I'm making a threatening gesture if I don't know what I might be threatening?"

"You'll know," Ariel replied, "if you make it to the top alive."

She refused to elaborate further.

Chapter 7

They made it up to Bloss's field alive, although not knowing the source of the danger, Bruce wasn't sure what sort of accomplishment it was. Cab said that he had to get back to town and file a report about Ted's accident for the State Police, and he pressed Ariel again for more information, and she assured him that she would explain it all, but that she had to confirm something first. He wanted her to come along with him, but she told him that she'd meet him there instead. "I'll be right behind you," she promised.

They watched as Cab climbed into his '99 Dodge Neon with the magnetic "Powderhole Constable" sign stuck on the door. Seconds later the car lumbered out of the grass, onto the broken macadam, and drove away. Ariel turned to the rest of them. "I need two of you to stay here, and one to come back to town with me."

They just looked at her. "And I need to finish my doctoral dissertation," Trish finally challenged. "And Bruce and Larry maybe need their mid-morning naps."

Ariel sighed impatiently. "I'm asking you to trust me. This is very important. Possibly a matter of life and death."

"Like Ted's death?" Bruce asked.

"Possibly," she confirmed.

"We don't even know you," Trish reminded.

Bruce thought she should earn their trust. "There's no satellite, is there?" he asked.

She looked at him, and it seemed as though those bright aqua eyes were scanning the synaptic connections in his head. She finally shook her head. "No, there's no satellite."

"Why the story, then?"

She shook her head again, more emphatically. "I can't tell you yet. I'm sorry."

"How can you expect us to trust you," Trish argued, "if you won't trust us?"

Ariel screwed her mouth in thought a moment.

"I trust you," Larry said out of the blue.

"You'd trust the devil if he looked like her," Bruce scoffed. Embarrassed, he glanced at Trish, who was looking at him with one raised eyebrow.

"Listen," Ariel offered. "I can't tell you everything I know, but I promise that I will at some point. In the meantime, I can at least promise not to tell any more lies. What do you say?"

Larry agreed before she'd hardly finished her proposal, but Bruce looked to Trish, who shrugged and nodded. Bruce turned back to her. "Are you really here to follow up about the power generator project?"

She hesitated the barest moment before replying, "No. In fact, I'm not associated with Penn State at all."

As she explained this, Ariel had lifted her foot onto a rock and was unconsciously rubbing her ankle. Bruce saw that there were red marks where Dagger's dog had indeed bitten her. He found this simple truth more meaningful than her earnest promises.

"Do you know the insurance agent that came through?" Trish asked.

"I know of him," she replied, then qualified it. "I do know him a little, but mostly I know about him."

"Who is he?"

"That's one of those things I can't tell you yet."

Trish nodded. "Fair enough. But he's somehow connected with Ted's death?"

Ariel seemed frozen, caught between internal loyalties.

"That's okay," Trish reassured. "I think I got my answer."

"Okay, then," Ariel said, pressing on with business, "who's going with me?"

"I'll go," Larry enthused, raising his hand like a student volunteering to clean the white board.

Ariel gave him a wry smile. "That's the spirit. Nothing like a little self-sacrifice." To Bruce and Trish, she instructed, "Don't go down into the falls, understand? I mean it."

"I think you've got us sufficiently scared about that . . . whatever it is down there."

"Good. You should be scared."

"Why do we have to stay here?" Trish asked. She didn't seem nervous about it, just curious.

"Your job is to keep guard, make sure nobody else goes down."

Bruce shrugged. "How are we supposed to do that?"

Ariel threw him a quick glance as she walked to her black rental, waving for Larry to follow. "You'll have to figure that one out for yourself," she said. "That's why it's a job."

"Where are you going?" Trish asked. "Or is that another secret?"

"To talk to the coroner," she replied as Larry got in.

"Hey! You told Cab that you were going to follow him to his house."

Ariel grinned. "Well, I didn't promise him that I wouldn't lie, now did I?"

She swung the door closed and drove off.

Bruce and Trish watched the car disappear behind a stand of trees, then looked at each other. Trish said, "What the hell is going on?"

An odd thought came to Bruce. "The SPF wants to have the falls declared an historical site or something, don't they?"

"More likely protected as a state park, and even that's a fat chance, or I should say *not* a fat chance."

"Well, if there is some kind of deadly monster down there, maybe you could go for the notoriety aspect. There's a state park in California where the Donner party holed up for the winter, and you know what happened there."

"Oh, yeah. You can't convince Americans to invest in a little Native American heritage, but give them cannibals or man-killing monsters, and they're all over it."

Trish remembered that they should check for ticks, and after they'd inspected each other's clothes and hair, they sat down in the shade. Bruce told Trish how the falls were their childhood playground, amusement park, and adventure safari ride all rolled into one. He and his friends had spent almost every day there in the summers. "No kids there now, thank God," Trish commented.

"Nope," Bruce concurred. "Video games and online streaming has sucked all the kids into their bedrooms. The only time they venture outside is for a comic book convention or a rave."

He asked Trish about growing up in Baltimore. Parts of the city was now gentrified, she said, but when she was small, it was gritty—a down-to-earth blue-collar working town. "Working people have an integrity that sometimes misleads the over-educated professional class," she opined. "They confuse the integrity for simplicity, honesty for naiveté."

They had lain back in the grass, and Bruce turned his head and looked at her. "You do realize that you're working hard to become part of the over-educated class."

She didn't even smile. She lay staring at the puffy cumulous clouds easing past against an otherwise brilliant blue sky. "It's ironic, I guess," she admitted after a while. "My father worked the docks all his life, a proud union man through and through. Still, he'd be proud that I've come as far as I have."

"How'd he die?" Bruce asked.

She turned her head to look at him. "He didn't die," she said, looking offended.

"But—"

"He just left."

She turned back to the impossibly white clouds. Bruce thought that she was done with the subject, but after a minute, she went on. "My mom became depressed. She'd always had bouts now and then that put her in bed for a couple of days, but when she turned forty, she went to bed and essentially never got back up."

"Was she, like, clinically depressed?" Bruce asked.

"Don't know. By then my Dad's insurance didn't cover much, and Mom didn't care enough to find out."

She didn't offer anything else, so after a few minutes, Bruce asked, "And that's why your dad left?"

"Eventually. I'd started college, and my aunt—Mom's older sister—took her in, which may have been a mistake. I guess Dad just got lonely. He met a woman—I don't even know her name—and moved out. I haven't heard from him since. He's ashamed, I know. I've tried to contact him, but he goes out of his way to avoid me. Our house, the house I grew up in, just sits there in southeast Baltimore, empty."

"That's a sad story."

She looked at him. "I guess we've both lost our moms and dads."

"We're orphans."

"Boo-hoo. Poor us."

At first Bruce thought that she was making fun of him, but her smile said it wasn't that

As a way of moving on, she commented, "Ariel looks like she'd be a hot catch."

"Not for me," he blurted.

Why did I say that? he wondered, since he'd been thinking that exact same thing ever since they'd found her standing above the fourth falls.

"Why not?" Trish queried playfully, then going on to list all the things he too found appealing about her: "She's beautiful, fit, independent, and obviously sharp as a whip. Of course, that last one can be a turn-off for some guys," she added, eyeing him curiously.

"That's not it," he defended. "I'm not attracted to dumb girls," he added, then mentally slapped his head.

"Well, that's commendable. So, what is it, then? Are you alienated by the woman's independence? Threatened by her athletic fitness? Ah, maybe you're actually intimidated by her beauty."

"Are you naturally a bully?" he shot back. "Or is there something about me that you feel needs whittling down?"

She just smiled at him, apparently pleased that she'd provoked him.

"Hey!" he cried, teasing, "you seem to find her so attractive, maybe you should find out if she's gay—no, unfortunately, you're Donald's gal."

He hadn't meant to add that. It was as if there was some evil part of him, out to sabotage the thinking, speaking part.

Trish turned completely on her side and gave him a serious look. "Who told you that?" she demanded.

Her intensity caught him by surprise. "Why, uh, Larry, I guess. He made it sound like it was general knowledge, like you and Donald were almost engaged."

"What?" she exclaimed, pushing herself up on her elbows. "Where in God's name did he get that idea? Jeez! You go out for drinks a couple of times with a guy, and the whole town concludes that the next step is to meet him at the altar, bulging with his child. What kind of hick town is this, anyway?"

Bruce held his tongue. For once that day, his brain functioned. Maybe it was that her distraught denial was something he was happy to hear.

They both jumped and spun around when the sound of footsteps suddenly appeared just below the lip of the canyon. Before they could get to their feet and move away, Dagger's floppy hat appeared, followed quickly by his face and sweat-soaked T-shirt.

"Jesus!" Bruce exclaimed. "You scared the shit out of me!"

Although sweating, the old man was breathing only moderately hard. "That effect has hounded me most my life," he remarked so dryly, Bruce wasn't sure if he was kidding.

Bruce saw that he was carrying something, a fancy case made of what looked like burnished steel. It was the size of a laptop case, but had two complicated locking latches, both of which were dangling, obviously having been broken from their fastenings.

Dagger set it on the ground. The way he handled it, it was obviously very light. "There's your meteor," he said simply.

Bruce looked at the case, and then at him. "What are you talking about?"

"I'm telling you that this is what fell out of the sky. Punched a hole in the roof of my chicken shed. Lucky there hasn't been any chickens in there for years."

Bruce glanced at Trish who just looked on mystified. "Why didn't you tell anybody?"

"I didn't find it 'till after I talked with Cab," he explained. "I figured it was mine, since it fell on my property."

"What's in it?"

"Nothin' that I can tell. It was busted open when I found it, but there was nothin' nearby, other than some foam packing. I think it busted open from the fall."

"But why keep it a secret?"

Dagger rubbed his chin. "I was just protecting my rights, is all."

Bruce shook his head. "But, why? What can it be worth? A few dollars?"

In answer, Dagger picked it up, walked over to a tree, cocked it like a baseball bat, and swung it into the trunk with full force. It bounced off as though made of solid rubber. "What do you think?" he asked, walking back over to them.

Bruce looked at the case. It wasn't even dented. "Titanium?"

"That's what I figure."

"I see," Bruce agreed.

"How much would it be worth?" Trish asked.

"Hard to say, exactly," Dagger said. "Maybe a hundred dollars."

"Probably more," Bruce guessed. "It just fell from the sky?"

"Yep."

"But, why are you bringing it to me? Do you want me to see if I can sell it for you?"

Dagger blinked and pulled his head back as if Bruce had offered him something putrid. "Hell no! I thought that other missy wanted it so bad."

"But why now? Why didn't you give it to us then instead of hauling it all the way after us?"

Dagger stared at the valuable gift from the sky a moment and then handed it to Bruce, who accepted it reluctantly. "I got to thinking, is all. Your dad must have given me a thousand dollars worth of trout over the years—retail, that is. Who was I to hoard this windfall—literally a windfall—that wasn't even mine a week ago?"

"But, Dagger. It's not me that's even after it. It's that other missy." Bruce reminded. He found that he always quickly fell back into the local dialect.

"It don't matter. She's your friend."

Bruce decided not to complicate the situation by explaining how that wasn't necessarily so.

The old man studied Bruce a few seconds. "Do you know why your dad brought me all that trout?"

Bruce tilted his head. "No. Dad never told me."

"You knew we served together in 'Nam, right?"

"That I knew. But that's about all I knew. Dad never talked about it."

"A lot of guys don't like to talk about that time, and for good reason. I was on my second tour—I'd made corporal. Your dad was green, a buck private just a few weeks in the jungle. We were on patrol when we was ambushed. It was a slaughter. Your dad and me, we somehow found ourselves holed up behind a log. The rest of the squad was gone, killed. The Vietcong stripped whatever they could from our buddies, but didn't realize we were still there alive. After a while, they left—didn't make a sound. One minute they were all around, and the next, nothing.

"Problem was, I was wounded. Not bad, but I couldn't walk. Worse, the ambush was the leading edge of an advance. We was now behind the enemy lines, if there were ever any lines in that God-forsaken land. Things got worse. I don't know if it was an infection, or just the festering jungle, but I got sick. Terrible fever. It was your dad kept me alive. For three weeks, we hid. He'd go out at night, go fishing in the river a quarter mile away. Before dawn, he'd come back, sometimes with a catch. We couldn't cook, no way could we make a fire with the Cong all around. So we just ate it raw.

"Now, you'd think a person would get sick to death of the same food day after day. Raw even. But it was the exact opposite. When you're starved, food—any food—is gourmet, as they say. Sick as I was, I'd wait for your dad to come back in the dark, my mouth watering.

"Well, I said it only got worse. And it did."

Here, Dagger paused. He stood there staring into nothing for so long, Bruce thought that maybe he was finished. But after a while he shook his head as though waking up and went on.

"One night, not too long before our boys found us, I heard your dad coming back, but a lot earlier than normal. I thought maybe he'd run into a patrol or something. Anyway, I whispered to him. I'd usually do that so he knew where I was and not step on me. But when I whispered, he stopped dead. Everything went completely silent. That's when I realized I was in deep shit—excuse the language, missy. Sure enough, next thing I know, a knife comes flashing down—I see it glinting in the starlight. The knife missed me by an inch, and the next thing I know, I'm fighting for my life— hand to hand. Scratching and punching. I thought I was a goner for sure, but sick as I was, I was fighting off this Vietcong.

"Now, those people are naturally small, but this one was almost tiny. I don't know how the knife got dropped, but in the end, I had my hands around his neck, and I squeezed. I was terrified and my blood was all pumped up. Anyway, I guess I had that super strength that comes at those times, but I think I actually broke his neck. In any case, he was dead."

Dagger stopped. He seemed spent, drained of life. Then Bruce noticed that his eyes were wet. He was crying.

"Here's the thing, Bruce." He choked a moment, stifling a sob. "You see, it wasn't a he at all. It was a woman. I'd killed a woman. With my own two hands."

The old man ran his forearm across his eyes, but without a long-sleeved shirt, he only smeared the tears across his nose and temples.

He took a deep, phlegmy breath. "Now you understand why your dad brought me those trout?" he asked, his voice sounded clogged and nasal. "It should've been me bringing him the fish, but that was your dad."

He laughed then, a choked laugh with a nose full of snot. "It seems kind of crazy now, like we was trying to relive that terrible time. But it wasn't that way. You can try to forget stuff so terrible like that, but it can't be done. You just end up pushing it down to fester. No, your dad was smart. That little fish ritual was sort of a way to remind us both that we'd come through it. We'd come through it, and could never forget it."

Dagger stood there, like that was an integral part of the story. The ending. The curtain call, only the audience was as much him as Bruce and Trish.

Then, as though a timer had rung, he looked at them, nodded, and a moment later was gone, back down the canyon pathway.

Bruce and Trish were silent. It seemed disrespectful somehow to talk.

"Oh shit!" Trish suddenly exclaimed.

"What?"

"We weren't supposed to let anybody go down there!"

Chapter 8

Bruce ran to the edge and looked down. Dagger had already disappeared into the pines. He ran down the path, calling. When he came to the lip along the top of the first falls, Dagger's head reappeared. "What's all the racket?" he asked loudly above the roar of the water.

"Ariel told us not to let anybody go down!" Bruce warned.

"Why?"

Good question. "It's dangerous!"

"Why?"

"She didn't say exactly."

"Not very convincing, then."

"I know! But she's serious."

"I don't doubt it."

"So you're coming back up?"

"No. I'm going home."

Dagger's head disappeared again.

"She thinks that whatever is down there killed Ted!"

The old head popped back up. "Ted Stickltow? That's why the copter?"

"Yeah. Lenny said he fell, but Ariel thinks that it was something down there."

"What's down there?"

"I told you! I don't know!"

The old man shrugged. "I'm not persuaded."

Bruce ran to the edge and watched the thin figure make his way carefully down the switchbacks and then disappear into the first plateau.

Half way back to the parking area he met Trish, who had started down to find out what was happening. "I wasn't persuasive," Bruce explained.

"I'm not sure I would be convinced either if I heard about an unspecified danger second-hand from a complete stranger in town," Trish said as they walked up the path back to the parking area.

When they stepped out onto the grass, Bruce put his fists on his hips and surveyed Bloss's alfalfa fields, large open squares, neatly bordered by stone fences choked with brush. "Nobody's going to listen to us," he predicted. "I don't know what Ariel was expecting."

"You wrestle them to the ground," Trish suggested, "and I'll tell them stories from the Old Testament."

"What's that supposed to achieve?"

"Scare them senseless."

"Stories from the Bible?"

"Everybody on Earth drowns except Noah and his wife; God waits until Abraham has his knife all ready to slit his son's throat— what a joker; God turns Lot's wife into a pillar of salt for looking back at a city that God completely destroyed—even children and babies. He seemed to particularly like to kill children, God slays one child in every Egyptian household before the Israelites leave—"

"Okay! I get it. Sheesh. You're morbid."

"I'm morbid? I'm not making this stuff up. I came home from Sunday school every week traumatized."

"I wouldn't criticize the Bible around Donald."

"I don't intend to do much of anything around Donald."

Bruce looked at her, wondering if there was some extended meaning intended. She quickly looked away, though, squatting down to examine a piece of shoelace. "I thought this was a little snake," she remarked.

He bent down next to her. "It does sort of look like one. Hey, didn't Donald say that the fake insurance agent guy was asking about some lost air baggage?"

"Yeah, I believe so. You think it's this case?"

"Sounds reasonable."

They both looked up when an engine suddenly revved in the distance. It was Larry's dented red Toyota. The clutch was beginning to slip, but he wanted to salvage every last bit of clutch disk surface before he had it replaced. Bruce had assured him that a new clutch would long outlast the rest of the car, but Larry's response had been that he preferred to be optimistic.

Bruce and Trish stood waiting until Larry pulled in next to her Forester. "Where's Ariel?" Bruce asked as his friend got out.

"Off to the coroner in Berwick."

"Did she tell you why?"

"She wants to know if the job is as icky as it seems, and whether he regrets taking it," Larry replied as he started hauling a collection of seemingly random junk from his backseat and dumping it on the grass.

"In other words, she didn't tell you any more than before."

Larry put his finger on his lower lip and pretended to contemplate this. "Oh, yeah. That was it."

"What's all this stuff?" Bruce asked.

He saw that the pile contained ski goggles, an old beat-up fencing mask, two tennis rackets, a couple of hooded sweatshirts, ski pants, wire mesh gloves, and even a cheap hooded mail tunic Larry'd picked up when for a couple of months he was enthused with the idea that he would tour the country as a jouster with a traveling Renaissance Fair outfit.

"Badminton armor."

"Come on, wise guy. Be serious for once."

"I am. Ariel told me to imagine that someone was going to whack a badminton birdie at me, and if it managed to touch me, I'd be dead."

"You're kidding."

"Nope."

Bruce surveyed the plunder. "Why not just the hood and some work gloves?"

"She told me to also imagine a tack sticking out the front of the birdie."

"Tennis rackets?"

"I didn't have any badminton rackets."

Bruce snorted, shook his head in consternation, and looked to Trish. She was eyeing the motley pile pensively, however. She glanced at him, and realized that he was looking for moral support in his scoffing. "Ted was throwing stones," she remarked.

"Yeah, but he was the one who was killed."

She nodded, still pensive. "Yeah, he was the one who would have gotten hit by the imaginary badminton birdie sporting the imaginary tack."

"And Lenny was watching him when he apparently fell. If somebody threw something when he lobbed the stones, Lenny would have seen it, unless it was really small."

Trish nodded reluctantly. "You're right. He'd have seen something the size of a badminton birdie."

"So, what are we supposed to do with all this stuff?" Bruce asked Larry.

"Ariel said to sit on it."

"Literally?"

"You know, she didn't say. I assumed it was, like, a figure of speech. But maybe she did mean to literally sit on it. Trish, you go first."

"Larry," she replied, feigning weariness, "someday you're going to make some wonderful woman completely miserable."

Larry whispered loudly to Bruce, holding his hand to the side of his mouth as though to hide what he was saying, "I'll take the other one. This one's too cranky. You can have her."

Bruce glanced at Trish nervously. Joking about having her was way over the top. Or, way out front. Something out of context, anyway.

She saved him further uneasiness. "Larry, if you can get Ariel to admit that she'd even consider going out with you—even for just a cup of coffee—I'll give you a hundred dollars."

"Whady'a know?" Larry crowed, rubbing his hands together expectantly. "Trish is going to pay for my date."

The three of them sat in the shade, trying to make casual conversation but really, just waiting

Enough time had passed for Bruce to get itchy about the whole situation when the sound of a car speeding along the narrow country road brought them to their feet. It was Ariel's rental Ford and it looked like the devil himself was after her as she braked hard and turned into the grass, her tires making little squealing sounds. Her demeanor as she stepped out contradicted the driving, however. Her face was serious but calm as she walked over to them.

"What did you find out?" Bruce asked.

"The coroner's still looking into it," she replied coolly. Too calm and cool, Bruce decided.

"This is one of those times that you can't talk to us, isn't it?" he asked.

Her mask cracked, and she allowed herself a little grin. "Yes, it is, at least for now."

They told her about Dagger, about how they couldn't stop him from returning home through the falls. She didn't seem greatly concerned. "You impressed on him the danger?"

"We told him that something down there had probably killed Ted."

Ariel waved it off. "That's all you can do. Everybody's free to get themselves killed."

She whistled and nodded knowingly when Bruce handed her the titanium case that Dagger had brought.

"Just about what you expected, eh?" Bruce suggested, probing.

She just glanced at him with a little nice-try-bub smile, then went back to examining the recovered artifact. She ran her fingers over the dense, high-quality foam padding that lined the inside of one half. Padding had obviously once filled out the other half as well, based on the evidence left by splotches of glue marks. She closed it and tucked it under her arm. "Thanks," is all she said.

Ariel glanced at the pile of Larry's junk, and he pointed out hopefully, "I brought the stuff you asked for."

She scanned it. "That should do it. Good job."

Larry beamed at the compliment.

Ariel then studied the three of them, looking at each in turn. The events of the morning had transformed her into the de facto leader. Maybe it was simply that she knew something that they didn't, and knowledge was power.

She was obviously now sizing them up, deciding on a task. Bruce had always prayed to be picked for pick-up baseball games, but he wasn't sure what he wanted now.

She was awfully pretty, though.

"Bruce," she finally said, "how are you with a tennis racket?"

"The varsity high school team was a lot of fun," he replied, holding his face as straight as she had.

Larry's, though, was screwed up in thought. "Hey! You never made the varsity team!"

Bruce shrugged, but he could feel his face growing warm at being caught in the lie. "I never said that I did. I played junior-varsity," he defended.

"Second string," Larry qualified. "Hey, I can play tennis too."

"Larry, the last time you tried, you hurt yourself."

"So you're going to crucify me for exuberant effort?"

"Roll up your pant leg."

"No."

To Ariel, Bruce explained, "He has a scar where he missed an underhand and took three inches of skin off his shin."

Trish spoke up. "Hey, you two. I wouldn't be so hot to volunteer until I heard what she has in mind."

Ariel smiled as if it hurt her face. "She's right, but Larry, I have an important job for you."

"Meaning you're not going to play tennis with me."

"I'm not playing tennis with anybody. I need you to go back to town and get Cab. If he's willing to come, then fine, don't say anything else. If you have to, though, tell him I know what killed Ted."

"Ah, come on. I'm always the errand boy—"

"Larry," she said forcefully.

That's all she had to say. She was the undisputed leader now. No one questioned her orders.

"Do you?" Bruce asked. "Do you know what killed him?"

"Maybe," she replied. "Just maybe."

ж ж ж

Ten minutes later, Bruce was cocooned inside a sweatshirt with the hood up, wearing the fencing mask, ski pants, and gloves. He felt hot and foolish in the summer sun. Ariel had donned Larry's mail—she was still pretty, even framed in the metal mesh head covering. She positioned the ski goggles in place and then handed him one of the rackets. She looked pretty silly too, fumbling with bulky gloves when the sweat was dribbling down both their backs.

"What's all this for?" he asked for the third time.

"In good time," she responded for the third time.

She reiterated her instructions to Trish. "You have to make sure nobody goes down."

"I'll tackle them if I have to," she replied.

Ariel looked at her through the scratched plastic of the goggles for a minute, then nodded. "Thank you. It's not just their safety that's at stake."

"I understand."

"Well, then," Ariel said, waving for Bruce to follow. "We're off to see the wizard."

Bruce heard Trish mutter from behind them, "Or be eaten by him."

Into the trees and halfway down to the lip of the first falls Ariel stopped, gazed up the path to make sure Trish hadn't followed, and then put down her racket and took off her gloves and goggles. "Okay, now listen," she started.

"You didn't want Trish to hear this," he interrupted. "Why not?"

Ariel sighed. "Bruce, you have to trust me."

"You don't trust her?"

"It's not that at all. I trust her as much as I do you. It's just that I have to keep as much secret as I can. I just have to. You can believe me or not, but I'm looking out for her. It's you I'm being reckless with."

She studied him a moment, maybe reassessing her choice, then went on. "What I'm about to tell you—and what you see down here—you're going to have to keep to yourself. Can you promise me that?"

He wanted to promise this beautiful woman that, and whatever else he could, but he also felt like he was somehow betraying Trish. "Can I at least be honest with her about that? I mean, just like what you offered—can I tell her that you've told me things and I've seen things that I can't reveal?"

Ariel was smiling at him.

"What?"

Her grin widened. "You didn't include Larry."

"Well sure, him as well. Of course. It goes without saying."

But he hadn't said it, and he felt himself blushing again.

She became serious once more. "If this thing is what I think it is, it will be about the size of a hummingbird, and it flies. In fact, you might mistake it for a hummingbird. Whatever you do, don't let it touch you—your skin, that is. That's what the tennis racket is for."

"To swat it. It's a bird swatter."

"Exactly. We have to watch each other's backs. If it attacks us, we want to stand back-to-back so that we can cover a full circle. If we do manage to swat it and disable it, don't touch it! Let me handle it."

"It's poisonous, isn't it?"

She shook her head. "I've told you as much as I can for now. But there's one other thing. I left an envelope under your jacket on the passenger's seat of Trish's car—"

"When did you do that?"

"Never mind." She pulled her goggles back on. "Inside the envelope is a name and telephone number. If anything happens to me, call that person and tell him everything you know."

Bruce's heart skipped a beat. "Wait! You left it in Trish's car so that she'd find it if—if neither of us come back up."

Ariel looked at him steadily through plastic lenses. "Yeah. That's right. Now we have to go."

She turned, but he reached out and grabbed her arm, and she swung around, surprised. "Who are you?" he asked.

She smiled. "All in good time."

He followed her down the path, over the lip, along the switchbacks next to the little cave, and on into the first plateau. Bruce found himself flinching at every slight movement and sound. *She said it would look like a humming bird*, he thought, *but how much like one? Exactly?* Every few seconds, he'd twirl around, certain that he'd heard something making a bee-line for his back. *I'm wearing all this gear*, he reminded himself. *It can't get to my skin. But what if it's small and I don't notice it? What if it crawls up inside his hood?* He began swinging the racket randomly back and forth, up and down and behind him as they walked along.

"I'll let you know when I think we're getting close," Ariel finally assured. "You're going to wear yourself out before we even get there."

He tried to be calm. How do you force yourself to be calm? he wondered. It's called yoga, he lectured himself. They had offered free classes at work during lunch. He should have taken some.

At the bottom of the third falls Ariel finally told him to keep an eye out, but they descended all the way to the top of the last falls before she paused. Here, the Nescopeck Creek disappeared, falling over a rock ledge to drop down a sheer vertical wall. A massive roar rose from below. Occasional ghosts of spray caught in the wind swirled up over the ledge and back along the creek. Above the lip of the falls the industrial heft of the sturdy, time-worn metal skeleton, the remnants of the bygone railroad, spanned the creek. The surface was rusting in large patches, but the heads of hundreds of rivets, each as big as a plum, still grasped and clasped the beams together. This is where Angie had stood just before she fell to her death.

Of course, Ted had died nearby as well—just a hundred yards or so upstream. But his death had been so . . . un-dramatic. He just fell down dead.

And that's when it finally came to Bruce. He made the connection, why Ariel had brought them all the way here to the trestle. "It got Angie, didn't it?" he called. He had to yell to be heard above the roar.

Ariel turned, and Bruce wasn't sure of her expression, half hidden behind the goggles. "Yes! Of course!" she yelled back.

And that's when Bruce heard it. It even sounded like a hummingbird.

Chapter 9

At the same time that Bruce heard the buzzing hum, Ariel shouted a warning. It had to be very close for him to hear it above the waterfall. But where the hell was it? He spun around and yelped when suddenly a ball of blurry, frantic motion hovered just inches from his face. The buzz was now a mad whine, like a thousand mosquitoes massed together into a small jar. His eyes focused, and he saw that there was a solid core to the thing—elongated, smooth, and black, but with a sheen, clearly manmade, maybe plastic. There was some definition: slanting lines on each side enclosing an even smoother, shinier surface—tiny windows. Windows, perhaps, but windows that were also eyes. Two jet-black impassive eyes gazing out at him. They slanted back along the curving surface, giving the gut-clenching impression of malevolence—of wicked, evil intent.

All of this had taken perhaps two seconds, but for that two seconds, Bruce was paralyzed, like a rabbit under the hypnotizing stare of a cobra. He blinked. Ariel was screaming for him to use the racket. The frantic whining little thing sidled to the left, and then to the right, studying his fencing mask, something new. Three inches in front of his nose was an awkward position to hit with his tennis racket. For a brief moment he considered swinging the racket straight up, squashing the little devil against the mask, but he sensed that the last thing he wanted to do was force it closer.

But his dilemma was solved when the tiny predator backed away and rotated. Bruce now saw that its body was the size of his thumb and tapered at each end. It was black, except for a design drawn in precise white lines that looked like stick legs running with curved, stylized feet. He also saw a needle extending from its snout, so thin, it was almost invisible. It had turned to face Ariel, who had seemingly lost her mind. She had yanked the hood off of her head, and had pulled one edge of it over her mouth, as though hiding a smile. More disturbingly, she was shouting words of a language that Bruce didn't recognize, although it sounded vaguely like the engineers he'd worked with from Delhi.

The hovering attacker apparently didn't find her antics humorous, for the whine of its wings surged up an octave as it accelerated, making a bee-line for her. Instantly, she whipped aside her mouth cover, threw her arms wide, and yelled, "Abort! Montana! Abort! Montana!"

It didn't abort, it made straight for her head. Bruce flinched involuntarily, expecting it to crash into her unprotected lower face, but at the very last minute, she swung her racket up. He had one quick glimpse of motion shooting upward. The deflection broke his spell and he sprinted to her. "Back to back?" he yelled, and she nodded and turned so that he could stand facing away from her.

He held his tennis racket in front of him. If the bastard appeared again, he'd be ready to smack it this time. He could hear the buzz, but couldn't tell where it was. It seemed to be above them.

"Oh, shit!" Ariel spat. "Damn, oh damn!"

Bruce followed her gaze upstream, expecting to see the malevolent little beast coming in low from that direction, but there was nothing, just the sun-drenched boulders bordering the rushing water. Then he saw motion, farther off—a man working his way along the path. It was Dick Armstrong.

Ariel was muttering, clearly debating her next move. Suddenly she shouted, "Go back! Run!"

Dick stopped, noticing them for the first time. But then he picked up his pace, hurrying forward. Bruce saw that he had a towel tied around the lower part of his face, as though ready to enter a burning building.

"Shit, oh shit!" Ariel continued to curse. She shouted again. "Sir! Go back! You're in danger!"

"His name's Dick," Bruce offered. He heard the buzzing sound change in pitch, and caught a flash of motion off to the left. He jerked his racket towards it, but it disappeared. It seemed to be cautious after having been launched once from Ariel's volley.

"Dick!" she yelled. "You're going to be killed if you don't go back, fast!"

He was closer now, and most of his face was hidden by the towel, but Bruce could see the pro-gun leader's eyes. They were fixed on Ariel with determination. He ignored her entreaties.

"Dick! She's serious!" Bruce yelled.

"I'm sure she is!" he called back, his voice muffled by the towel. "Lenny discovered your connection with the military. That's why you killed Ted."

"I didn't kill Ted, Dick. But I know what did, and it's going to get you if you don't leave now!"

"You'd like that, but you're not going to intimidate me."

Bruce noticed that the buzzing had disappeared. He relaxed a tiny bit, but remained wary that the lethal little beast might still be up to something.

"Dick," Ariel pleaded, "at least take off that towel. Do it now!"

"That's it, isn't it!" he shouted, almost hysterical now. "It's a gas!"

"It's not a gas, Dick. And even if it were, cloth wouldn't stop it. Come on, take it off now before it's too late!"

But it was already too late. The wings beat so quickly as to be nearly invisible, and if Bruce hadn't been expecting it, he wouldn't have noticed the black thumb-sized body from this distance, no farther than Lenny would have been from Ted, certainly not as far as Donald was from Angie. Dick heard it, though. His head jerked up, and the beast darted to the side, playing hide-and-seek with the man's line of sight. But the game ended as soon as it had started. The hovering menace seemed to disappear in a flash of motion, and a second later, Dick slapped his shoulder, pulling his hand away to stare at it, probably surprised that it was empty after such a penetrating sting. He turned his furious glare back to Ariel. "What the hell have you done?"

She didn't respond. There was nothing to do but wait, and it came quickly. He gave a little jerk, as though he'd fallen asleep for an instant and woke with a start. He put his hands to his head and took a step, but it was never completed. He crumpled to the rocks, as good as shot clean through the heart.

Bruce gave a little involuntary cry and started forward, but Ariel caught his arm. "Not yet," she said. She nodded towards the fallen man.

The towel had fallen away, and Dick stared emptily at the sky as the killer bird hovered a foot above him, staring back.

"What's it doing?" Bruce whispered.

"Face recognition," she replied absently as she watched intently.

"It's seeing whether it knows him?" Bruce asked, feeling a horror at the potential cold-blooded sophistication.

She threw him an annoyed glance. "Never mind. Forget that."

How do I forget something on command? he wondered.

When he looked back, the beast was gone. "Come on," Ariel said, and ran the hundred feet up the creek to where Dick lay motionless.

Bruce thought that she was going to see what she could do for him, but she didn't even look down, just stood with her finger pressed against her lower lip looking off into the distance, her pose of contemplation.

When Bruce squatted down next to fallen man, she told him not to bother, which he greeted with some relief, since he wouldn't have known what to do anyway.

He'd known Dick all his life, a dominant figure of authority, a man that the citizens of Powderhole naturally deferred to for guidance. And now here he lay, dead. The body lying twisted among the rocks looked like Dick, but with life gone, the corpse appeared horridly fake, like a macabre mockery left behind as a warning by the little flitting bundle of evil.

"It's the face coverings, isn't it?" he challenged. The question was out almost before he'd put together the common denominator—Angie's scarf and Dick's towel, and Ariel had mimicked one to draw its attention.

She didn't answer. She just gave him a look that said don't push it, bub.

His adrenaline was boiling, though, all capacity for cool analysis temporarily disabled. "It's some kind of drone, isn't it? Some kind of assassin weapon."

He might as well have called her a dirty whore. She spun and had his sweatshirt twisted up in her fist before he could even begin to react. "Shut up!" she growled, anger contorting her face into an ugly mask of passion.

But to Bruce it was simply confirmation. "It is, isn't it!"

She stared at him a moment, then let go of his shirt. She seemed to have accepted the inevitable. "Knowledge is power, but it can also be dangerous. Bruce, you have to stop asking questions. You have to trust me. You have to believe that I'm trying to do the best thing—the right thing."

Her earnest plea finally penetrated his panic. He nodded, suddenly feeling tired. "Okay."

Her anger had dissipated as quickly as his anxiety. She smiled a tight truce and put her hand lightly on his arm. "Thanks. I know that it must be frustrating, but believe me, I'm trying my best."

Her smile, strained as it was, presented such a contrast that Bruce wondered why he'd done anything to anger her in the first place.

"The military connection he referred to was DARPA," she explained. Bruce had to think a moment before remembering what Dick had accused her of. "The agency has been partially funding the General Aerospace project, then they pulled in Penn State."

Bruce had the sense that she was giving him a bone. No, more than that maybe, perhaps doing what she could to keep the connection between them from breaking.

"I thought you said that you weren't really part of the Penn State project," he replied, trying to remember if she'd actually said that.

"I'm not. I dug up the DARPA relationship on my own."

"In preparation for the part, pretending to be part of the Penn State project."

She shrugged. She didn't want this line of inquiry to go any further. She suddenly glanced around anxiously. "Come on, we'd better get out of here before it comes back."

"Where'd it go?"

"After a kill, it's programmed to immediately hide, but I don't know for how long."

"Programmed? Then it is a machine—a drone."

"Bruce," she said in a warning tone.

"Right. Knowledge can be dangerous."

But he'd said it, and she hadn't denied it.

ж ж ж

"You went to the coroner to see if he'd found poison in Ted, didn't you?" Bruce asked.

They'd made it up to the bottom of the second falls without another sign of the drone. If Ariel had an idea of what she was going to do next, she wasn't sharing, so Bruce was probing.

She glanced at him, and shook her head at his tenacity. "Actually, no. If the coroner had found poison, then I would have known that it wasn't . . ."

"The drone."

She sighed in exasperation. "Let's refer to it as 'the danger,' shall we?"

Which means that a drone is exactly what it is. "So the poison of the dro—the 'danger' is, like, short-lived. It breaks down or dissipates?"

"Very good, Sherlock."

"Hmm, you got the coroner to talk to you. That was a good trick."

She didn't fall for the bait. "Yep," was all she'd say.

Bruce knew that he wouldn't get any more in that direction. He remembered the marking. "I noticed that there was a symbol or something on the side of the . . . danger. It looked like running feet."

Ariel furrowed her brow. "I saw a marking, but it looked like a teardrop."

Bruce couldn't imagine how she would have interpreted a teardrop in the upside-down V stick legs he'd clearly seen. But it was surprising that either of them had noticed anything at all in the excitement.

More importantly . . . "You're not familiar with the markings on it?"

"No, I've never—" She stopped short and glared at him. "Nice try. I think we'd better hold the questions for now."

She stopped beside the rapids of the second falls and stood peering into the tangle of dead tree branches, the obstacle course through which they were about to pick their way. Bruce strained to see the blur of drone wings, and took a cautious step back, but what he heard was the thumping and crashing of something much larger. He saw motion and jumped back with a shout before recognizing a human face. "Donald!" he shouted. "Jesus! You scared me!"

The handsome man stepped into the sunlight. He looked at Bruce curiously. "Why?"

Bruce realized that someone was shouting a short distance farther up the rapids. It was Trish, calling for Donald.

"We're going up," Ariel explained, waving for Donald to turn around like he might be a bothersome fly.

"Where's Dick," Donald asked Bruce.

He glanced at Ariel, not sure what to say.

"He's down there," she reported, gesturing vaguely down the creek. "He's dead."

Donald's eyes nearly popped out of his head. "What! How?"

"He was stung by a bee," she said. Her response was so assured and convincing that Bruce had to remind himself that she was lying.

Donald wasn't buying it. "What did you do to him?" he growled. He took a menacing step towards her, but she held her ground so that they were nose-to-nose, or nose-to-chin.

"Donald—" Bruce started.

"You shut up!" he barked, pointing a finger at Bruce, but keeping his eyes fixed downward on Ariel. "What did you do?" he repeated to her.

"I did nothing to him. Why would I?"

"Stickltow found out that you're with the government."

"Because of the DARPA funding? I have nothing to do with them, but even if I did, what do you think DARPA is? Some secret branch of the CIA? They're a bunch of scientists who don't know which end of a gun the bullet comes out."

Donald stepped back and looked at them both. "Where is he?"

"Down along the creek—but you're not going down there."

"Like hell, I'm not. You're hiding something."

"You'll be killed, too, if you go down."

"Is that a threat?"

"Not in the least. Just an absolute prediction."

Trish's shouts were getting closer, but she seemed lost in the jumble of fallen trees. "Over here!" Bruce yelled.

Seconds later, she appeared from among the dead foliage, swiping irritating twigs away from her face. "Damn you, Donald!" she scolded.

He turned to her. "Are you in with these two?"

"In what?" she asked, glancing at Ariel, as though for guidance.

"Killing Dick."

Trish went instantly from sweaty and annoyed to shocked. "Dick's dead?" she repeated, looking at Ariel now with alarm.

The mysterious woman just nodded.

"Is it the same . . ." Trish started.

"Same what?" Donald demanded, his suspicion confirmed.

Trish glanced from him to Ariel, clearly at a loss. "The same thing that got Ted," she replied, but her tone was questioning.

"Yeah," Ariel answered. "It was a bee sting."

"A bee sting?" Trish repeated.

"Yes. Killer bees. And if we don't get out of here, they're going to start picking us off."

"Screw you guys," Donald snarled. "I'm gonna see what happened to Dick," he said and loped off down the creek.

"You should stop him," Ariel said to Trish.

"Donald!" she called, running after him.

He stopped and turned. Bruce sensed that he wanted to be talked out of it.

"Don't go," she begged.

He looked at her defiantly, but his eyes were pleading. "Why not?" he asked. The question challenged more than just the purported danger lurking below the falls.

Trish hesitated just a moment. She glanced at Bruce, and he imagined that she was asking forgiveness. "Because I care about you, Donald," she finally blurted.

He stood up straight and nodded slowly, as though this was the critical piece of information he'd been waiting for. "Fine. But we're going to get to the bottom of this yet."

Donald returned and led the way back through the jungle of twisted branches. Trish followed, and as soon as she was immersed in the foliage mass, Ariel caught Bruce's arm. He turned to find that she had her finger to her lips. "Remember—" she whispered.

"I know," he whispered back, cutting her off. "Don't worry. I won't say anything."

"Are you straight with the bees? We saw one sting Dick, right?"

He nodded and sighed. "Yeah, I got it."

She let go of his arm and nodded for him to follow the other two.

It seemed to him that she'd kept her hand on his arm longer than necessary. He told himself that it was just his imagination. His mind was as jumbled as the intertwined twigs he was thrusting out of his way. The death of first Ted and now Dick lay underneath all his thoughts, dreadful and dreaded, like a rotting footbridge upon which he was stepping fearfully, but with no alternative.

Above that frightful foundation danced conflicting pulls. He felt resentful that Donald had forced Trish's admission, overplayed as it may have been, and disappointed that she had cooperated. But the touch of Ariel felt like a subtle, maybe unconscious, invitation.

He stopped. Had he heard something? He held up his hand for Ariel to stop and be quiet behind him. There was just the rush and gurgle of the rapids. But suddenly, as though materializing out of thin air, something buzzed past his head, and he cried out and threw his arms over his head. Thoughts of love and sex evaporated under the scorching glare of death by poisonous sting.

"It's a dragonfly," Ariel said.

Bruce's heart settled slowly from his throat back to his chest.

Chapter 10

When they got back up to the parking area, Donald immediately sped off to tell Cab about Dick. Bruce was glad to have him gone.

"What got up his butt?" Larry asked, watching Donald's Camaro speed away.

"Dick's dead," Bruce explained.

Larry stared, open-mouthed. "How?" he finally asked.

Bruce glanced guiltily at Ariel. "A bee sting."

"A bee sting?" Larry repeated, incredulous.

"Killer bees," Ariel qualified, taking off the mail jacket.

"You knew about the bees before you went down," Trish said to Ariel. "That's the reason for the Halloween getups?"

Ariel nodded as she pulled the mail hood off, allowing her silken, blonde hair to fall seductively across her face and shoulders.

"How did you know?" Trish asked, suspicious.

If Ariel picked up on the skepticism, she didn't let on. "The coroner."

"I thought you said that he was still looking into it," Trish objected.

"I wanted to be sure before I caused unnecessary panic," she replied.

"Wait a second," Larry protested. "I've read about killer bees, and it's not like they're actually poisonous or anything. They can just be more aggressive." His eyes went wide with alarm as he realized that he was arguing with a beautiful woman. "But, you know, that's just what I've read."

"No," Ariel agreed, "you're correct. These aren't really killer bees, at least not the kind you've heard about. These are genetically synthesized versions that have been created specifically as a terrorist weapon. And they are very lethal."

The alarm that had opened Larry's eyes wide was now replaced with apprehension that left him gaping. "Seriously?"

Ariel shrugged as though she didn't care one way or another if he believed her.

Bruce wasn't sure whether Trish was buying it so easily. She watched Ariel carefully, as though waiting for a fatal slip.

"Who would do this?" Larry squeaked.

"Al-Shabab," Ariel replied, looking him square in the eye.

"Al-Shabab?" he repeated, aghast.

She nodded. "Out of Somalia."

"Those bastards!" he exclaimed, punching his fist into his open palm.

She shrugged.

Trish nudged the titanium case lying in the grass, with her toe. "I presume the bees were dropped in this?" she asked.

Ariel gazed at the case a moment, then looked at Trish. "Yes."

Trish finally gave in to her doubts. "Wait, you're telling us that Al-Shabab has just made a terrorist attack on America?"

"No, that's not what I'm telling you. This is probably just an experiment. They want to see how effective this batch is."

Trish struggled with the outlandish information. "How do you know this?"

Ariel sighed. "I'm really sorry, but—"

"I know, you can't tell us. Shit."

Trish wasn't discounting what Ariel said, just expressing frustration at the situation. She looked at Bruce for confirmation of the maddening state of affairs.

Bruce just shrugged. There was nothing else he could do. He wasn't prepared to blow Ariel's story. He trusted that she had an inside scoop, and just prayed that she was on their side in whatever this devilment entailed. But he very much hated being part of a deception against Trish—and Larry—and his face felt hot with shame.

Ariel declared that they needed to get back to town, and nobody disagreed as they threw wary glances towards the opening in the trees to the path, Trish and Larry watching for genetically fabricated monster insects, and Bruce for the insistent buzz of artificial wings.

Their effective leader also instructed that Bruce should ride with her—they'd meet at Cab's house, where they would presumably find Donald spouting about murder plots. Larry suggested that maybe he should leave his car and ride along with her as well, but Ariel shook her head without replying. Trish was looking at Bruce as he climbed into Ariel's rental car. She seemed curious about the riding arrangement, but he wasn't sure whether it was because she suspected the truth—that he and Ariel were in cahoots—or if she was wondering whether Ariel desired his company. Although he hated to admit it, Bruce was hoping that it was the latter.

Ariel cleared that up as soon as his door was closed. "Are you sure you've got the story straight?" she asked.

Nope. He was there because of the cahoots.

"Well, let's see—we weren't attacked by some man-made drone with a poisonous needle for a snout, but by Frankenstein bees that Somali terrorists somehow managed to deposit in the Pennsylvania countryside so they could see how many people the little buggers killed."

"Other than the unnecessary hyperbole, that'll do—except that we agreed not to refer to it as a drone."

"Because that's exactly what it is."

She didn't answer, concentrating instead on pushing her rental car faster than was safe for the country road.

"What're you going to do when we get to Cab's place?" he asked. "He's probably already called in the State Police. They have to come from Hazelton—probably be here within the hour."

She waved it off. "That's fine."

But Bruce sensed that it wasn't fine, that she was worried about facing a six-foot, square-jawed, no-nonsense trooper in a crisp gray uniform.

"You promised not to lie anymore," he said. It was still difficult risking her disapproval.

She glanced at him, and he wasn't sure if her look was annoyance at him or the situation. "I'm not happy about that," she replied, leaning into a turn that forced Bruce to push against the console to keep from ending up on her shoulder. "The—what we found down there—that changed everything. I hope Trish and Larry will forgive me." She threw him another glance, checking his reaction. "Bruce, you have to believe me, it's for their own good."

"And not yours?"

She took a deep breath. "I didn't say that. I am trying to . . . contain the situation—that's why I'm counting on you to play along and keep the truth under wraps for the time being."

"How do I know that you're not lying to me?"

She chewed her lower lip a moment, then threw him a sympathetic look. "You don't, at least not absolutely." She reached over and put her hand on his arm, like she did at the bottom of the second falls. "Bruce, all I can do is ask you to trust me. I've let the other two slip away, but I promise—I promise that I'll be straight with you." She gave him a searching gaze that lasted so long, Bruce was terrified they'd catapult off the road. "It's you and me, Bruce. We have to stick together and count on each other. Can we do that?"

It sounded so phony, so scripted. Her hand still lay lightly on his arm, and the warmth seemed genuine.

"Okay. Fine. But we have to come clean at some point. Trish and Larry have to know the whole story."

She smiled and put her hand back on the wheel. "Of course."

"Promise?"

"Yes. I promise that as well."

Bruce sighed and then gasped as she ran through a stop sign at the beginning of town. They hadn't established when "at some point" would be, but he decided not to push it.

Ariel stopped short in the middle of the street near Cab's house. "Shit!" she uttered, frantically putting the car in reverse and backing away half a block.

"What's up?" Bruce asked, peering around for some clue, wondering if maybe she'd seen one of the drones

"It's Walker," she replied. She glanced at him, her brow furrowed in worry. "He's—the insurance investigator."

"The man with the red hair."

"Yeah," she replied distractedly.

"How do you know he's here?"

She nodded, indicating through the windshield. "That car has Virginia plates."

He searched and found it, a black Chrysler 300 parked in front of Cab's house. These people had a soft spot for black cars. "You recognize the car?"

"I recognize the parking sticker on the windshield."

A man in a suit stepped out of Cab's front door and stood on the porch. He looked up the street in the opposite direction, and then turned and looked directly at them.

"Ah crap," Ariel, said. "Time to face the music."

She slowly pulled forward as the man stood and watched them. She spoke to Bruce, but didn't look at him, staring straight ahead. "Now you have to play along—" she started.

"But, I don't understand—"

"Shut up. If Walker finds out that you know about the drone, I'm not sure which will be more dangerous, him or the drone itself. All you know is what we've told Trish and Larry—Ted and Dick were killed by bees. Do you understand?"

"Yeah, sure. But this guy doesn't have red hair."

They were close enough to see that the man had hardly any hair at all, and what he had was dark brown.

"That's not Walker," she explained. "Now keep your mouth shut if you can."

She pulled up to the curb in front of Cab's house. The man came around and opened her door. He seemed trim and fit, and if not for the nearly bald head, could have had a career in Hollywood. Perhaps to distract from his dome forehead, he wore a dark, neatly-trimmed beard. He didn't say anything. He just stood waiting for her to get out.

"How's it going, Bert?" she asked pleasantly as she stepped out.

He just nodded in response.

"Walker inside?"

Bert sighed, as though bored with her questions. "Yeah."

"How's his mood?"

"Fine, Miss La Rochelle. It's always fine."

Bruce understood the unspoken meaning. *You should know I'm never going to actually answer a question like that.*

Bruce assumed he should follow, so he got out as well. Bert glanced at him, but then ignored him. He could now hear that Cab was talking loudly inside the house. In fact, he was shouting. Bruce couldn't hear the other end of the argument, and it sounded as though Cab was shouting to himself.

"We'd better go in and find out what's brewing," Ariel suggested brightly. She might have been talking about a party they were late for.

Bruce followed her across the lawn, up the porch stairs, and through the front door, which she opened without knocking. Bert brought up the rear.

The constable was standing in the middle of his living room, facing a large man sitting sprawled comfortably on the sofa. The man had close-set eyes and broad, sagging cheeks, reminiscent of a late stage Nixon—the ugly duckling opposite of handsome-Bert. Although his doughy, mottled complexion suggested many years of neglect to proper diet, his hair was full and youthful. It was also red.

Cab stopped mid-shout and turned when they came through the door. "Finally!" he shouted at Ariel. "I thought you were going to follow me!"

Nobody paid attention to his protest because Walker spoke. "You've created quite a mess here," he said calmly, addressing Ariel. The quiet voice belied an inherent power—his perfectly modulated voice somehow rendered the simplest observation a commanding directive, and his beady eyes held your gaze like they had physically grasped your eyeballs.

"Have I?" Ariel replied. Her tone was still light, but Bruce thought he detected a trace of tension.

Walker waved his hand across the room, taking in Cab and Bruce. "You've involved citizens."

Citizens? Bruce thought. *What is he? A member of an invading army?*

"I've involved citizens?" she shot back, her light tone hardening. "Have I been reconfiguring outside approval protocol?"

"Have I?" he asked.

She looked at him out of the corner of her eyes. Bruce could tell that she was boiling. "Come off it, Walker. The jigs up."

"The 'jig' has hardly begun, my girl."

Bruce thought that she'd throw a punch at the diminutive address, but she held her temper. She turned to Cab. "Have you told him?"

"You mean about Ted? Oh yeah, I—"

"Fine," she shot back, cutting him off and then turning back to Walker. "Now there's another one dead—Dick Armstrong. What the hell?" she asked, leaving the ugly man to interpret the rest.

He lifted his hands in mock-horror. "The good constable tells me that you've been poking around the old hermit's place."

"What are you implying? That I'm the cause of the men's deaths?"

He merely lifted his hands again. His meaning was clear.

Bruce assumed that the reconfiguring referred to the drone. He had the idea that Ariel was somehow not under Walker's direct authority, at least not in a formal hierarchy. It was impossible, though, not to be influenced by his natural authority.

Cab had had enough. "Everybody just shut up!" he yelled, and they all looked at him. "I don't know who you folks are, but I've got two dead townspeople, and I'm going to get some answers one way or another. You tell me what's going on right now, or I'm calling the Sheriff. So, what is it?"

Walker glanced at Bert who stood at the door, apparently guarding it—whether from people entering or leaving, Bruce wasn't sure.

"It's killer bees," Ariel blurted.

"What did you say?" Cab asked.

"It's a special breed of bees that can kill with one sting."

Cab just stared at her, wide-eyed. Walker watched her as well, but his expression was one of curiosity.

"Where'd they come from?" Cab finally asked.

Ariel threw Bruce a quick here-we-go glance. "Somalia—Al-Shabab terrorists. They've been developing them in secret. They've apparently decided to test them here, in Powderhole."

Cab stared at her, transfixed. He finally turned to Walker, who just lifted his palms and shoulders in a gesture indicating that maybe she shouldn't have spilled the beans, but there you are.

"That's ridiculous!" Cab declared. "How did they get here?"

Ariel returned his incredulous stare with calm assurance. "They were dropped in a titanium case from the air. That's the meteor that Dagmar reported."

At this, one of Walker's eyebrows inched up ever so slightly. "You've recovered the case, then?" he asked.

Ariel nodded.

His eyebrow inched up a couple of millimeters more.

She shook her head. "Just packing foam," she replied to the unspoken query.

"Hold on!" Cab yelled. "We're talking about killer bees. Are you serious?"

Ariel nodded solemnly. Bruce found her false sincerity disquieting.

"You believe that they killed both Ted and Dick?"

She nodded again.

"Well, holy hell! We have to call the FBI!"

Walker shook his head dismissively. "They'd just call us."

"Who the hell are you?"

Walker just returned Cab's stare.

"Well, whoever you are," Cab went on, "you're just sitting around. The next person might get killed any minute."

Walker took a deep, impatient breath and heaved his bulk to his feet. "We've got it under control, Constable," he said.

Cab shook his head. "I don't think you do! I'm calling the Sheriff. I'm going to ask him to call the governor and get the National Guard in here!"

Walker snorted and laughed. "You think you're going to get the National Guard here with a couple of phone calls?"

"I've got to try," Cab affirmed with determination as he stalked out of the room.

Walker nodded to Bert, who had quietly moved to follow Cab. Walker's flunky called to Cab, and as the Powderhole constable turned around, Bert grabbed him with one hand by his wrist, and the other by his neck. "Take it easy," Bert cautioned.

At that moment the front door burst open, and Donald stepped through. He was holding a shotgun in both hands. He held it up proudly to show Bruce. "They didn't stash all the guns in the vault," he explained with a smug grin. "Leslie kept one behind." Donald then seemed to notice Cab, and reflexively lowered the tip of the barrel towards Bert, who also operated on reflex and a handgun appeared as if by magic in his right hand. "Put it down," Bert warned.

"What's going on?" Donald asked, genuinely confused.

"Put it down, Donald," Cab instructed, his voice strained from the neck-hold.

Bruce had gone hunting in his youth enough to know that after a while handling a shotgun became second nature—your hands knew what to do. When relaxing from a firing position, you naturally set the safety switch. For convenience, this is usually placed near the trigger. So when Bruce's finger automatically moved to push the button, Bert misinterpreted the motion.

Constrained in the small room, the gun shot seemed to explode like a bomb. It took a moment for Bruce to recover from the shock, but when he did, he saw that Donald had fallen to the floor. A red splotch on the tan shirt over his heart broadcast the horror. The fourth citizen of Powderhole was dead.

Chapter 11

Bruce stared at Donald lying dead on the floor. He'd known Dick and Ted all his life, but they were from another generation. Bruce's gut reasoned that if Donald could die, then anyone of the gang—Larry, Trish, or he, himself—could be next.

A part of him registered that Ariel and Walker were talking. Ariel had uttered a nasty expletive, and Walker had cursed the stupidity of the young man, but their emotional reactions lasted all of ten seconds. Bruce turned to find Walker speaking to Bert about what to do with Donald's body, and Ariel was holding the dazed Cab by the elbow, talking urgently. Her words were soft and Bruce didn't catch the gist. Bert motioned for Ariel to help him with Donald, and Walker led Cab away into the kitchen and closed the door behind them.

Bruce was left to stand in the middle of the living room as Bert and Ariel half carried, half dragged Donald down to the basement. A fog gummed up his thinking, and he wondered for a moment what they intended to do with him down there before realizing that they were simply getting him out of sight. Bruce was suddenly overwhelmingly tired, and he sank down in Cab's recliner in the corner. His hand shook as he reached out to ease himself in. Despite the August warmth, he felt cold, and pulled Cab's comforter over him.

It slowly dawned on him that these people—Walker, Bert, and yes, Ariel—were above the law, or at least considered themselves to be. They had to be with some agency of the government, something clandestine.

He didn't mean to spy on them, but when Walker came out from the kitchen behind an ashen-faced Cab a few minutes later, the dough-faced operative didn't notice him tucked away in the dark corner. "Your job now is to keep people out of our way, understand?" Walker said.

Cab nodded dumbly. He was blinking a lot. He'd been the constable in Powderhole for years, and in all that time, the only deaths he'd ever had to deal with were accidental or suicides, and there weren't many of either.

Walker put his finger against Cab's chest and held it there. "You can be useful as the constable. You'll want to stay useful, understand?"

Cab looked at him and the blinking stopped. He nodded.

"Now go outside and make sure nobody comes in. Somebody may have heard the gunshot. Your gun went off accidentally, right? Nobody was hurt."

Cab frowned. "I don't have a gun."

Walker waved it off impatiently. "Useful, remember? Use your head and play along. Now get out there."

Bert appeared in the basement doorway, and Ariel came up right after him. Walker said to Bert, "Time to seal it. Tell Mike," and gestured towards the door.

"How did you know to come back?" Ariel asked Walker after Bert left. She was all business, focused on the situation.

"You showed the coroner your ID."

"I had to, otherwise he wouldn't have cooperated. The remnant juice would have completely dissipated if I'd waited any longer."

"Well, he called the FBI after you left."

Ariel just nodded. That Walker would find out about that call was apparently a given.

Bruce figured that the "juice" was the drone's poison. She'd probably had to guide the coroner in the specifics of the test to detect any trace remnants.

"Where's the case?" Walker asked.

Ariel hesitated, as though deciding what to say.

"You're not going to give me trouble, are you?" he asked, but it was more of a rhetorical question, a warning.

She shook her head. "It's in the car, I'll get it."

Walker took his phone from his pocket and punched a call as she went out the front door, then put it to his ear. "Mike, it's me," Walker said. "Have you found it?" He stared out the window as he listened to the response, then said, "It's going to be a metal box about the size of a small closet with a door, usually mounted on a cement base. It's probably right off the highway." He listened. "Well, call me when you find it—and nobody leaves, understand? Nobody."

A closet-sized metal box near the highway. What could that be? A stash of high-powered weapons? It seemed improbable.

Ariel came back and handed the titanium case to Walker, who immediately opened it and then looked at her. "Where's the other half of the foam?"

"Wasn't there when the old hermit gave it to us. It must have fallen out."

Walker stared at her a moment. Bruce thought, *These people spend a lot of time deciding who's telling the truth.* He finally nodded and closed the case.

"You did reconfigure it, didn't you?" she asked.

He didn't answer.

"Look," she urged, "we've got a terrible mess here, and our imperative is to contain and clean—you know that. You have to let me help you."

He took a deep breath and blew it out slowly, staring out the window again as though making sure the answers weren't sitting on the lawn. He finally nodded. "It wasn't actually me, of course."

"But you specified it."

He puckered his mouth, seeming to have difficulty admitting it, but then nodded again.

"I guessed you had—I'd pretty much concluded it, actually. But I couldn't get the details. Your crew's very loyal."

Or scared shitless, Bruce thought.

"You've created a real monster," she declared.

That seemed to snap Walker out of whatever doubts or regrets may have been weighing on him. "I finished the design," he stated.

"It looks like you added back all the behavior that was ruled too risky."

"Risk equates with gain."

"We don't deal in risk. We can't afford any more slip-ups, not after Benghazi, not after El-Masri."

Under the Bush administration the CIA had held and tortured Khlaed El-Masri, a German citizen, in Afghanistan for four months before finally admitting that they'd made a mistake. So Walker and Ariel were CIA. Or maybe not—maybe the President just didn't want any more clandestine operations blowing up.

"I've created an operative that is truly effective," Walker refuted. "The risk would have been doing the job half-assed. That's when you get caught. Effective is getting out undetected after a clean kill. Failing that, the next best thing is getting out without getting caught. The unit has to return, that's the imperative. Its program now makes that possible."

"By allowing it to be aggressive to the point of malicious."

Walker shrugged his agreement.

"Well that aggression has wiped three civilians."

Walker just stared at her, refusing to support what he probably viewed as a damning admission.

"You also extended the needle," she noted.

He shrugged again.

"You know, it's figured out that it can get through clothes now. That's how it took out the last civilian."

Walker sighed, feigning fatigue with her interrogation.

Ariel added her own sigh, one of exasperation. "What I don't understand, though, is why you tried to transport it off record. That was just stupid." She seemed to be working up a head of steam. "It fell off the copter! You strapped it in along with loose baggage! Are you nuts?"

"Risk equates with gain," he repeated.

"And risk can screw you to the wall!" she yelled.

She stopped and took a calming breath. "Well, like I said—the jig's up now. You have to call the office. We need all the help we can get."

He stared at her and shook his head ominously. "Not until I recover it."

"Why? You think that's going to somehow get you out of trouble? You know you're in a shit-load of trouble."

He looked at her. Bruce could almost see the options and contingencies spreading like tree branches in his brain. He shook his head again. "I have to see it through. It's my mess."

Ariel returned his glare. She didn't seem to be buying it, but she let it go. "It wouldn't abort," she said. "You obviously changed the code word, it's no longer Montana."

He shook his head. "It's still Montana, but I added an adjunct—a visual, something not obvious."

Walker's attention was drawn by an argument outside. Bruce could hear Cab's authoritarian tones, balanced by an equally determined woman's voice. The argument got louder, approaching the door, and Cab's commands changed to pleading. Trish burst through the door, followed by Cab, with Larry bringing up the rear, smiling at the entertainment.

Walker put up his hand to halt the mob, then pointed his finger menacingly at Cab. "I told you. Stay useful, or else. Now get out of here, all of you."

Cab turned to Trish, as though seeking her help.

"Who the hell is this?" Trish demanded, pointing at Walker.

"They're here to help," Cab explained. "But we have to stay out of their way."

"Help?" Trish, asked. She turned to Ariel. "Is this true?"

"Yeah," Ariel replied. "Please do what he says."

"And I say 'Out!' " Walker ordered, herding them towards the door. "Nobody else comes through that door, constable. And I mean nobody."

As Walker was slowly pushing the three back, Bruce decided he'd better come out of hiding. When he stood up, Ariel's head snapped to the side, her eyes wide with surprise, and then her brow furrowed. She glanced at Walker, but he was still occupied with his purge. She looked back at Bruce and shook her head the tiniest bit in warning and motioned for him to step forward.

Trish wasn't taking her forced exit willingly. "At least tell me if you're here to help with the bees."

At this, Walker stopped and held up his hands. "What did you say?"

"The bees!" Trish repeated angrily. "What are we going to do about the killer bees?"

Walker turned and gave Ariel a menacing look. "They know about them," she said.

Walker's gaze had locked on Bruce. "Where was he?"

"Upstairs," Ariel lied. She looked at Bruce for support.

"I had to go to the bathroom," he explained, joining in the lie.

Walker didn't like it, but Trish and Larry obviously posed a greater threat. "Did they see . . .?"

"No." Ariel replied.

"See what?" Trish asked.

"The bees," Ariel replied. To Walker, she said, "I told them."

"What about him?" he inquired, tilting his thumb towards Bruce.

"No," Ariel said, practically jumping on his words. "He didn't see them either."

Trish and Larry exchanged glances. Bruce caught Trish's eye. Walker was still looking at him, so all he could do was look at her. But she seemed to get it. She gave a little nod, and glanced at Larry to make sure he understood as well.

"You're either with the government or Al-Shabab," Trish said to Walker, "and I'm going to take a wild guess that it's not Al-Shabab. So, which part of the government?"

Walker seemed to be deciding whether to answer. "The FBI," he finally replied.

Bruce looked questioningly at Ariel, but she shook her head the tiniest bit.

Larry was watching Cab curiously. "Hey, man, you okay? You don't look so good."

"He's just shaken up," Ariel explained for him. "The bees," she elaborated.

Trish pointed at the carpet where Donald's blood had soaked in, leaving a dark patch in the dark blue nap. "Cab, what happened here? It doesn't look like water," she observed, squatting down and reaching out to touch it.

Walker blocked her with his foot, and she fell backward. "Hey! What the hell!" she exclaimed.

Ariel gave a little groan of exasperation. "It was for your own good," she quickly assured, stepping forward to help her up. "It's—" She glanced at Cab, who was just staring stone-faced. "It's battery acid," she finished. "It would burn you."

"Cab!" Trish admonished. "You have to get that up! Or at least dilute it with lots of water. It's going to eat right through the carpet."

They all looked at Cab, but he'd checked out. Bruce wasn't even sure the man was listening.

"It's already ruined," Ariel said.

"Still—" Trish started.

"Enough with the carpet!" Walker barked. "It's not important."

Trish was surprised at the harshness. "How about Dick? Is that important?"

"Dick?" Walker asked impatiently. "The last one wiped?" he asked Ariel.

She nodded.

"Wiped?" Trish repeated, aghast. "Is that what the FBI calls it?"

Walker just looked at her and cocked his head, annoyed at the trivial concern. "Killed," he corrected. "Dick was killed. Is that better?"

"Well, what about him?" she insisted.

"Don't worry about him. He's dead."

"We can't just let him lie down there! Animals will eat a human corpse, you know. I can't believe you're so callous. If this is how the FBI works, I'm writing my Congressman."

Walker's response was delayed as his phone chimed in his pocket. He turned away and pulled it out.

Bruce watched Trish as she waited impatiently to get back on Walker's case. He was impressed. The gal had spunk. He found this appealing. Maybe the average man expected women to be docile, but if so, he figured he just wasn't average.

"—just hold tight," Walker was saying into the phone. "But keep the access sealed—and I mean tight. Tighter than your sphincter will be if you let anybody through."

Bruce thought that this sounded ominous. What were they sealing? Maybe access to the falls. Somehow he wouldn't have taken a bet on that.

To Bruce, Trish said, "I'm going home. Give me a call later, or stop by."

She turned to leave, but Walker grabbed her upper arm with a grip so tight she cried out. "Ow! What the hell?" she protested, twisting loose.

"Where do you think you're going?" he asked.

She glanced at Bruce, incredulous at the man's boorish behavior. "Unless this is a formal FBI interrogation, I don't think I have to answer that. But I will because I'm nicer than you. I'm going to tell my mom and step-father to stay in the house with the windows closed, and I would think you'd be spreading the news to everybody to do the same."

"No," is all Walker said.

"You don't care if more people are killed by the bees? This takes the cake!"

"No. It would just cause unnecessary panic."

"It should cause panic! One sting and you're dead! That's panic-able!"

"Be quiet."

"I won't be quiet! You have a responsibility—"

Walker slapped her across the face, and she stood staring, shocked, holding her stinging cheek.

"I said, shut up!" he shouted, his bread-dough face finally taking on some color. "Christ! Did you tell anybody else about them?"

She wagged her head slowly, still obviously shaken.

"What about the dead man—Dick. Did you tell anybody about that?"

She wagged again.

He turned to the rest of them. "How about everybody else? Has the information left this room?"

There was silence for a few seconds, then Larry cleared his throat.

"Who'd you tell?" Walker asked him.

"My mom. I called her."

Walker stared at him, and Larry seemed tensed, ready for a smack across the face. "Like Trish said, they have to stay safe in their houses. It's my mom!" he added.

Walker took a deep breath and held it a moment, then took his phone from his pocket, dialed, and put it to his ear. After a moment, he spoke. "Okay, do it. Make sure you get all the cables. When you're done, try calling me back. If the service is out, then just stay at the barricade. Otherwise you'll have to jump on the cell tower as well."

Walker jabbed at the phone, and slid it back into his pocket.

Bruce now understood. His company—his former employer—developed high speed digital switches that were used as part of the country's broadband communications network. He'd become familiar with the basic components of the internet and cell phone infrastructure.

"You told him to take out the local remote terminal," Bruce guessed, amazed at the seemingly irrational destruction.

Walker just glared a warning at him.

But Bruce was so astounded that the warning didn't properly register. "That's probably the backhaul route for the town's cell towers—there's two, by the way. So, taking out the terminal effectively cuts off both land lines and cell links—all traffic with the backbone."

"Bruce, what they hell are you saying?" Trish asked.

Bruce suddenly felt a cold chill. The glare from Walker now loomed as a very real threat. But he'd already spelled out the situation. There was no use holding back the final inch. "They've cut off all communication with the outside world," he stated, looking around the room. Trish and Larry were confused, but Ariel seemed resigned and worried, like when the passenger in your car tells the cop standing outside your open window that, yeah, you're coming from a party where there was lots of booze.

Suddenly the front door burst open, and Jack Weitzel, who owned a small dairy farm up the valley, burst through. He came up short at the crowd inside, but his eyes found Cab standing off to the side, still in a daze. "Cab! What's goin' on? There's a roadblock on both sides of the highway loop. I can't get out of town!"

Cab finally spoke up. "We know, Jack. You're just gonna have to be patient. We have a . . . problem."

The farmer shook his head in consternation and took his own phone from his pocket, opened it, and looked at it.

"It's dead," Bruce assured.

The man looked at the collection of people filling the room. "What the hell is going on?"

Bruce was wondering the same thing, and feared that he was going to find out.

Chapter 12

"I say we take a peek," Larry urged for the second time.

"Go ahead," Bruce replied. "Let me know when you're ready so I can stand in the corner, away from the storm of bullets."

His friend continued to punch the pillow. He'd been doing that absentmindedly for the last ten minutes. "This is kidnapping, you know," he reminded them. He was anxious and bored.

"Yeah, you're right!" Bruce agree, feigning outrage. "I'm going to tell the FBI—wait a second—they are the FBI!"

"Still," Larry insisted, punching harder, "they can't just, like, disregard the constitution."

"Larry," Trish reprimanded, "you're going to ruin that."

He tossed the pillow back on the bed, presumably the guest bed, since this didn't look like a master bedroom.

Walker had told them that they had to stay in the room until he came for them. He'd said that he was going to wait outside until one of his agents returned to take over. He'd warned that he couldn't take responsibility if they so much as poked their heads out. Bruce guessed that he would have locked them inside if that had been possible, but bedrooms lock from the inside. Walker probably would have locked them in the basement, except that there was a dead body down there.

Bruce felt like punching something as well. He was still a little nauseous over Donald, and to have to keep it from Trish and Larry—on top of the whole bee and FBI fabrications—was just tearing him up. He felt like a traitor. As they were being corralled up the stairs, Ariel had thrown him a surreptitious serious little nod, a reminder to keep quiet.

And that was the real crux of the problem: he wasn't sure if he even trusted her. She sure seemed to be on the same side as Walker, despite their spats.

"You don't actually think there's anybody out there, though, do you?" Trish asked Bruce.

He shook his head. "I'm sure Walker and his goons have better things to do than guard us."

"Better things?" she questioned.

"Okay, more important things—or more consequential things."

"Maybe we should take a look," she suggested tentatively.

Bruce shrugged. "Sure. Larry, go stick your head out."

At that moment, though, they heard footsteps outside, and they looked at each other, surprised and alarmed that they'd been considering venturing out.

The footsteps faded down the hall.

Bruce suddenly made a decision. "Listen guys, I . . ."

Trish and Larry were looking at him, waiting.

But then he flopped the other way. There was a reason Ariel didn't want them to know more. Walker could be dangerous. He was clearly protecting the real source of Dick and the others' deaths, and he hadn't flinched when Donald was killed right in front of him.

But there was more to it, and Bruce had to admit this. He wanted to stay in the good graces of Ariel. Not because he thought she was the voice of justice and reason here—he couldn't wrap his head around that decision—but because she was a beautiful woman. He felt ashamed to admit that, even to himself, but it was true.

"What did you want to tell us, Bruce?" Trish finally encouraged.

He looked at each of them in turn—Larry, his friend since as long as he could remember, whom he knew like a brother, and Trish, a new friend, but one who it seemed he'd known as long as

Larry. He felt a complete rapport with her, as though their thoughts clicked together like meshing gears. *Like she was a soulmate.* Oh geez, he'd sworn he'd never use that tired term.

He couldn't deceive them any longer.

"Guys," he started again, "I know some . . . things."

They just watched, patient and trusting.

"Ariel asked me to keep them to myself."

His friends words came on top of each other as Larry said, "Tell us!" and Trish said, "Be careful."

"Once you tell us," Trish went on, "you can't take it back. And she obviously has a reason for keeping it secret."

Bruce chewed his lip. "Oh Christ," he muttered. "it's not just abstract stuff about the dangers down at the falls—"

"Dangers beside the bees?" Larry cried excitedly.

"—it's also something really personal," he said, ignoring Larry. "Really, really personal."

Trish claimed that she hadn't actually been dating Donald, but how could she not be horrified at the killing?

Trish put her hand on his arm, just like Ariel had. "Bruce, you have do what you think is right. It's okay if you can't tell us. We trust you—right, Larry?"

"Sure! But tell us anyway!"

Bruce sighed. "Larry, sometimes you act like a kid, you know that?"

"You're probably right. Now tell us."

They stopped and looked at the door as the footsteps returned and halted just outside. The door opened and Ariel stood there looking at them a moment before stepping inside. "I'm not sure if Bruce has told you anything," she said, "but he knows a few things that I've asked him to keep to himself for now."

Trish looked at Bruce, and he wondered if his face was as red as hers.

"I need to borrow him for awhile," she went on.

"It's okay," Larry urged. "You can tell us everything. Particularly the other danger down at the falls."

Trish hit Larry in the chest with the back of her hand, and Bruce said, "I didn't say anything—he's just guessing."

Ariel hardly acknowledged it. "You two have to stay in the room, though."

"Walker's not here, is he?" Trish guessed.

After a moment, Ariel shook her head. "But I'm asking you to stay in the room anyway. It really is for your own good."

Trish held up her hand for a pause. "Ariel, something very serious is obviously going on here. I don't think there's any bees, otherwise I'd already have been out that door warning people." She turned to Bruce. "Do you want us to stay here?"

He felt himself being torn—skin, bone, and organs—right down the middle, from the little tuft of hair in the middle of his forehead that refused to lie flat, all the way down to his crotch.

He nodded. "I'm sorry."

Trish put her hand on his arm again, her touch gentle. "Nothing to be sorry about. We trust you."

Bruce looked into her brown, soulful eyes, and felt his torn organs melting.

He resolved that he would earn that trust.

But not right now. First he'd have to see what this capable, beautiful, and enigmatic woman wanted from him.

Ariel closed the door behind him as they left and led him down the stairs to the living room where Donald had been shot. "Walker's gone off to retrieve the drone," she explained quietly.

Bruce shrugged. "Good. Retrieval sounds like the right thing."

She wagged her head a little. He wasn't getting it. "He went alone. He insisted that he go alone. He claims that the other two agents—Bert and Mike—need to man the roadblocks in-and-out of town, and that I need to stay here to keep an eye on you three."

"Which I'm guessing you don't intend to do."

"Correct."

"You're going down after him aren't you? It's too dangerous for him to go alone."

"Yes, but not because he's in danger—which he definitely is—but because I'm suspicious. He was too adamant about me not going along."

"I have to tell you," Bruce confessed, "I don't really get it. You and he are obviously on the same team—same secret government agency, whatever—but he hasn't seemed to trust you from the start. Hell, you two seem like adversaries."

She nodded, gesturing for him to follow as they left the house and walked to her rental car. "You're right—we're both part of the same . . . agency, but not exactly on the same team. A few years ago Congress set up an oversight department within the agency—"

"I don't remember that," he said as they got into the car.

She glanced at him as she pulled away and drove down the street. "You're still assuming we're part of the CIA, but you wouldn't have heard about it in any case. Anyway, select congressmen get to peek inside some of the secret stuff that goes on behind the curtains."

"Now that sounds dangerous."

She smiled. "I'll hang onto my personal opinions about that, but whatever the congressmen's competencies, it's better than no accountability at all."

"So, you're presumably part of this oversight department."

"That's right. My colleagues are mostly desk jockeys, doing electronic investigation, which is essential, no doubt, but that's not for me. After I got my degree, I realized that I couldn't spend my life sitting in a chair all day long."

"Degree?" Bruce inquired.

She waved it off, as though it wasn't relevant. "Law. I've had my eye on Walker for nine months now. He's 'old school', you get the job done by whatever means necessary—the end justifies the means. I think he's used to the times when clandestine meant that whatever you felt you needed to do would be kept under wraps. The office would clean up after you, and if you could still finish your mission, then you got a promotion—cold war mentality."

"I can see how his generation would need some oversight."

"Not everybody's like that, not at all. But he has old friends in key positions."

"And he's obviously not happy about having someone—a kid, in his eyes no less—looking over his shoulder."

"Exactly. Anyway, he tapped into one of his crony contacts to access a new highly secret weapon—"

"The assassin drone."

"I wince every time you call it that."

"Because it's true?"

She ignored his probe. "It was so secret, in fact, that I couldn't even find out what it was, at least not directly. I had to piece together mostly inferences. At first I thought it was some kind of special gun, but then I began to glean that it comprised a poison delivery system, and that it could fly. I knew that a whole lot of effort had been invested in programming it, so it was a safe bet that it was an automated device, pretty intelligent. The picture wasn't complete, though, until it was hovering in front of my face down there."

"Both you and Walker came specifically to talk to Dagger. It was because he'd reported a meteor, and you knew that Walker had tried to transport it by helicopter."

She took her eyes from the road a moment. "You heard the whole thing?"

"Uh, yeah. Are you going to have to kill me now?"

"No," she said, way too seriously. Bruce sat looking at her, not sure how to take this. But after a few seconds she looked at him again and grinned. "You thought that was a possibility?"

"Well, not you, personally."

She nodded agreement, but it was a qualified agreement—an agreement that she wouldn't have to kill him. "What about Walker?" he asked. He tried to make it sound casual, but it came out a bit squeaky.

She shook her head, but there was no grin now. "Not for the things that you overheard."

"Yi!" he exclaimed. "That's not exactly a reassuring answer. There is information he would be willing to kill over?"

She shook her head forcibly. "Don't worry. There's nothing you heard—or will hear—that's as valuable as that."

"But he would if necessary."

"You know I'm not going to comment on that." She glanced at him again to make sure he'd heard her.

He'd guessed that she wouldn't. Maybe this was the biggest secret of all—just how far the inner sanctums of the government would go to keep other secrets secret.

"There's one thing I don't get, though," he went on. "Why'd you come to Powderhole when Walker had already checked it out?"

"For one thing, he was still looking farther along the transit route, meaning it was still lost. For another, he'd given it less than a day here. I thought he might have missed something. And there was Angie's death. He discounted that too quickly."

Bruce nodded. It made sense. "But you knew that it was dangerous, assuming it survived the fall from the copter. Otherwise we wouldn't have been wearing the Halloween outfits when we went down."

"Sure. Of course."

"And that it was even more dangerous because of his re-programming."

Bruce was fishing, and she knew it, as demonstrated by her annoyed glance.

"You heard that as well," she noted.

"You're still not going to kill me?"

"Give it up, already."

"I gathered that he programmed it to be more aggressive so that it could get away after its—job—without being caught. That's the worst thing that can happen, isn't it? Having the enemy capture your assassin."

"Sure. Without the assassin—human or otherwise—in your possession, the assassination, or attempt, is just hearsay. No matter how damning the evidence, the political advantage to holding up the actual culprit for all to see has no comparison."

"Gary Powers," Bruce suggested.

"Exactly. When the Soviets shot down his plane and captured him, it was a huge embarrassment for the US, and torpedoed Eisenhower's talks with Khrushchev. And that was just a spy mission, not even an assassination."

"I'm surprised, then, that Walker had to arrange this aggressive behavior reprogramming on the sly—I'd have thought that it would have been welcomed from the get-go."

She shrugged. "You could also use a nuclear bomb to take out a dictator."

"Ah, collateral damage could be bad publicity."

She twisted her mouth to the side in disapproval. "Partly that, sure, but there are people in the agency that actually place a value on human life. On the other hand, it is part of the government."

"Meaning . . .?"

"Meaning the place is infested with politics. There was a faction, Walker's crony friends, that wanted more aggressive behavior, but the conservative group—the more careful group—had the ear of the President and won out. I believe that this drone mission was supposed to prove the viability of the aggressive approach. It was a huge risk, though, breaking from program directives by secretly reprogramming the drones. The old-school cronies were worried enough that they put a monitor on Walker. I'm sure he doesn't even know this."

"Spies spying on their own spies?"

"Sure. Never trust, always verify. I doubt Walker would be surprised, though, that his friends set up a watchdog to look after him."

Bruce considered this. "You said that the drone is probably pretty sophisticated—intelligent is the word you used."

"Yeah, that's right," she replied, waiting for the rest.

"Intelligence implies learning from experience."

"Okay, so?"

"You already noted that it's figured out that its needle can pierce most clothing."

"Yeah—what're you getting at?"

"Just that Walker's trying to recover it, but the drone's getting more dangerous, more difficult to capture by the hour."

"He doesn't have to capture it 'alive.' "

"The abort sequence."

"Right."

"Uh-huh. What about us?"

"What do you mean?"

"Do we know the abort sequence?"

She didn't say anything as she pulled into the grass parking area next to Walker's Chrysler. She turned off the engine, took out the keys, and looked at him. "No. He didn't tell me the last part."

"The visual part."

"Yeah."

"So, what about us?"

"You mean if it attacks us?"

"Ye-ah," he replied letting his exasperation show. He knew that it was fear.

"We're going to stay out of sight. The idea is not to have it attack us."

"That is a good idea. But what if?"

She lifted her shoulders, and he had the sense that she was considering this, and the fact that she didn't have an immediate answer inflated his fear by half. "We do our best," she finally offered.

"Our best," he repeated, dispirited. "What if we . . . damage it? You know, in defense?"

She considered this a moment longer. "So be it."

"Are you sure? Because I have to tell you, I don't intend on spending a lot of effort trying to capture it. Not when one kiss drops me dead to the ground."

She nodded, more sure. "They made three drones. If this was the only one, then it would be a completely different story."

"Really? Because they, like, broke the mold?"

"Yes."

"You're kidding."

"No. They didn't destroy the design intentionally. It was bureaucracy at work. That last government budget shutdown triggered an automatic failsafe process set up to protect all highly secret development. The contracted vendor tried to avoid it, but by the time the request went up the command chain, and permission trickled back down, most of the design files were indeed destroyed. They're frantically working to re-produce the design, but for maybe a year, these three prototypes are all they've got. But that assumes that they have a sample—one of those three—to reverse-engineer. Otherwise, it would probably be more like two or even three years."

He chuckled mirthlessly as they got out of the car.

"What's so funny? The endless comic relief of governments in inaction?" she asked.

"The irony of it. They force a full federal shutdown over battles that are supposedly about saving money, and then waste billions because of it."

"I just work for them, I don't set policy," she said.

Bruce thought of something else. "You pulled your hood over your mouth when you drew the drone away from me, but you yelled to Dick to take the towel *away* from his face—what was that all about?"

It was disconcerting how quickly her face contracted from an open smile to a tight storm of agitation. "Forget about that," was all she said, then went to the back of the car and opened the trunk.

Bruce stood in silence, surprised by her reaction. He had to know, though. "That's one of those things Walker might kill over, isn't it?"

She didn't answer, and didn't nod, just gave him one piercing glare.

Suddenly, a boom whumped in the distance. It would have been alarming if it wasn't so familiar to Bruce. It carried him back to his youth, roaming free among the fields and forests surrounding Powderhole.

"What the hell was that?" Ariel demanded.

"A farmer," Bruce said.

"That's how they butcher a cow?"

He smiled, glad to have her distracted from her anger. "Stumps. They use dynamite to clear new acreage."

She shook her head as she tossed her bag in the trunk and slammed it closed.

Even now, years removed from the carefree life of a rural kid, the startling blasts somewhere in the near distance could carry him through time and distance to an imaginary battlefield. Battles had changed in the decades since the Great War, however. Roaring B52 bombers had been replaced by smart cruise missiles.

Bruce stared off at the opening in the trees where the path began its long descent to the Susquehanna. Bygone battles, fought in theaters of massive conflict had evolved to cat and mouse forays, where stealth was king—guerilla terrorists embedded in the population and secret countermeasures hidden from public view.

When the value of the countermeasures depended on secrecy, and that secrecy was threatened, the battle could turn 180 degrees.

Walker and the drone—two dangers, two evils—dancing around each other, and God help anybody who got in their way.

Chapter 13

"I feel naked," Bruce confessed.

Ariel glanced at him. "You're not naked. I can see clothes."

"Ha, ha."

He had felt silly and encumbered in the ski pants and fencing mask, but now as they came to the end of the tangled thicket below the second falls, he would have paid handsomely to be back in the hot clown outfit. As difficult as the mass of foliage debris was to navigate, he assumed that it would be equally difficult for the drone. The rush and gurgle of the rapid-flowing water could camouflage the buzz of its approach, and he constantly scanned back and forth, forward and behind, until he was making himself dizzy.

Ariel noticed the nervous swiveling. "Don't worry—if it sees you and decides you're a danger, there's probably nothing you could do about it anyway."

"That's supposed help me stop worrying?" he asked.

"It should," she replied, as she squatted just beyond the tangle of limbs and peered down the creek. "Worrying about something you can't control is just wasted brainwaves."

"They teach you that in secret agent school?"

"I think I learned that in first grade," she answered and waved for him to follow as she carefully made her way back into the trees. "And 'secret agent' is so sixties," she added.

"What would you call yourself?"

"A government employee."

"Fine. Call yourself whatever you want, but the only reason the word 'secret' isn't included is because it's too secret."

She'd apparently had enough of the repartee, for she remained silent, stepping quietly through the ground cover along the boulders bordering the creek, keeping ever watchful of the open expanse ahead. After a few minutes, she held up her hand, and he stopped. "Hear that?" she asked.

He did. Somebody was blowing a whistle, two or three toots, and then a pause for some seconds before repeating. "It doesn't sound like a call for help," he observed.

"It's not," she replied. "It's a call for attention."

She moved on before he could query her. She moved more quickly, seeming unconcerned about being heard. Bruce had to scramble to keep up. "It's Walker, isn't it?" he asked when he managed to get close to her.

"Yeah," she replied curtly. She didn't want to talk, she wanted to make progress.

After a while, she gave up the pretense of staying hidden, and moved out onto the path again. Bruce hesitated before following. If it sees me, there's probably nothing I can do about it.

She was gone! He realized that she'd literally sprinted off alongside the creek, nearly dancing atop the mass of boulders. He took off after her, resisting calling out for her to wait up. Rational or not, he couldn't help tensing his back, waiting for the sting of death.

He caught her at the top of the third falls. She was looking down the waterslide, and must have heard him approaching, since she held up her hand behind her for him to stop. "What is it?" he whispered.

He thought that she hadn't heard him over the sound of the water. But then she pointed, and he saw him. Walker was below, sitting against a boulder beside the catch-pool at the bottom of the slide. He had his knees pulled up to his chest, and his arms tight against his sides. He continued to blow the whistle. It looked like the beefy man was just amusing himself while keeping warm.

"He's using the rock to cover his back, isn't he?" Bruce asked.

Ariel gave a quick nod.

"Is the drone programmed to come to a whistle?"

"No," she said impatiently. "It doesn't need to be."

Walker suddenly stood up.

"Here goes," Ariel muttered.

Bruce couldn't see the drone, but Walker held up his hands, palms out, fingers tilted towards each other, as though warding off something invisible. Then Bruce discerned a fuzzy ball the size of an orange floating five feet in front of his hands. He heard Walker call out, "Montana," over and over, each time louder and more determined than the previous. The words echoed among the rocks, so that a multitude of Montana's merged together into one earnest chorus.

"Why doesn't he use the visual cue?" Bruce asked, ready to burst from tension.

"I don't know," Ariel replied, clearly as apprehensive.

Suddenly the indistinct ball of hyper-beating wings disappeared in a smear of motion upward. Bruce held his breath, and a second later, Walker jerked, trying to slap his back, but unable to reach. He whirled around, flailing at the air, but the drone seemed to be gone. Then he put his arms down and stood very still a brief moment before collapsing to the ground.

"Good God!" Ariel hissed and ran down the uneven path.

"Wait!" Bruce cried. He had the opposite urge—run in the other direction and hide. "Damn," he muttered and ran after her.

Ariel reached the fallen man seconds in front of him, but she just stood looking down at the victim. When Bruce arrived, out of breath, he understood why. Walker wasn't dead—he wasn't even unconscious. He lay there completely still, but a stream of angry curses filtered up from his downturned face. He rolled over and looked up at them. "What the hell are you doing here?" he growled. Bruce had the sense that the two of them were a mere annoyance. The man responsible for re-programming the drone was truly pissed off at his creation.

"Are you okay?" Ariel asked, astounded.

"Oh shit, yeah," Walker replied, patting his torso. "Vest," he said in explanation as he got up on hands and knees, and then, grunting with effort, stood up shakily.

Bruce guessed that he meant a bullet-proof vest, though Walker's bulk made it hard to tell.

Walker continued to curse, and Bruce realized that it wasn't the drone but programmers behind it he was so furious with. The expletives were vivid and exotic—and thus distracting—but Bruce gathered that a "stupid shit-head Christian meathead," presumably one of the drone's programmers, had committed some kind of double-cross. Walker seemed fixated on the double-cross, and Bruce wondered if this programmer was maybe some kind of mole.

Bruce could feel his back tensing again. "Maybe we should leave," he suggested.

Walker absorbed his presence for the first time. "Why the hell did you bring him?" he asked Ariel. "Did he see it?"

Uh-oh.

"Look," Ariel said seriously, "maybe we should get out of here. I'll explain everything once we're safe."

Walker waved off her concern. "It'll stay hidden at least ten minutes. That was a big mistake bringing him along—"

He froze, eyes wide.

Bruce heard it, too. The high-pitched whine was approaching again, coming in very fast. Walker started to turn, but jerked and screamed. He slapped his neck, but his hand came away empty. He looked at them and horror swelled in his eyes. "Fuck!" he said, and slumped to the ground.

The incessant buzzing was still there, loud and very present. Bruce wanted to run, but he wasn't sure in what direction. Then he saw the drone—it was motionless, floating over Walker's now lifeless face. Seemingly satisfied, it rose a couple of feet and zoomed away, the miniature chainsaw buzz fading quickly until it was gone, merged with the rushing sound of water.

"He's dead?" Bruce asked unnecessarily, staring at the lifeless hulk.

"Oh, yeah," Ariel concurred. She had squatted down next to Walker, and was pushing against his side as though trying to wake him up.

"What are you doing?" Bruce asked, aghast that she'd be so cavalier with a corpse.

"Shut up and help me," she said, grunting against the weight.

"Help you what? What're you doing?"

"Roll him over! Don't be so dense!"

He gave up trying to understand, knelt down next to her, and shoved. When they'd managed to roll hundreds of pounds of flesh and bone a quarter turn, Ariel reached with one hand underneath and extracted his wallet. "Okay," she said, letting her load drop. "Let's get the hell out of here." She took off at a trot up the path.

With one last glance at the sightless eyes, Bruce took off after her, his ears straining for the distant buzz of returning death.

He caught up with her a minute later. "You don't want anybody to get his ID," he guessed.

"Brilliant, Sherlock," she shot back.

"Hey!" he objected. "I didn't ask to come on this horror safari!"

She sighed and glanced at him as they made the top of the third falls. Walker lay in the near distance below them, an inanimate contribution to the lumpy contours of the boulder landscape. "Sorry," she said. "This has just gone all to hell. God-damn that Walker!" she exclaimed.

"Why did it come back so soon?"

She just shook her head, disgusted. She was scanning the area below the waterslide that they'd just left. "This is what happens when you let crony cowboys run their own private show unchecked."

"You mean the re-programming," he offered.

She sighed again. "Yeah. This is probably why the conservative faction decided to pull out the motivation loops in the first place. They predicted this."

"Motivation loops?"

She shot him a quick glance. "You're the engineer. You tell me."

"I'm hardware, not software," he explained. "But it may be AI components. You can program a computer to do almost anything—pattern recognition, trend prediction, even psychological analysis. It could have a hundred sophisticated algorithm sub-tasks, but the hard part is to decide what tasks to do, and how to correlate the results, what the next rational course of action should be."

"It's programmed with a mission," she reminded him. "It already knows what it's supposed to do."

"That's fine if the whole sequence of the mission is predictable. But what happens when something goes off-script? It needs overarching guidelines to give it perspective when analyzing options."

"Motivation," she concluded.

"Walker told you that its imperative was to return from the mission without being caught, and you accused him of making it aggressive to the point of being malicious."

"That's great, Einstein, so what do you think recursive reinforcement is?"

"That's part of its programming?"

She shrugged. She either didn't know, or didn't want to commit to the fact.

"Recursive reinforcement," he repeated, mulling. "It sounds like maybe it's modifying its own operating parameters based on the results of its actions."

She was looking at him knowingly.

"It's learning!" he concluded.

"Now you know why it came back so soon."

"It's able to change something as basic as that in its programming?" he questioned.

"For only a hardware engineer, you're on a roll."

"Holy shit!" he concluded.

"Indeed," she agreed. "We'd better get going," she added, but immediately grabbed his arm. Her eyes were pure alarm.

Then Bruce heard it. The sound that set his spine tingling. "Where is it?" he whispered, trying to peer in all directions at once. The damn buzzing whine was hard to locate among the echoes.

He could tell by her continued swiveling that she didn't know either. She gave up and searched the ground.

"What are you doing?" he asked. Raw panic urged him to run for his life.

"Find a club," she ordered. "A stick."

He looked, but he only saw flimsy twigs buried between the stones. Ariel had found a foot-long branch that looked half rotten. He realized, though, that the drone wasn't exactly a muscular wild beast. He finally settled for the largest twig he could find, which was hardly thicker than a pencil, and barely as long as Ariel's decrepit club. He debated whether to run into the trees for something substantial, but Ariel cut short his indecision. "Back-to-back!" she called.

Bruce guessed that she now had the drone in sight, and he scrambled over to her, stumbling and nearly falling, then turned to press his back against hers. He was gasping for breath. His lungs seemed paralyzed.

A moment later it arrived. It whirled around them once, just a flick of motion, and a rasping burr of angry wings. And then, as though forming out of thin air, it was a hand's width in front of his nose. The black unliving gloss of window-eyes stared at him. He could see the glint of the needle extending towards him, pointing an uncaring finger of death at him. He felt the breeze from its wings blowing in his hair.

And then it was gone, but not departed. The whining sound of flight had moved behind him. Bruce imagined it was studying Ariel in the same fashion.

"It's not sure what to make of us," she said quietly. "It's never seen a person with two heads."

Bruce knew that it wouldn't take long for it to decide to attack. Its motivation was still the imperative. It had probably concluded by now that witnesses—all witnesses—were dangerous. "Should we club it?" he asked.

"If you can."

Not exactly confidence.

They seemed doomed. Bruce couldn't imagine the drone just giving up.

His mind raced madly for some angle—an approach that would give him the advantage. The whine modulated, and an instant later it was back, hovering in front of his face. He slowly lifted his twig and then swiped. The drone danced away deftly, and was back in exactly the same position before he'd even finished his swing. He might be smarter than the evil little devil, but it could literally run circles around him when it came to speed. He knew that the bastard's little brain was clicking along at a million tiny micro-thoughts a second.

Damn it, it was a machine. It couldn't really think, not truly. It could learn, though. That was the damnable part.

But—learning came with its own risks. Venturing outside the predictable bounds of the program led into unknown territory, where dangers could come at you from unexpected directions.

The thought quickly flowed into a plan.

"It's attracted to covered faces, isn't it?" he asked.

Ariel didn't answer.

"Hey! Do you want to die? Now's not the time to worry about secrets. Is it, or isn't it?"

"Yes, it is."

"Okay. I have an idea. Pull up your shirt and cover your face."

"What are you—"

"Just do it! Please. Unless you have another idea."

"Okay," and a moment later, "it's done."

Sure enough, the drone whipped around to check out the activity, and Bruce took a deep breath and twisted around so that his stomach was pressed against Ariel's back. "Keep your arms in," he instructed, and reached slowly around on each side of her.

The drone hovered in front of her. He knew that it was surely his imagination, but Bruce would have sworn that the whirr of beating wings had risen an octave, the drone's version of an angry growl.

He raised his left hand, slowly, slowly. The drone rotated slightly to face it. The bare flesh felt pathetically vulnerable, like he was putting his head in the lion's mouth. He flexed his fingers in random contortions, hoping that this would confuse the little brain, at least for the moment. As his left hand reached its position, fingers wiggling away, he slowly raised the right one, the one holding the twig. At this motion, the drone rotated in that direction, but, holding his breath, Bruce flicked the fingers of his left hand at the little inanimate beast. It danced up and away, and when he pulled his fingers together into a fist, it returned to the precise same position. He flicked again, and again the drone swooped up, out of the way. By the third time, the drone was catching on, and it merely moved off to the right side and back again. It was learning.

This was it. The fourth time had to be the charm, because he knew there would be no fifth. He flicked the fingers of his left hand and simultaneously swatted down with the twig.

The result was astounding. The drone was gone. Not gone, but no longer in their face. The smooth whir of hyper-wings had degraded into a jumbled mash of sputters, clicking, and wildly modulating buzzing as it bounced and flopped its way around the rocks at their feet. Bruce could hear the metal tinkle of the deadly needle bouncing off the stones. He'd obviously damaged one of its wings.

Ariel jumped away, shouting, "Get back! Don't let the needle touch you!"

Bruce did as instructed, hardly needing her urging.

"What'll we do?" he asked. He had to practically shout above the racket of the micro-machine's floundering.

Ariel ran into the woods. A moment later, she returned with a leafy branch that she must have pulled off a tree. She approached the crippled monster carefully and swung the branch down, over the bouncing chaos. She got it. From underneath, they could hear the madly beating wings flailing at the leaves, cutting them to shreds. Seconds later, it bounded up and out, once again flopping about like an over-sugared five-year-old at a birthday party.

Leaves obviously weren't going to work. Bruce started to pull off his T-shirt, but realized immediately that it would be impossible to throw it accurately. He needed something heavier. No time for modesty. He unbuckled his jeans and yanked them off, losing his balance in the process and falling painfully on his tail bone. When he stood up in his boxers, Ariel grabbed one pant leg, and handed him the other. They walked over to the frantically struggling assassin, one on each side, and simply dropped the pants on top.

This did the trick. The jean material was too heavy for the drone's wings to lift. It lay under there, immobile. The rattling racket had ceased. Only slight movements of the cloth indicated where it was trapped.

Bruce lifted his foot to stomp on it.

"Whoa!" Arial yelled. "I wouldn't do that."

He looked at her. "Don't tell me you want it alive."

She shook her head and approached it. "The needle could pierce your shoe." She chose a large rock, lifted it, and brought it down on the tiny movements of cloth.

Bruce found the crunch extremely satisfying.

Chapter 14

"I can't walk around in my underwear!" Bruce protested.

"I still need your help," Ariel said, as she used her stick to carefully lift his jeans off the smashed drone.

"What's that supposed to mean? Why can't I help you with my pants on?"

She peered at the remnants of deadly miniaturized technology. "I need you alive." She prodded it with the tip of her stick, as though making sure it wasn't faking.

This gave Bruce pause. "Because of the poison?"

"They don't call you Sherlock for nothing."

"You're the only one. So, you think the poison may have, uh, gotten on the inside of the jeans?"

He was looking over her shoulder. Other than obviously damaged wings, the little torpedo-shaped device looked intact. No, he saw that there was also a crack running down the length.

"I don't know, but do you want to take a chance?" She didn't wait for an answer. "What do you think powers it?"

Now that he thought about it, it seemed almost miraculous. The most sophisticated battery technology known might keep it in the air for ten minutes. Even if it had some means to charge itself between flights, he'd already seen it outlast any known power storage.

At least, any power storage mechanism that would be available for public use.

"Do you think it's, like, radioactive?" he asked, feeling an urge to move a few dozen steps back.

"I have no idea," she answered, "but I can confidently assume that whoever developed it wouldn't have been told to put health and safety at the top of the list."

"Right."

Even if it didn't use plutonium or some other radioactive material, anything that stored that much energy in such a small package could essentially be a bomb waiting to be triggered. They were lucky that it hadn't blown up in their faces—or blown their faces off.

"Here, help me," she instructed.

Bruce held the disabled drone in place using her stick while Ariel began carefully rolling up the pants leg. "Wait," he said.

"Why?"

He prodded the little robot back and forth. It seemed extraordinarily light, as though made of just paper. "The symbol," he replied, pointing.

She leaned in and took a close look. "You saw little running legs," she recalled, "and I saw a teardrop, but we were looking at different sides—two halves of one symbol." A symbol that could only be seen when looking down from above. "It looks like . . . isn't that the symbol for female . . . or maybe life?"

She moved aside so he could lean closer. "I don't think so. It looks familiar, though, sort of like alpha. I think I can feel the gamma rays burning my face," he said, sitting back, then jumped up when he felt cold stone through the thin cloth of his underwear.

"I think you're imagining that."

"Maybe, but I don't want to find out."

Ariel continued rolling it up into the pants leg, and then the rest of his jeans, until she had a ball of cloth, which she picked up and cradled under her arm. "Let's go," she said, starting up the path.

"Er," Bruce noted, "you're holding it, like, a foot from your . . ."

"From my what?"

"Your ovaries."

She stopped and looked down at her potentially radioactive package. "You're right. You want to carry it?"

"Hell, no."

He heard something. Faraway voices. Voices arguing, in fact.

"Shit!" Ariel cried. "Don't we get any breaks?"

"What's the problem?"

He'd be happy to see people—thrilled, in fact. Five minutes ago there were two dangers to his life, and now both were gone. *I want to celebrate.* That thought was immediately followed by shame. No matter how much of a jerk he was, Walker didn't deserve to die.

"This!" she exclaimed, holding out the ball of denim. "That!" she yelled pointing down the falls, presumably meaning Walker's body.

"Right."

A nasty mess to clean up.

"It sounds like they're coming down," he said.

Ariel dashed into the trees, returning empty-handed.

"You gonna remember where you stashed it?" he asked.

"Good point." She studied the terrain. "That dead tree leaning against the other one," she decided, pointing.

The arguing voices became louder and more distinct. Bruce could now tell that one of them was definitely Trish, and the other sounded like Leslie. Looking up the creek through the sparse brush hugging the sides, he saw that these two had indeed emerged from the debris tangle of the second falls . . . and that more people were emerging after them. And more.

"Judas Priest!" Ariel exclaimed. "Your friend was supposed to stay put. It looks like she convinced the whole town to commit mass suicide."

Bruce couldn't make out the words, just the tone. "Sounds like she's trying to stop them."

At least a dozen men had followed Trish and Leslie through the debris tangle, and more were coming through.

"A cattle prod, that's what we need," Ariel muttered, starting off at a trot in their direction.

Bruce followed close behind. She'd want to intercept them as far from Walker as possible.

As he got a better view, Bruce saw that everybody except Trish was carrying a gun—rifles and shotguns, mostly, although Leslie had a pistol—a high-end Glock—which he held ready to shoot at a moment's notice.

When they saw Ariel approaching, they stopped. Trish seemed relieved to see them. Her eyebrows went up, though, when she saw Bruce in his underwear.

"What's the meaning of this?" Ariel called in a commanding voice.

"You tell us!" Leslie called back.

Bruce stopped short when the angry little man lifted the pistol with two hands. Ariel paused just a moment before continuing on.

"Put the gun down, you idiot!" Trish yelled. "Can't you see? She's not armed!" She reached out and pushed his hands down. He let them stay down, but kept the gun ready.

"You're interfering with a government investigation," Ariel warned as she reached them and stood directly in front of Leslie, the obvious leader. A half dozen more men had arrived, and the mob had spread out, possibly to provide wider coverage, but more likely just to hear better. Three or four whom Bruce thought of as Leslie's cadre—men who, although not nearly as radical, nevertheless took every opportunity to proclaim their patriotism, implying that yours was wanting—stood closest to their excitable leader. They held their guns ready, while the rest of the men, farmers and factory workers, cradled the barrels of their rifles and shotguns in the crook of their arm, the traditional method of carrying a gun at rest.

Leslie leaned forward belligerently but Ariel refused to back off, leaving their noses practically touching. "Your game is over, comrade," he snarled. "Now give up or die."

Ariel came even closer and spoke into the twisted face. "Put the gun down, or you will be arrested for interfering with a vital government operation."

"I don't think so," he snarled, and lifted the pistol so that the tip rested against her belly.

"Jesus Christ, Leslie!" Trish's shout hardly registered with Bruce as a flash of motion ended with one of Ariel's arms around

Leslie's neck, and the other clenching his wrist behind his back. He still held the gun, now pointed off behind him.

"Take it," she instructed.

Bruce didn't realize at first that she meant him. Leslie's cadre were pointing their rifles at Ariel. One of them swung his to aim at Bruce's chest.

"Take it before he drops it!" she ordered. "It could go off."

Bruce reached in and grabbed the barrel. The pinned assailant struggled to hang on to his gun. "You filthy traitor!" the scrawny man yelled and a second later, the gun exploded—at least, that's how it seemed to Bruce. But Leslie had let go, and Bruce stepped back holding the pistol.

"Anybody hurt?" Ariel asked. She was met with shocked silence. "You better hope not," she said into Leslie's ear. "Do you have it?" she asked Bruce. When he confirmed this, she let Leslie go, pushed him away and then took a step back in case he tried to take a swing at her. She faced the armed cadre with a steady stare. "Put them down," she ordered. They looked at Leslie who shook his head, and they remained in firing positions.

Bruce glanced at the other dozen or so men. They stood looking at their feet, not happy with the way things were going. He handed the pistol to Ariel, but she waved it off. He didn't know what to do with it, but wished he could get rid of it. Holding it felt like he was challenging the cadre, drawing their fire.

"Where's Walker?" Leslie demanded, rubbing his neck where Ariel had pinned him.

Ariel gestured vaguely down the creek, but didn't explain. Instead, she asked, "What the hell do you think you're doing down here? Do you think you can shoot bees with rifles?"

"The rifles are for you and Walker," he replied. "And him," he added, pointing at Bruce. "We know there's no bees. We're on to your game."

Ariel glanced at Trish.

"They didn't get that from me," she explained. "Leslie just figures that everything you say is a lie."

Bruce noticed that Trish had positioned herself closer to him. She was taking sides.

"Damn right!" the disarmed leader acknowledged. "Lying through your teeth."

"What 'game' am I supposed to be up to, then?" Ariel asked.

Leslie glanced at his cadre. They were his audience. "Terrorism," he replied confidently.

"I'm a terrorist," Ariel repeated, derisively.

"Yep."

"Are you insane?"

Leslie's eyes went wide with fury. "You watch it, bitch!" He glared at her.

Ariel shook her head incredulously. "Look, I'm with the federal government, part of a security department. So are Walker and his men. There were bees, but we've taken care of them. Now we have some business to deal with, and if you'll just stay out of our way, we'll be gone, and you can get back to your own business."

Leslie sneered. "Lies, all lies. The government wouldn't take a whole town hostage."

"What in God's name are you talking about?"

"You know goddamn well. Your comrade's have blocked all the roads and cut the telephones. But you miscalculated. You figured that all Americans were lily-livered liberal sheep. Wrong, commie!"

With this, he took a step forward, but stopped when Ariel lifted her pert little chin and clenched her fists in front of her.

"You killed Ted and Dick," he continued, "because they were on to you. Now Donald's missing—you've probably got him tied up somewhere. Al-Shebab, hell. You're probably one of them yourself!"

"You really are insane, aren't you?" Ariel taunted, and Leslie came at her. This seemed to be what she was after as she grabbed one of his wrists and landed a fist on his jaw. Bruce guessed that this was for the others, his cadre. She wanted to establish that she wasn't some frail little girl to be pushed around. A couple of deft moves later, and she had the commie hunter on the ground, but she quickly stood back to let him get up.

Just then, one of the cadre shouted, "Les!"

All the men had turned their attention to the tangle of debris, and even the farmers moved their shotguns to positions ready for firing. Bruce heard it. There was something coming through the jungle of tangled gray limbs. A final thump, rattle, and shake of leaves, and Jessie, the pizza delivery boy, stood frozen, staring at a dozen gun barrels pointed at him. "Oh, shit," he whispered.

"God damn, boy!" one of the farmers admonished as he let his barrel fall. "You almost got yourself killed!"

The teenager glanced around, reconnoitering the situation until his eyes found Leslie, and he went over to him. Ariel didn't intervene when the two stepped away to talk in lowered voices.

Trish was standing next to Bruce, and he suddenly had an overpowering need to explain about Donald. He wanted to tell her before his body was discovered in Cab's basement. He hesitated, though, fearful of her reaction. Instead, he opened with, "We heard an explosion before. That was Leslie blowing the vault, wasn't it?"

She nodded, rolling her eyes. "He was way too gleeful about it. The man had a whole crate of dynamite. He's completely destroyed the bank building . . . listen, I want you to know that we stayed in Cab's bedroom like you asked. Leslie showed up with Cab. He seemed to be in shock—"

"Cab, not Leslie," he guessed.

"Oh, yeah," she said. "He seemed cowed by Leslie, like he was fine that somebody else was taking charge."

Bruce knew why Cab was dazed. He had to tell her about Donald.

"Anyway," Trish continued, "Larry and I tried to stop them, but Leslie is like a little bull. He'll just bowl you over."

"Actually," Bruce said, "I think terrorists capturing Powderhole would be the high point of his life." He decided to start with a smaller confession first. "Listen, Trish. Ariel made me swear silence, but I think we're past that now. Those bees she's been talking about—"

"The ones that don't actually exist," Trish added.

Bruce paused and nodded. "That's right, they don't. But her fib wasn't too far off. There really was something like a bee that could kill you."

Trish was studying his face, catching every clue available. "What is it?"

"It's not what it is, it's what it was—we . . . killed it. I probably shouldn't give you too many details yet—"

"Of course," Trish chided, but a little grin peeked through. She didn't really blame him.

And that's when Bruce found out that he'd waited too long. "Okay!" Leslie called to the group, breaking his huddle with Jessie. "Here it is! We've broken out!" He waited dramatically, baiting the farmers and factory workers. "We got the terrorist who was blocking the north highway—"

"What do you mean, you 'got him'?" Ariel barked.

Leslie was all sneer. "We killed him! He's dead!" He basked in that a moment. "Fred got it too, unfortunately, but we managed to get somebody out, going for help."

"You mean Fred Simmons?" one of the farmers asked.

"Yeah. Too bad," Leslie replied, not seeming at all broken up by the news.

"Jesus!" the farmer exclaimed, absorbing the shocking turn of events. They all looked on with furrowed brows. This was way beyond what they'd bargained for.

"But there's more!" Leslie cried. "We found Donald in Cab's basement!"

The group stood waiting, guessing the drama wasn't done yet.

"They shot him!" Leslie cried like a preacher finally hitting the point of the sermon. "They shot him and tried to hide his body down in a dark basement! Ted, Dick," he enumerated, ticking the dead men off on his fingers, "and now Donald! They're blood-thirsty murderers!"

The man had a gift for firing emotions, Bruce decided. He could see why his cadre were loyal followers, and why otherwise peaceful working men could be induced to action.

Trish gasped, looking at Ariel and then Bruce with horrified eyes. "Did you . . . did you know?"

How could he explain that it was an accident? That he certainly had no part in Donald's death? That he was about to tell her!

He didn't have a chance to even try. "Hey!" one of the farmer's off to the side yelled. He was holding his cupped hand to his ear. "You hear that?"

"What?" Leslie asked, irritable at being interrupted.

The farmer looked at them, mystified, but also alarmed. "I think it's a . . . bee!"

A blur of motion zipped over the group and disappeared as it arced away beyond the other side.

The sound of the mechanical wings was all too familiar to Bruce. "Holy shit!" he exclaimed, in awe. "There were two!"

Chapter 15

"No, not two," Ariel rasped, almost a growl, stepping close to Bruce and Trish. "I think there's three!"

"Three?" Bruce repeated, feeling the hairs on his neck raise as he tried to peer in all directions at once.

She looked angry, but as though she'd half expected this disastrous turn. "The packing. In the case. I thought it was odd that Walker was so intent on finding out what happened to the top half."

Ariel pulled him down into a squat, maybe to reduce their target area. Trish followed suit beside them, watching them intently.

"I don't get it," Bruce confessed.

Ariel flashed a little irritation. "The packing would have been form-fitted. It would clearly show that it was made to transport three drones." She glanced at Trish. "You're now sworn to secrecy," she added, without waiting for agreement.

"Where are they?" Bruce wondered. "Why don't they attack?"

"They're probably reconnoitering. Don't worry. They will."

"How do you know?"

She shook her head, a little acknowledgement of the pickle they were in. "They wouldn't have shown themselves otherwise."

Bruce blinked. Three of them. Three brothers. Identical triplets. No, not quite identical. "The first one was the alpha," he stated.

Ariel looked at him, a question.

"The symbol," he explained. "Alpha is used to indicate the first item of something."

"So, these two are, what? Beta and Omega?"

"Beta and Gamma," Trish corrected.

"Beta and Gamma," Ariel repeated, looking up and around, waiting for the inevitable.

All the others—Leslie, his cadre, and the rest—were standing. They huddled in small groups muttering and glancing around, not realizing that they made large, easy targets. Everybody now had their guns up and ready.

Everybody except Leslie, that is. The frantic leader was calling for them all to listen up. "There's no bees! I told you! The whole story's just a distraction."

"I saw it!" one of the farmers shouted.

"It was probably a humming bird—"

"No flowers down here," the farmer reminded. No nectar meant no humming birds.

"A swallow, then! I don't know and I don't care! But there's no God damn poison bees! Forget about them!"

The farmers continued to argue, and Ariel leaned in close again. "With luck, he'll be the first one to get it." She seemed charged, excited. "This explains everything," she enthused.

"Everything?" Bruce questioned, having no idea what she meant.

"Walker! Everything!"

Bruce hated to play the dummy, but she was giving him no choice. "Sorry, I don't get it."

She shook her head. "S'okay." She didn't really expect him to. "I couldn't understand why Walker would insist that he come down alone—it didn't make sense. Extra eyes and ears would be invaluable. The son-of-a-bitch was in deep shit, and he knew it."

"Because these were the only three prototypes."

"Right on, Sherlock. He was desperate to get at least one back intact."

"These are the only three in the whole world?" Trish asked.

Ariel stared at her a moment. Bruce thought she might be willing Trish to disappear in a puff of smoke. "You're sworn to secrecy," she reminded.

Trish just grinned sardonically.

"They destroyed the design," Bruce explained. "They need at least one prototype to reverse-engineer them." He looked quickly at Ariel, but she seemed to accept that Trish was now in on the whole game.

The men suddenly began shouting. Between the gurgle of the creek and their yells, Bruce couldn't hear the drone, but he saw the flick of motion. The thing was fast. It seemed to be everywhere at once. It didn't seem possible that it could cover so much ground. No! There were two! They'd both come to attack.

Leslie stood gapping, jerking his head in seemingly random directions, trying to get a glimpse of the frenetic assailants. He spun his gaze to where they huddled, squatting, and locked eyes. He finally understood that the "bees" were real. He ran over. "Give me my gun," he demanded.

Bruce was still holding it by the top of the body—holding it by the handgrip would be too much like using it.

"Guns are no good!" Ariel barked. "You'll never hit them. Tell your men to run into the trees. It's hard for the bees to maneuver in there."

The shouts suddenly rose in volume and pitch. One of the men had fallen to the ground. Even if they ran immediately, Bruce knew that it was now a matter of how many of them the drones would get before the rest could escape. Hell, maybe the drones would hunt every last man down, even in the trees. He had the fleeting thought that he wanted the men to stick around as easy targets so that the three of them would have time to get away.

Leslie was panicking. He lunged and grabbed the pistol, and Bruce let him take it, afraid it would go off again if they struggled. An angry burr zipped past just over their heads, and Leslie swung the pistol and fired off a shot. He might as well have been shooting at the moon.

But the shot energized the rest of the men, and they began swinging their rifles and shotguns in wide arcs, trying pathetically to track the impossibly quick flyers.

"No!" Ariel shouted. "Run, God-damned it. Run!"

They ignored her. Leslie held his pistol in both hands, swinging it back and forth, his eyes wild with terror. He tried to track one of the drones that had arced wide and came in towards the group of men in an almost straight line. He fired and Bruce was horrified to see one of the men jerk and fall. Leslie froze in shock. He'd shot one of his own men.

"Damn it!" Ariel cried. "It's a slaughter house!" She stood up, cupped her hands around her mouth and yelled, "Montana!" Then she called again, this time so loud her voice cracked.

"What are you doing?" Bruce hissed.

"We have to do something!" she croaked. "We can't stand by and watch them be picked off one-by-one."

Bruce thought that sacrificing themselves wouldn't go a long way towards saving anybody, but he held his tongue as Ariel continued shouting the abort code.

Suddenly one of the drones was hovering ten feet in the air before them, staring through black glass eyes. Ariel got to her feet. The other drone zoomed in, and took up position another twenty feet behind its brother.

"What now?" Bruce asked quietly. The desire to sprint away was like a force beyond his control. He had to concentrate to keep his feet planted under him.

"Pray," she replied.

She slowly lifted her hands, palms out, then tilted the fingertips towards each other. She was copying what they'd seen Walker do from a hundred feet away. "Montana," she intoned.

It hadn't worked for Walker—why would she think it might work for her? Prayer was indeed the only recourse left.

That thought tickled something in the back of Bruce's head, like little shutters opening to a shelf he'd forgotten existed. Walker had railed against the Christian software programmer. Bruce had thought that Walker was accusing the man of double-crossing him, but what if he hadn't been? What if Walker was simply repeating the programmer's visual part of the abort?

"Two fingers!" Bruce hissed.

Ariel's only indication that she heard was a deepening furrow of her brow, but she curled her ring and little fingers down, leaving the first two fingers lying across each other—a double cross.

The drones remained in their attack positions. It wasn't working.

Ariel wasn't forming a very distinct cross, though. With both hands tilted together, it was more like a double X.

Bruce knew that the drones would swoop in to deliver lethal jabs any second. All three of them could be dead before Bruce explained to Ariel. Show, don't tell. "Montana!" he cried.

Ariel threw him a glance but kept her position. He stepped forward, and the closest drone angled to face him. "Montana!" he called again, and raised his hands, palms out, but he held one set of double fingers upright, and the other across it, at a right angle.

"What are you doing?" Ariel whispered.

"A double cross," he replied.

The drone moved to the side, placing itself directly in front of him. The glossy black eyes were inscrutable, but Bruce imagined programmed decision trees inching towards invoking the kill routine. The other drone had disappeared, maybe taking up a position behind them.

It wasn't working. I'm dead, he thought.

He was making a double cross. What else could it be? What if his first impression was actually correct? What if Walker really was accusing the programmer of double-crossing him?

From another shelf in his mind, one that hadn't been accessed since he was a kid, the idea of double-crossing someone formed another image. For a while on the playground, they'd had this silly idea that it was okay to lie to somebody if you said it while holding your hand hidden behind your back with . . .

"Montana!" he shouted in desperation, and moved his hands apart, crossing each middle finger over the forefinger, the secret recognition sign early Christians made to each other. Two hands— a double cross.

The world seemed to pause for an eternal second. Even the gurgle of the creek seemed to freeze. And then, as though somebody had hit the play button on the remote, the constant angry burr of the drone's wings modulated, falling in pitch as the drone sank slowly to the ground. As soon as its belly touched the sand, the blur of wings coalesced into four shear, fragile membranes which slowly folded back against the body, leaving just a little toy torpedo, much too small to seem at all dangerous. Even the lethal delivery needle retracted until perhaps a quarter inch was left protruding.

He'd done it. He'd done it!

Ariel wasn't clapping him on the back with congratulations, though. Bruce turned around, following her gaze. The other drone was indeed behind them, and had moved in closer, the same attack position.

"Do it," Ariel encouraged.

"Montana!" he called as he lifted his hands to deliver the visual abort command.

He never finished. The heart-stopping blast of a gunshot exploded right behind him. He jumped, and then another shot sent urgent echoes bouncing off the rocks of the canyon.

It was Leslie. He stood holding his pistol with two hands, pointing it at the ground in front of him. He squeezed off a third shot, and this time, something nicked against Bruce's pant leg. It looked like a piece of black plastic.

"God damn you!" Ariel cried, throwing herself bodily at Leslie so that they both toppled to the ground. It was too late, though, if she was trying to save the disabled drone. It lay in the sand, a mangled tangle of carbon composite shell and fantastically intricate electronics and micro-machines. Its guts were revealed, and they spoke of impossibly complex technology.

The immediate danger wasn't Leslie, however. Bruce had turned back to the third drone, and it was gone. His skin crawled along his spine, waiting for the prick of death. He heard the distinctive burr of drone wings. It was distant, though, barely audible. Ariel had gotten to her feet, and he pointed. She followed his gaze. The drone hung in the air a hundred feet away. It watched them a moment, then zipped off, gone in an instant.

She whirled back towards Leslie who was picking himself up, rubbing his elbow. "You stupid little shit!" she exclaimed. "Who the hell do you think you are?"

He sat back on his butt and lifted the pistol to point at her. "The one with the gun, commie."

"Big shit, big shot. You going to shoot me? You already toasted one of your own guys."

This shut him up. He chewed his lower lip, glancing at the man lying on the ground. Two other men were kneeling next to the fallen man. He called over, "Is Henry . . ."

One of the men said "He's alive. You got him in the hip. We need to get him to a hospital."

"What about Clarence?" Leslie called, turning his attention back to Ariel in case she tried anything.

Three other men were clustered around somebody else. One of them replied, "No. Clarence is dead." He seemed amazed, as though this was the most astounding news. "No marks. Just a tiny sting on the back of his neck."

Leslie took a deep breath and let it out, blowing between pursed lips.

Ariel had gotten down on her hands and knees before the obliterated drone. Using a little twig, she prodded the splayed pieces back together into one pile. Bruce guessed that she was going to wrap up the remains as they'd done with the first one.

"What is it?" Leslie asked, peering cautiously, ready to jump back if it started to move.

"You don't need to know, and you don't want to know," Ariel replied without looking up. "Trust me. The best thing you can do is take care of your men. Get the hell out of here as fast as possible."

Leslie was recovering from his shock. "You'd like that, wouldn't you?" The sneer returned. To the men he called, "I told you!" They glanced over. "They're terrorists!"

Ariel had pushed all the various pieces together. She pulled her shirt off over her head—leaving a lot of bare skin and a bra—folded it twice, and made as though to wrap the pile in it.

"Hold it!" Leslie ordered.

"Shut up," she replied calmly.

Leslie's mouth was set in a tight, hard line as he raised his pistol and fired into the air.

Ariel stopped. She sat back and looked up at him. "You are an asshole, aren't you? You have no idea what kind of trouble you're making for yourself."

"Cut the tough talk. Your commie comrades can't help you now." He glanced at Bruce, who was going to protest, but decided it didn't matter.

Ariel studied Leslie, sizing him up. "Are you even aware that the Soviet Union fell apart decades ago?"

His sneer never faltered. "Once a commie, always a commie."

She shook her head slowly, amazed at the stupidity. "Was it communists that brought down the twin towers?"

He gave a quick shrug. "Same thing."

She snorted. Almost to herself, she muttered, "Forget the terrorists, the real danger's the flag-waving patriots."

"Enough!" he yelled. His cadre of four had moved closer, leaving the dead and wounded for the others. Leslie nodded his chin at one of his men. "Carl, pick this thing up. You can use her shirt to carry it."

The man stepped forward, but Ariel jumped up and put her hand against his chest. "No! It's dangerous!"

Carl pushed her aside, but stood looking down at the mass of inscrutable disassembled science.

"She's lying," Leslie said. "Look at it. It's smashed all to hell."

"No!" Ariel persisted. "It's . . ."

"Pick it up," Leslie said.

Carl reached down.

"It's the poison," she finally blurted. "It could be leaking."

"Do it," Leslie said. "Just be careful with that needle thing."

Carl scooped his fingers under the pile, but Bruce could tell that he was being extra careful, taking no chances in the event that she wasn't lying. He lifted it gingerly in cupped hands, and waited while Leslie took Ariel's shirt from her and held it out. Carl dropped the pieces into the shirt, but then held one hand up in front of his face, peering at the palm. "I think I got something on my—" He stopped and blinked. "Oh shit," he mumbled and swayed, unsteady.

"Damn it!" Ariel muttered, and grabbed him by the arm. "Come on! You have to wash it off!"

Carl only had to stagger a few steps to reach the creek, where he fell heavily to his knees and plunged both hands into the water. He shook them back and forth in the flow, and then shook them some more. Ariel dug out a handful of mud and sand, lifted the man's hand from the water, and slapped the goop into his palm. She rubbed it around, and then plunged his hand back into the water.

"Am I going to . . . die?" he asked.

"If you were, you'd be dead already. But you'll be pretty sick for a day or two."

Leslie had hastily dropped the shirt and drone wreckage to the ground, and was wiping his hands on his pants. Ariel stomped up to him. "Have you had enough? How many more men do you want to lose?"

Leslie started to reply, but she held up her hand, cocking her head to the side.

Bruce heard it. The sound was barbed wire pulled through his head, in one ear, and out the other.

Chapter 16

Ariel moved away from Leslie and Carl, turning her complete attention to the sky and the trees that surrounded them like the walls of a cathedral. She seemed enraptured, enthralled by a miracle about to descend from the heavens. She waved Bruce over. "This is our last chance. We have to capture this one intact."

"Or what?"

Her hopeful glow turned sour. "Or these bumpkins will find out that the flip side of terrorists can be just as nasty."

Bruce wasn't sure he understood. "You're talking about our own government?"

She wagged her head in slight irritation. It seemed that she'd said more than she liked.

She turned back to Leslie. Quick as a cat, she had the front of his shirt balled in her fist, and her face inches from his nose. "Stay out of the way, mister, or I'll shove that damn gun right up your ass."

She let him go with a little push, and returned to scanning the sky, while Leslie glanced around, taking in the reaction of his cadre to their leader being manhandled by a slight woman wearing just a bra.

The burring sound became more distinct, and Bruce finally saw the third drone. It watched them from twenty feet in the air, almost hidden among the dense cover of a maple tree, a little ebony core surrounded by a fuzz of hyper-motion. The needle caught the sun and winked evilly at them.

"Montana!" Ariel called, holding her arms out as if to prove she was not armed.

The drone immediately tilted and zipped down, stopping in attack position.

"Bruce," she said softly, "make sure Leslie stays put." Then she repeated the verbal keyword and brought her arms to the front, fingers of each hand crossed.

Bruce looked at Leslie, who returned a defiant glare, but remained still.

When he looked back at Ariel, nothing had changed, except that whereas previously the drone would hold rock-steady when waiting for the abort code, now it swayed back and forth, up and down, in nervous little twitches. It looked exactly like it was trying to make up its mind.

The abort wasn't working.

Bruce couldn't tell what Ariel was doing wrong, but clearly the drone was going to kill her any second. "Montana!" he cried, holding up his crossed fingers exactly as he'd done for the second assassin.

The drone seemed to consider this a moment, and then suddenly it was a foot in front of Bruce's face. The tip of the death-delivering needle was poised inches from the bare skin of his face. It was not going to abort.

"Montana! Montana!" Ariel shouted from a dozen feet away, but the drone ignored her, considering instead the best place to plant its lethal kiss.

An explosion rocked the world, and Bruce felt the hot blast of shotgun pellets fly past his ear. The drone was gone—no, it had just moved three feet higher. Another blast rang out, and the drone was now two feet to the right. The drone must predict the path of the discharge from the position of the barrel, he guessed—it couldn't actually react to the flight of the supersonic pellets. Could it?

Behind him, he heard Ariel struggling with Leslie, but he kept his eyes on the drone, death poised to strike. He wanted to shout to Ariel to leave Leslie be, the maniac's shots might not bring down the drone, but they were at least distracting it.

Bruce yelped when a rain of pellets suddenly spattered across his head and neck. No, that couldn't be. Where was the blast of black powder? And he surely wouldn't still be standing if he'd taken a shotgun blast in the head.

"Run!" Trish yelled.

Bruce realized that the drone had moved again. It was much higher, maybe twenty feet up. He glanced around and saw Trish, just as she cocked her arm and threw another handful of sand—this time almost straight up at the hovering little devil. Brilliant! She couldn't actually hit the lightning-fast machine—she probably didn't expect to—but a handful of sand spread much wider than a volley of shotgun pellets, and the fragile drone wings were vulnerable.

The drone wobbled and the smooth burr of synchronized wings sputtered a moment as a grain or two found their target, then it disappeared in a streak, arcing up and off to the right. Bruce intuited that the tiny silicon brain would decide to take out the most disruptive impediment first. "Duck!" he called.

Trish must have figured the same thing, for she threw herself down just as the drone whizzed by where she'd been standing. It only took a second for it to return to hover above the prone woman, looking for the best place to jab.

That second was all that Bruce needed. He'd grabbed a hasty handful of sand and threw it as he ran towards her. It wasn't sand, however, but mostly mud, and it splattered darkly across Trish's back. The unusual human behavior caused the drone a moment's pause, just enough for Bruce to find quality ammunition, and the hovering assassin was forced to retreat upward.

"Come on!" Bruce called. "Everybody! Throw sand!"

Ariel joined in immediately, and soon most of the other men were tossing handfuls skyward. For several minutes, it rained dirt along the flats between the second and third Powderhole falls, with throwers pausing only to work grains of sand from their eyes. He noticed that the only ones not contributing were Leslie and the three remaining members of his cadre, who stood off to the side talking, holding their hands up to shield from the raining dirt.

"Hold it!" Ariel finally shouted. "Stop a minute!"

She waited until the last grains pattered down and held her hand up for everybody to keep quiet, listening. They peered in every direction, but there was no sign of the drone.

During the barrage, the Powderhole farmers and factory workers had migrated into a loose mass around Ariel, Trish and Bruce, leaving Leslie and his cadre, along with the sick and fallen, to themselves. Ariel seemed to have abandoned any hope of keeping the true details of the drones secret, and spoke freely with Bruce as the others stood listening, continuing to scan the sky for incoming.

"It's ignoring the abort code," she said.

"Maybe we're doing something wrong?" Bruce wondered, more hope than reason.

Ariel shook her head. "I don't think so. The second one reacted immediately once you figured out what the double-cross really meant. No," she shook her head again, exasperated, throwing Leslie's group an angry glance, "it's decided that the abort code has been compromised. The final straw was probably when dumbass obliterated its brother."

"You think it's . . . like, scared?"

She looked at him as though he might be joking. "Of course not."

"Of course," he agreed. He was embarrassed that he'd suggested that. "Its motivation loops are just trying to stay one step ahead of potential subversion. After all, why would a legitimate abort be followed by the unit's destruction otherwise?"

She just nodded after his lecture. Maybe he could still make an intelligent remark. "There must be some way to disable it."

She shrugged. "There may be some backup abort code, but I wouldn't have a clue. It's probably so secret that nobody knows it."

He wasn't sure how that could be possible. "I don't understand—"

"I was kidding. It might take an act of Congress to get it, though. And I'm only half kidding there. There's no phones for me to even start the process."

Leslie was walking over to them. "Okay, where's Walker?" he asked.

Ariel sighed. "Give it up, already. We have a serious problem, and I need to get word out to call in help."

"We have a problem, all right, and it's you. Now, where's Walker?"

Ariel stared at him a moment, then replied, "Down below. He's dead—killed by one of his own drones."

Leslie returned her stare, chewing his lower lip. Without taking his eyes from her, he said loudly, "Abe, go down and check it out. See if she's telling the truth."

"Me?" Abe responded.

"No, the other Abe—of course, you."

"Uh, I don't know, Les."

"Oh, Christ. The Tally-ban Soviet thing is gone. Take Chuck along if you're chicken."

"Oh, no," the other cadre member protested. "No way."

As they continued to argue about it, Ariel took Bruce by the elbow and led him aside. "It's coming to a head here," she said softly. "We have to clear everybody out, but we can't let them get hold of any of the drones, even if they're smashed."

Bruce nodded with little enthusiasm. "I understand. It's a matter of National Security. The spy goons need to protect their secrets."

Based on her pursed lips, Bruce figured that she didn't like his response. "I don't think you do understand. I have a responsibility to protect restricted government information, sure, but that's not the main reason we have to keep the drones secure."

"The world will find out that we use weapons of micro destruction?"

She ignored the dig. "Walker's cronies are going to quickly realize the hot water they're in. I'm not sure how far they'll go to contain the situation."

"You think that they'll, like, kill to protect it?"

He didn't at all like that she had to consider before answering. "I wouldn't think so—actually, I don't know. I wouldn't rule it out."

Bruce blinked. Apparently the danger that Walker represented hadn't died with him. "This isn't going to be easy with our deluded vigilante," he noted.

She looked sideways at the volatile little man waving his arms and cursing his troops to action. "Small man, big ego," she mused.

Leslie broke from his little group, waving them off in defeat, and strode over to Ariel and Bruce. "Let's go," he ordered.

"Where are you going?" Ariel asked mildly.

"Not me, 'we.' We're all leaving. Going to contact the proper authorities."

"I am the proper authority," she reminded.

He spat. "Nice try. Now let's go," he repeated. He started to take her by the arm, but apparently thought better of it, probably remembering the previous manhandling she'd delivered. Instead he held up his pistol at them.

"Are you kidnapping us?" Ariel asked. "That's a serious felony, you know."

"Let's call it a citizen's arrest," he replied, shaking the tip of the gun impatiently.

Ariel walked straight over to where Leslie had dropped the demolished second drone and squatted down, carefully wrapping her shirt around the scattered pieces. When she'd collected it together, she tied the shirt ends together, making a compact bundle to carry and stood up.

"Give it to Abe," he ordered.

"No," she said, shaking her head. She held the bundle in both hands as though it was a bowl that she didn't want to spill.

"Abe!" he barked, "Take it."

The man was uneasy. He held out his hands.

"Take it, I said!" Leslie commanded.

Abe just looked at his leader, begging for relief.

Leslie lifted the pistol and pointed it at Ariel. "Give it to him!" he yelled.

She just watched him levelly, waiting.

"Hand it over!" Leslie cried, the desperation growing.

"I can't do that," she finally responded quietly. "I have a responsibility to—"

She never finished her explanation. Leslie's pistol jerked in recoil as the shot exploded, and Ariel jerked back in concert. She bent over, and then lifted her head to look one last time at the mad little man. Bruce saw blood running down the bare skin of her stomach. She staggered backwards, splashing into the creek, but then stumbled and fell headlong into the water. Everybody stood frozen in horror as she floated away in the current. Nobody moved even as she reached the falls and her limp body slipped over the rim, launching off on a ride down nature's waterslide. A moment later, the tight little cloth bundle followed her over.

Chapter 17

Silence hung over the verdant canyon, and then, as though sharing a signal, the men began jabbering all at once. Leslie stood frozen in shock, though, staring at the spot where Ariel's body had disappeared over the lip of the third falls.

Bruce suddenly felt his stomach heaving, and he bent over and puked. The vomit poured from his mouth like a geyser, and acid burned his nose. He fell to his knees as his guts heaved some more, even though there was nothing left to give up.

He felt a hand on his shoulder. It was Trish, her face all sad concern. "He's gone mad," she said simply.

Bruce nodded. That's all he could manage.

He took a deep breath. He realized that he'd been holding it, and the air brought some clarity. With Trish's help, he got to his feet. Leslie was chewing his lower lip, watching the men mill about nervously. Bruce walked over to him, and the skinny man turned to face him, his pistol cradled in his hands like a carpenter might hold his favorite hammer. In the movies, men often drop their guns after they've murdered for the first time, but Leslie hung on to his, perhaps finding comfort in the cold power it gave him.

Bruce saw panic and desperation in the man's eyes, and he knew that he had nothing to say to the killer, nothing that would in any way be heard. Instead, he turned to face the alarmed crowd of Powderhole men. "Have you had enough?" he shouted, and they fell silent, morose eyes turned to him, waiting. "Guns!" he yelled like it was a curse. "They're made to kill, and today they've done their job."

It had been just one man that had done all the shooting, but nobody dared challenge him. "Go home before anybody else dies!"

The men looked at each other and one made a point to break his double-barreled shotgun and extract the two shells. Others pulled clips and worked bolts to unload chambers. Two men handed their guns to others and reached down to pick up the wounded man who Leslie had shot in the hip. They discussed quietly what to do about the dead man who'd been stung by the drone, and they decided to leave him for the time being as they shuffled away single-file into the foliage debris, working their way slowly back up to the road. Carl, the cadre member who had contacted the poison while handled the smashed drone, went along, helped by a fellow cadre.

Leslie watched them a moment, his nose wrinkled in disgust. "Chuck! Abe!" he called to his remaining cadre.

The men turned reluctantly. They seemed resentful that he was pulling them back.

"Let them go," Leslie sneered. "They're nothing but dumb farmers anyway. We don't need them."

One of the two men silently pulled the clip from his rifle and turned and walked away.

"Chuck!" Leslie called. "Where the hell you think you're going?"

"Home!" the man yelled without turning.

Leslie's mouth worked, his teeth grinding in anger. He lifted his pistol and fired into the air.

Chuck stopped, stood a moment, and then walked on without saying anything.

"Screw him," Leslie growled. "The pussy." He looked at Abe, the only one remaining. "You want to pussy out too?"

Abe stared at him, bitter and maybe even hating him for the situation, but unwilling to buck up and stand down.

"Okay, then," Leslie said. "We'll take these two in ourselves."

"Take us where?" Trish challenged.

Bruce put his hand on her shoulder. "Let's just go with him," he said, the vision of Ariel's body floating away still vivid in his head.

She shook his hand away, but then nodded. "Fine," she said to Leslie. "But you're going to burn, you little weasel. That gun doesn't make you a bigger man. It just shows how small you really are."

Leslie looked her in the eye, and raised the pistol so that it was pointing between her eyebrows. "You want to say that again?" he asked.

The words were delivered in a calm, cold voice. This frightened Bruce more than the spittle-flying rages.

It must have scared Trish as well, for she shook her head in little nervous jerks.

"Okay, then," Leslie went on in the same cool tone. "If we can keep the insults to ourselves, maybe we'll all make it back to town alive."

"Not all of us," Bruce whispered, too quietly for their abductor to hear. Drops of Ariel's blood lay scattered at their feet.

ж ж ж

"I thought Leslie had a crush on you?" Bruce asked just loud enough for Trish to hear.

Leslie and Abe were behind them as they climbed the path up and out of the falls, huffing and puffing, creating their own sound camouflage.

"Amorous goals take second place to God and country, I guess," she replied. She glanced back to make sure the murderous little man hadn't heard her insult.

Bruce still felt ill, hardly able to believe Ariel's fate, but the shock was wearing off enough that he could focus on one thought at a time. "You saved my life back there," he observed.

"You mean when I threw the sand?"

"Yeah. The drone was about half a second away from jabbing me."

She lifted her hands in a little shrug. "I didn't realize it could come after me."

Or maybe you did, he thought.

"Besides," she went on, "you returned the favor."

He smiled. Her pale blue fleece jacket was smeared with the mud he'd thrown. "I think I ruined your clothes."

She looked at her jacket and waved it off. "Better to be alive with dirty clothes than . . ."

She left it at that.

Than like Ariel, he thought.

"In any case," she started again, "some people are worth it." She gave him a quick side-long glance, then grinned, looking at his bare legs. "And muddy clothes are better than none at all. How in God's name did you lose your pants? Or maybe I shouldn't ask?"

"I—uh." Bruce realized that he had a dilemma. "Actually I can't tell you . . . at least not yet. But it was innocent."

"Innocent," she repeated, unconvinced.

"Really," he insisted. It was unsettling defending his behavior. "The reason I can't tell you—"

She shook her head. "No. I'm not questioning you. I was just thinking about the whole idea of innocence. Life can be so . . ."

"Complicated," he offered.

"Complicated and fuzzy."

"Fuzzy as in knowing the right thing to do?"

She sighed. "Yeah. Sometimes you wonder if there even is a right thing."

"Sounds pretty pessimistic."

She gave him an are-you-serious look. "What exactly do you find optimistic in this whole thing?"

After a few steps, he offered, "Well, we're going to be away from the falls soon."

"Death canyon?"

"They may have to rename it."

She glanced back at Leslie who was still struggling, falling behind, and based on his nervous glances over his shoulder, not happy about it. "We'll still have him to deal with," she whispered jerking her eyes towards Leslie.

Bruce waved it off. "His insanity will evaporate once we're back around normal people," he assured.

Leslie called for them to stop. They waited while he and Abe caught up.

"Cab's probably waiting at the top," Leslie said.

Bruce waited for more, but the vigilante just stared at them. He seemed to be agitated and distracted, as though suffering from a fever.

"Fine," Bruce finally said. "I guess you can turn us over as captured terrorists. Hopefully he'll have his handcuffs with him. Hey, does he even have handcuffs?"

Bruce's irreverence had no effect on Leslie.

"It was self-defense, you know," Leslie said. He looked back and forth between Bruce and Trish, seeking confirmation.

"You mean when you murdered Ariel?" Trish challenged.

She might as well have slapped him. His pallid cheeks burned red, and his eyes bulged. "She was going to kill me!"

"With what? A shoe?"

"That weapon! That poison flying thing!"

"The thing you broke into little pieces?"

"Even broken, it still nearly killed Carl! It was still dangerous!"

"It was all wrapped up."

Leslie wasn't getting anywhere. To Abe, he said, "Go on up. I'll be along in a little while."

Bruce and Trish exchanged glances. They'd both heard Leslie say that "he" would be along, not "we."

Abe must have understood Leslie's degree of desperation. "Nah, Les. I'll stay and we can all go up together. You know, in case that bee-thing comes back."

Bruce could have kissed the man, or at least encouraged Trish to.

Leslie was frustrated and flustered. For a moment Bruce thought that he might just go ahead and off them right there in front of Abe. But some vestige of sanity won the day and Leslie stormed off up the path.

They followed, and Bruce tried to thank Abe, but the man wanted none of it. He told them to shut up, that they'd let Cab take care of things from here.

When they finally emerged from the trees onto the parking area, Cab and Larry jumped up from where they were sitting in the grass, and Larry trotted over. "Hey! We heard shots, and the other guys said that people were killed down there—a woman, they said. What happened? Trish, thank God it wasn't you!" Larry blinked, taking in the implication of this. He seemed to have no expression. "Was it . . ."

"Ariel," Bruce confirmed. He glanced at Cab. "Leslie shot her."

"It was self-defense!" Leslie shouted. "She was going to kill me!"

Cab swayed, his face ashen, and Bruce grabbed his shoulder to steady him. "You okay?" Bruce asked.

"No. No, I'm not okay. What the hell?"

It was a question that expected no real answer.

"Somebody had to take charge!" Leslie shouted. He was on a rampage now. "I was right, you know! I told you! They have deadly weapons down there—they killed George! They were threatening the whole town!" He looked to Abe for support, but the man just stared at him, neither agreeing nor contradicting. "God damn it!" Leslie yelled. "I just saved the town!"

He jabbed his finger into Cab's face. "You have to arrest these two."

Cab reached up and swatted Leslie's hand away. He then sat down heavily on the ground, placed his elbows on his knees, and put his face into his hands. They all watched him, unsure what to do.

"I just wanted the town to feel safe," he muttered from under his hands. His voice was muffled, so it was difficult to tell if he was mad or maybe crying. "Keep the punks from defacing the school with graffiti, maybe settle a domestic argument or calm a drunk."

He was silent, just sitting there like a defeated version of Rodin's The Thinker. He might have fallen asleep, except that he occasionally kicked his foot, making a little rut in the grass.

"Cab!" Leslie finally called. "Come on! People have been killed. You have to arrest them!"

The constable finally dropped his hands, apparently ready to get back up, but Leslie was too impatient to wait, and snarled. "Do your job, dammit!"

Cab froze. Some threshold had been crossed. He looked up at the irritating little man with eyes both beaten and defiant all at the same time. With a clenched jaw, he jabbed his hand into his back pocket and took out his wallet. He yanked a plastic card from a slot and handed it to Leslie, who stood gazing at it in surprise before taking it. He looked at it, and then at Cab. "This is your constable ID," he said.

"It was, you mean. I quit. You're so hot to handle things, you try being the constable for a while."

Cab then got to his feet with a tired little grunt and walked off slowly to his car.

"Cab!" Bruce called, but the tired man just waved him off without even turning around. A minute later, he was driving away, leaving Bruce, Trish, and Larry to face Leslie and Abe.

Larry said, "Guys, I'm sorry, but there's something I have to do."

Without another word, he sprinted off, not up the road, but towards the trees. It was fortunate that he didn't give Leslie more warning, since by the time he had time to react and raise his pistol, Larry was far enough away that his shot went wide.

Before Leslie had a chance to get off another one, Bruce clubbed his hand down. Leslie immediately turned and Bruce found the tip of the barrel under his nose. The smell of burnt powder filled his head with an expectation of imminent death. The world froze. After five beats, Leslie finally lowered the gun, but then pointed it at Bruce again as he bent down to pick up Cab's ID card, which he'd dropped. He considered a moment, then told Abe to open the back of his RAV4. "Get in," he ordered, looking at Bruce and Trish.

"In there?" Bruce asked, pointing at the small luggage area behind the back seat.

"Yeah, get in."

"There's no room for both of us. Trish can sit in the back seat."

"No. I want Abe to keep an eye on both of you."

"Leslie, come on. Be reasonable. What do you think we'll do—"

"Get in!" Leslie yelled. His hands were shaking.

The man was close to breaking. Bruce crawled into the back of the crossover SUV without another word. Trish climbed in after him, and it was indeed a tight fit. It took Abe two tries to get the hatch door closed. Bruce had nowhere to put his arm, so he simply let it rest across Trish's shoulder. She didn't seem to mind—in fact, she let her head fall against his shoulder and sighed. It could have been a sigh of resignation at their questionable fate, not necessarily satisfaction at being held by him.

They talked in whispers on the way into town, and Bruce gave Trish an update about what had happened to him and Ariel before she arrived. "But, what was up with Larry?" he asked. "It's not like him to run scared like that."

"No clue."

"Did he say anything earlier?"

She shook her head, then gave a little shrug. "Before Wyatt Earp and his posse showed up, Larry was just pacing back and forth, looking off to the south, at the ridge."

"That's the direction he ran."

"Yeah, what's in that direction?"

"Nothing. Just the west end of Bloss's fields and then the ridge. It's all woods, too steep to farm, but a lot of guys go deer hunting up there in the fall."

"Larry is a mystery onto himself," she concluded, wiggling her head to find a more comfortable spot on his shoulder.

"He's eccentric."

"A euphemism for nuts." She seemed to consider that a moment. "Or maybe a good friend with a colorful character."

Whom you can always trust, Bruce added to himself, with a mild wave of guilt. He decided that there was no reason to keep any more secrets from her. "Listen, I'm . . . I'm sorry I didn't tell you about . . ."

"Donald?"

"Yeah. I was trying to do the right thing."

It took a moment for her to answer, and when she did it was qualified. "It's not like I was emotionally attached to the guy," she replied. "But it's a horrible shock, and it seems . . . I don't know—creepy, that he was lying down there in the basement and you knew it and didn't say anything."

"I would have—I really hated that I couldn't."

"You think you really couldn't? Tell us, I mean."

He thought about it. "I trusted her, I guess. It seemed important enough, so yeah, I guess I really couldn't."

It was her turn to mull this over. "Do you still think your trust was justified?"

"Yeah. In fact, even more so. Everything she did was in line with what she claimed she was trying to do."

"But where does that leave things? I mean now that she's . . ."

"Dead? Who the hell knows? There's still one last assassin drone lurking down there, and her colleagues—or Walker's cronies—are going to want real badly to get it back. In fact," he said, suddenly remembering the last conversation with Ariel, "she warned that there'd be trouble if any of them, even the smashed ones, got out. I'm thinking that maybe she would expect me to go down and . . ."

He could barely think about it, let alone say the words.

"Capture the last drone?" Trish said for him. "Well, that sounds like suicide. I doubt she'd want you to go that far."

"Maybe," he agreed, mostly because he wanted to believe her. In his heart of hearts, he knew that Ariel might indeed have wanted him to risk his life to capture it. She'd given hers.

They came to the outskirts of Powderhole, where the old Rinehimer farm had blossomed with a little scattering of upscale houses on larger lots, then passed the small, cookie-cutter ramblers—the layer added after WWII—and finally the old core neighborhood at the center of town. Through it all, they saw not a single person. It was like Chernobyl, a place where, in an instant, everyday lives had stopped.

Word must have spread: deadly bees and the town under siege by either terrorists or their own government, or both. Families had gathered together their broods, closed the windows, and locked the doors. The oppressive effect of disaster and abandonment was bolstered when they passed the half-collapsed bank building where Leslie had blown up the vault.

The town—which was the people, after all—had effectively disappeared. Bruce had hated the idea of coming home with his career tail between his legs, but now the possibility that there could be no home town to return to was an idea that he found deeply disturbing.

And Ariel was dead—and Donald—and Dick . . . and Walker.

He had a hard time grieving over Walker.

Chapter 18

Leslie stopped in front of the town hall, and Bruce saw that not all the people of Powderhole had hid away in their homes. The parking lot was half full, and he heard muffled voices inside as Leslie escorted them along at gunpoint. When their captor threw open the front doors, Mort's voice was filling the hall with heartfelt entreaties and proclamations. Leslie's brother had taken a couple of business law courses at the community college, and according to Larry, felt that this qualified him to provide legal advice whether requested or even welcomed. The obese man leaned ponderously with both hands on the podium as he boomed forth his authoritatively delivered advice, like William Jennings Bryan in a modern-day Scopes trial.

Mort stopped mid-sentence when the four of them came through the door, but held his braced position, probably finding it too cumbersome to move. Somebody had brought Donald and laid him across four chairs on the platform behind Mort. They'd covered the body, but Bruce recognized his shoes. One of Leslie's cadre member, Chuck, sat next to the corpse, as though guarding it. The two dozen or so people clustered near the front would have already been provided a rundown of the events.

"Ah!" Mort announced, "here they are now! Two remaining culprits!"

Not suspects or alleged criminals, Bruce thought, but flat-out "culprits".

Leslie prodded Bruce and Trish forward, past the gawking townsfolk and up onto the platform, where Abe quickly brought two chairs and set them next to Donald's body. Bruce sat down, resigned to wait and see where it all would go, but Trish refused. "What is this?" she demanded, sweeping her arm to take in the entire hall.

Mort turned his thick neck to look at her. "Pretty obvious, isn't it? A town assembly, tasked with formulating a plan."

"Who tasked you? How?"

"By referendum vote."

She held out her hand, gesturing at the small audience. "This group? What? Like, less than one percent of the population? Besides, a referendum vote is referred to the electorate by standing elected officials."

Mort hated her for besting him in his field of self-appointed expertise. Bruce could see the smoldering fire that burned in his piggy little eyes.

He side-stepped her challenge by asking Leslie, "Where's Cab?"

His brother came to him and they talked quietly. Leslie showed Mort Cab's ID card, and the business student took it and laid it on the podium in front of him. He gazed at the small gathering a moment, and then proclaimed, "Cab has ceded his authority to Leslie." He held up the ID card as proof.

"That's ridiculous!" Trish shouted. "A constable can't cede his authority!"

Mort gave Leslie a knowing look, and his brother in turn looked at Abe, who stood up reluctantly and faced her. "Sit down, and keep quiet, how about it?" he said to Trish.

Bruce could see that she was about to explode. "Look," he said quietly, "they're going to do whatever they want. Logic and reason aren't part of their game. They'll hang themselves in the end."

He wasn't at all confident about that last part, but it seemed like a good thing to say.

Mort turned his large bulk so that he could more comfortably address them. "Let's proceed", he announced formally. "Bruce Weiss and Patricia Bauer—"

"Adelina," Trish interrupted. "My last name is Adelina. What the hell is going on? Do you think this is some kind of court of law?" she challenged.

The hate in Mort's eyes flared. "Of course not. It's—" he paused the barest moment, "a police investigation."

"Oh, yeah," she said, feigning remembrance, "that ceded authority thing."

"Abe . . ." Leslie warned, and the de facto bailiff in turn held up his finger in warning at her.

"Excuse me," she continued anyway, "but aren't you forgetting certain guaranteed rights?"

Mort sucked in a labored breath and let it out. "Fine, fine. You have the right to remain silent, and anything you say can be used in a court of law. Now—"

"Oops! You forgot the lawyer part. Kinda important, you know?"

His mouth worked, like he might be struggling with a sour plug of chewing tobacco. He stopped and one eyebrow went up slowly. "You're not under arrest, so Mirinda Rights don't apply."

Trish smiled at him.

"You think this is funny?" Mort shot through clenched teeth. As a chubby kid Mort would flail into anybody who laughed at him.

"It's Mir-an-da Rights," she corrected, "not Mir-in-da."

"That's what I said."

"Sure," Trish replied agreeably.

"It is!" he bellowed.

She didn't respond, other than returning his glare with an innocent gaze.

Bruce leaned over and whispered into her ear. "Maybe we should just play along. Between Mort's temper and Leslie's gun, things could get dicey."

She nodded, but he could tell that she was one arrogant power play away from pushing back again.

Mort folded his hands over the elephantine girth of his torso, composing himself. After a moment, he asked, "What organization are you—both of you—with?"

"What kind of stup—"

Bruce cut her off. "What do you mean? Like, what college did we attend?"

Mort glanced quickly at the cluster of mostly men in the chairs, the audience he was playing for. "I think you know very well what I mean."

"No. I honestly don't. If you're implying that we're, like, with the government or something, we're not."

Bruce looked at the faces in the chairs. Some of these were people from his parents' church, people he'd known as long as he could remember. They were all familiar, though, nobody in Powderhole was a stranger for long. They seemed scared, but also sympathetic. He was a home boy, after all. He'd gone off to the wild culture of California, but in their eyes he was still "the Weiss kid" tearing down the street on his bike.

Some of the women were looking at him oddly, though, and he remembered that he'd lost his pants. He crossed his legs modestly, but that only seemed to accentuate his bare legs.

"I didn't expect that you'd talk about your own organization so easily," Mort went on, "but as long as we're on the subject of the government, what part did it have in this attack on our town?"

Bruce's mind whirled, trying to sort out what was already general knowledge, and what Ariel would want him to keep under wraps.

"Well?" Mort pressed.

"Walker."

"What about Walker?"

Bruce saw Cab ease in through the front doors and quickly take a seat in the back, what seemed to be his usual default location in any town gathering. He noticed Betty Stickltow sitting nearby. She watched sourly, ready to erupt into invectives.

"Walker was with the government," Bruce replied, distracted, wondering why Cab didn't just step forward and end this whole charade.

"We already got that," Mort said, glancing at Cab and seeming annoyed at his arrival. "Why don't you start at the beginning?"

"Like . . . what beginning? Me arriving at Avoca Airport?"

"The attack!" Mort yelled. "Anything relevant to that!"

The people gathered in the hall were leaning forward, all ears, hungry for any news.

"The attack . . ." he started, stalling while his brain spun freely. "The, um, poison bees are apparently, like, not really bees."

This much was safe, he reasoned.

"That's not the beginning!" Mort rebuked, his voice rising again.

"Right. The beginning. Er, let's see . . . Trish here, and me—and Larry—went down the falls to look for Indian artifacts—arrowheads."

It had been just that morning, but it seemed like a week ago.

"Fine. What then?" Mort asked.

"We, uh, met up with Ariel."

That wasn't giving anything away.

"You say you 'met up' with her. That implies a pre-arranged meeting."

"No! It was just by accident. We didn't know her before that."

This was hard to believe as well. So much had transpired in so short a period of time, Bruce felt that he'd known her as long as Trish. He reminded himself with a little shock that he'd known Trish only one day longer.

"Bruce, it's no use lying. We'll find out the truth sooner or later."

"If you're not going to believe him, then why bother asking?"

It was Cab, speaking loudly from his seat in the back. Good ol' Cab.

Mort glanced at Leslie, who shrugged. "Why are you here, Cab?" he asked.

"Why's anybody here?"

"We're here to plan how to protect this town—something you failed to do in your former position."

Mort emphasized "former."

"That may be," Cab replied. "But that don't mean you can take over the law."

Mort glanced at the people seated in front of him, as though making sure they weren't abandoning him. "Cab, you're not the constable anymore. You gave that position to Leslie."

"Now, wait a second. Just because—"

"You're just another citizen," Mort rode over him in his dominant bellow. "And it's pretty clear that we would've had to take away your badge, anyway, based on how badly you screwed up—"

"There ain't no badge," Cab said.

Mort pretended to be surprised. "What?"

"I said that a constable ain't got no badge, you fool. He ain't no sheriff."

"That's for sure! You were no sheriff, not even close. Not if a sheriff does his best to protect his community. Cab, you should be ashamed of yourself. Poor Donald here was shot right in front of you, and you didn't do anything. You didn't do anything to stop it, but worse, you went along with the perpetrators."

"That ain't true," Cab said, but his voice had fallen in volume.

"Cab, you should be happy we don't take you into custody. You're the fool, Cab—you're the fool!"

Mort held his position of righteous defiance as Cab slowly got to his feet and went to the front doors. He turned to the room. "I admit that this whole thing is way over my head. I admit that. But you get your dander up, you get all riled, and you'll do something you're going to regret. I guarantee it. Violence only brings more violence."

He opened the door and started to leave, but Mort called out, "Cab, you're pathetic!"

The former constable paused a moment, but then left without responding.

Mort turned with satisfaction back to Bruce. "Now, then—"

"Just one minute, Mortimer!"

It was Stickltow. She'd gotten to her feet, and her face was blazing with fury. "You halt this childish game this very instant!"

Mort stared. Stickltow had always ranked her students, from favorites like Donald down to the bottom of the barrel, the Larry's and Mort's. Mort raised his head slightly in defiance. "This is not one of your classrooms, Betty."

He'd spat her first name, it's use a declaration of the fact that they were both adults now.

"You may no longer be my student," she cried, anger turning her words into a screech, "but you are still an ass!"

Mort's mouth worked as he ground his teeth together, searching for a response.

"Pettiness!" she yelled, waving her arm to take in the entire hall. "Small-minded meddling! Vanity and arrogance! I am guilty, the same as you, and what has it gotten me? My Ted and my Donald— gone! I . . . I—" She couldn't manage any more words, swatting her hand at all of them instead, resigning them to their ignorant doom. She turned to the door, slowly following Cab out into the fading afternoon sunlight.

Mort waited until she'd left. He composed himself. She obviously still wielded some remnant of authority over him, but she was gone, and the hall was once again his. Bruce would have begged her to come back if he could.

Mort turned back to Bruce. "I believe that you were about to tell us the truth about meeting up with Ariel?"

"I've already told you, we met for the first time this morning down at the falls."

The inquisition master glanced at his audience, in control again, making sure they understood that he wasn't buying this, and neither should they. "We can come back to that—what happened next?"

"We took her to see Dagger."

"Why?"

"She wanted to talk to him about the meteor he thought he saw."

"Just like Walker had done," Mort observed, throwing a victorious smile at his audience.

"That's right," Bruce agreed, "just like Walker had done."

"Why did Ariel want to talk to him about that? Why would Walker?"

"We didn't know."

This was the truth. At that time, they didn't know.

"Bruce, you're not helping yourself in the long run by lying."

He raised his hands in submission. It was what it was.

"What did Dagger have to say?"

"Nothing, really. Just what he told Cab. He'd changed his mind about it being a meteor."

This was the truth also, Dagger hadn't given them the case until later.

Mort waved it off. "So, what happened then?"

"We came back to the falls and found that Ted . . . had died."

"Had been killed, you mean?"

He was about to agree, but caught himself. "We didn't know how he died. We weren't there when it happened."

"You weren't," Mort reiterated skeptically.

"That's what I said. We heard the helicopter on the way back."

Mort sighed, as though he was trying hard to be patient, but being mightily tested. "Then what?" he asked, his tone implying that they shouldn't expect anything useful.

"We talked to Cab, and then came up."

"Then what?" Mort intoned in a voice that he might use on a stubborn little child.

"Ariel left, and we . . . we waited for her to come back."

"Ah. And where did Ariel go?"

This was it. Up until this point in the story, he'd been innocent of protected information, and so was able to tell the truth. He looked at Trish, but she was no help. He could see that she was lost in anger, just completely pissed off that this buffoon would be allowed to bully them.

He took a deep breath and let the grenade drop. "I'm afraid I can't tell you that."

Mort feigned shock, but Bruce could tell that he was overjoyed. "You can't?"

"That's right, I can't."

"Why not?"

Bruce searched for some way to explain. "I can't even tell you that."

The sympathy in the faces of the Powderhole people he knew had dissolved. Their fears were free to set the agenda. The only item on the table now was the safety of them and their families at any cost—even if it meant setting aside abstractions like protected rights.

"Well," Mort exclaimed, placing both hands on the podium like a preacher delivering the key point of the sermon, "is there anything else you can tell us?"

His interrogator was facing the small gathering with his back to Bruce, but he assumed that Mort was referring to him. "Um, let's see." He glanced at Leslie, who was watching him closely. *What the hell.* "I can tell you how Ariel died."

"Mort!" Leslie yelled.

His brother looked at him with surprise. Leslie hurried over and spoke quietly into his ear, then waited a moment while Mort recovered from the shock of the information. They fell into a heated debate full of waving hands and hissed whispers.

Trish had had enough. "Hey!" she called. "Are we going to get on with this kangaroo court, or do you two want to retire to the judge's chambers and reconvene the jury later?"

Mort threw her an angry glance, but quickly wrapped up the flustered deliberation and gestured for his older brother to return to his seat. "Leslie tells me that the supposed poison bees were actually some kind of little flying robot."

Bruce shrugged and gave a little nod. That much was already known.

"These things are deadly," Mort stated.

Bruce just stared. No sense handing the bastard every little tidbit.

"In fact," Mort continued, "just touching one, even one that's been smashed, can be lethal."

Bruce saw where this was going. "That's a gross exaggeration."

"Carl was nearly killed by just touching one."

Mort waited, but Bruce said, "Are you asking me questions, or just telling us Leslie's story?"

Leslie jumped up. "It's no goddamn story! It's the truth!"

Mort tried to calm him, but Leslie was erupting from pent-up anxiety. "She was going to kill me! She threatened me with that . . . poison thing—"

"And that's when you shot her?" Bruce yelled. He wanted to make sure that got said early.

"She was going to kill me, goddamn it!"

Bruce was on his feet as well, now. "Whatever she had was wrapped up in her shirt. If one touch was lethal, then how could she be holding it herself?"

"She was trying to kill me!" he repeated.

"She was ten feet away! You murdered her in cold blood!"

Bruce had taken a couple of steps forward, and Leslie now rushed him. Bruce held up his fists, ready for a fight, but found himself looking into the barrel of Leslie's pistol. That seemed to be happening a lot. Eventually it was going to go off.

"Leslie!" Trish called from behind Bruce. "This time there will be no question that it's murder, and you'll get the electric chair, guaranteed."

"Les," Mort admonished. "Don't make it worse. It'll be okay."

Leslie's jaw muscles bulged and pulsed, but he finally lowered the pistol. He couldn't resist, though, giving Bruce a shove with his elbow as he turned to go back to his seat.

One of the men in the audience—Bruce couldn't remember his name—stood up. "Shouldn't we be talking about what we're going to do now? Seems like all this stuff can wait for the proper law. If Tom really got out through that roadblock, then help should be on the way. In the meantime, what do we need to do now?"

The man remained standing, making sure his question was addressed.

Mort nodded. Bruce could well imagine that at this point the two brothers would like nothing better than to end the public debate. "There's three dead bodies down in the falls—"

"Four," Trish reminded. "Ariel makes four."

"But it's going to get dark in an hour," Mort continued. "Unless somebody wants to volunteer to go down, I say that we just lock our doors for the night and wait for that help to arrive."

A voice called out from the back. "Leslie's the new constable. Shouldn't he be dealing with it?"

The little man's stored anxiety hadn't been completely depleted. "Go to hell, Fred! You want to say something? You come up here and say it to my face!"

Mort held out his hand, calling for peace. "Let's all just go home and stay safe."

"What about Bruce and her?" the man standing asked, gesturing at Trish.

Mort glanced at them and then at his brother. "We'll take care of them until help arrives. Don't worry about that."

Bruce didn't like the sound of that. He looked at Trish, and she too seemed scared. An innocent phrase like "take care of" could have a completely opposite meaning.

Chapter 19

The sun was low in the west when Bruce and Trish again squeezed into the hatch area of Leslie's RAV4. When Bruce asked where he was taking them, Leslie told him to shut up. Abe had already gone home, and Mort took his place in the passenger seat. Bruce felt the small SUV list heavily to starboard when the younger brother eased his bulk in.

"I don't like this," Trish whispered.

"It'll be okay," Bruce said. "Leslie might be an excitable hot-head, but Mort's not stupid."

"Oh, that's great, my life is in the hands of Jabba the Hutt."

"At least you won't be chained to the floor in a bikini."

"How do you know?" she asked with mock seriousness.

"This could be good—you could strangle him with your chain."

"That would be worth the bikini."

Bruce and Trish sat pressed together, silent, as their two captors talked in hushed whispers in the front. Bruce could only make out a few words here and there, but it sounded like they were discussing Donald, how he was "useful." Bruce thought this a bit odd, considering the guy was dead.

"They're going to Cab's house!" Bruce whispered, as they turned onto the constable's dead-end street.

"That's a relief," Trish replied, and Bruce could feel her relax.

Sure enough, Leslie stopped in front of Cab's house, and Bruce waited for one of them to open the hatch. Leslie got out and trotted off to the front door, and Mort jiggled his way laboriously out onto the sidewalk, but then just stood waiting, ignoring the two squashed in the back. A minute later, Leslie came back and talked to his brother. Bruce heard him say that Cab had agreed to go. A minute later, the constable came out carrying his jacket. As he walked past the RAV4, he glanced in and saw the two of them jammed inside. "I'll be back before too long," he said through the glass. To Leslie, he asked, "Did they say how soon they'd be there?"

Bruce didn't hear the answer, but Cab nodded and started off.

"Where're you going!" Bruce called, despairing at the turn of events.

Cab came back. "Word apparently finally got out, and the state troopers are on the way. I'm going out to meet them at the north highway. I'm sure they'll have some questions about the two dead bodies there." He held out his hand, palm up, to Leslie and said, "You can't have it both ways." The self-appointed constable handed over the ID card, and Cab added, nodding towards the SUV, "You're going to let them out of there, right?" and then walked off, muttering something about more bodies littering the town than fast food wrappers.

"Do you think it's true?" Trish whispered hopefully.

"Sure," Bruce lied, then said, "Maybe."

He suspected that the two Stooges had actually made it all up to get rid of Cab, but he decided to keep that to himself.

Leslie and Mort waited until Cab drove away before opening the hatch. Bruce wasn't surprised to find Leslie once again brandishing his beloved pistol. The little man followed them inside, and Bruce noticed that he kept glancing up and down the street, as though wary that somebody might see them. Once inside, Bruce and Trish sat down on the sofa, but Leslie waggled the pistol at them. "Uh, uh. Down in the basement. Both of you."

Bruce and Trish exchanges panicked looks.

"Come on, move it!" Leslie ordered nervously.

"Why?" Bruce croaked. It was all he could manage.

"Never mind."

Mort tried to reassure them. "It can be locked from the outside," he explained.

"What if we refuse?" Bruce asked. He was terrified of what would follow them down there.

In answer, Leslie moved the pistol so that the tip of the barrel was pressed against Trish's temple. She sat perfectly still, staring at Bruce.

He feared Trish would call Leslie's bluff and dare the little twerp to do it. But she was not so stupid, and waited in terror.

"Okay," Bruce said quickly, holding his hands up in surrender. "Okay. Take us to jail."

As they filed down the narrow stairs into the damp darkness, Mort called after them, "Ironic that you'll be sharing the same space as Donald's last moments."

Bruce didn't even try to explainin that Donald had actually expired prior to the basement. You don't pick at an open wound.

From the blackness below rose the musty smell of mold and old cardboard. Leslie flipped the switch at the top of the stairs, and the basement revealed itself under a single bare bulb. An oil furnace filled one corner, and the rest of the space was cluttered with battered boxes, some showing water stains along the bottoms.

Bruce froze when he saw two large cardboard boxes side-by-side, still slick and wet. This must be where they'd laid Donald. He looked away in case Trish should follow his gaze.

His heart was pounding now. Their captors hadn't made any actual threats, but the malevolent intent was evident in the nervous glances they exchanged. The danger was almost palpable.

"Stay here," Leslie ordered and went back upstairs.

"Like there's any place for us to go?" Trish noted, glancing around. Her horrified gaze froze on the two boxes, but she didn't say anything.

"Hold it!" Bruce whispered, lifting his hand for her to be quiet. He heard voices, but they didn't seem to be coming from up the stairs.

Trish stepped around the boxes to the furnace, where sheet metal ducting sprouted and headed off to various destinations. She listened a second, then put her ear against a short one that mated to the low ceiling above their heads—what was probably a floor vent in the room above. After a moment she waved him over.

Ear to the duct, he heard it, Mort and Leslie talking in the kitchen above them. "—you sure nobody else saw it?" Mort was saying.

"Well, everybody saw it, but at that point all they could see was her holding it," Leslie replied.

"But it was all wrapped up in clothes, like they said?"

"Yeah, sort of," Leslie reluctantly agreed, then became irritable. "All they saw was that Carl nearly died from just touching it, and she was going to hit me with it."

"She was, like, holding it above her head to throw it?"

"No—sort of—I don't remember exactly, but Chuck and Abe will go along with that. The others were too far away to see exactly, anyway. It looked like self defense, god dammit!"

Leslie's outburst was loud enough to hear through the floorboards.

"Take it easy," Mort cautioned. "I believe you, but look, the only way this makes sense is if these two are the only ones who know that it wasn't self defense."

"Well, it was self defense. She was going to kill me."

They were quiet for a few seconds. Mort finally said, "If that's really true, then there's no need to do this."

"No, we have to! They'll lie. They'll make it sound like she wasn't going to hit me with it."

There was silence again, and then Mort said, "Okay, Les. Do it."

"You sure Cab's place is best?"

"Yeah, I think so. Donald was killed here, and the forensics will be more confused. Besides, Cab's would be the most likely place to be holding terrorists."

"You just make sure nobody comes in," Leslie cautioned, and then the floorboards creaked as bodies began moving.

Trish looked at Bruce with her hand over her mouth in horror. "He's going to—" she started to say, but couldn't bring herself to finish.

Moments later, the door at the top of the stairs opened, and Leslie's feet and legs and then torso descended. He stopped at the bottom, watching them warily, as though prepared in case they might charge him. Bruce considered this for one brief second, but saw that Leslie was holding not just the pistol he'd been carrying all day but another as well, one in each hand. Whereas the former was fairly new and had a handle clip that held over a dozen bullets, this latest entry was older, actually a revolver.

"Over there," he said, motioning with one of the guns for them to move to the side.

"Leslie, look," Bruce began. "This is crazy—"

"Shut up!" he yelled. Then, more softly, "Just . . . shut up."

Bruce could see that the man's hands were shaking, the tip of the pistol waving up and down in a little dance.

They stepped around the cardboard boxes as he had indicated. Trish gripped Bruce's arm as though afraid he might run away.

Leslie kept his eye on them and walked over to the furnace where they'd been standing listening. He turned, lifted the old revolver towards the stairs, and the basement exploded with the shot. Bruce jerked reflexively, and he heard something tick on the floor next to him. The bullet had ricocheted off the stone wall behind the stairs and bounced off the beam above his head. Leslie shot again, and this time the wooden stairs thumped with the impact. He checked the revolving chamber, and motioned for them to step back to the furnace, backing away so that he could watch them.

Then Leslie held the revolver out to him, handle first.

Bruce just looked at it.

"Take it!" Leslie cried, nearly hysterical.

He met the man's frantic stare and said, as calmly as he could manage. "Leslie, if I take that gun, you're going to shoot me."

Leslie's mouth seemed to be trying to say something, but was having trouble with lips that weren't cooperating. Bruce guessed that this was throwing him off, diverging from the mental script he had created. Leslie's mouth relaxed, and he grabbed Trish by the arm and pointed his Glock pistol, his warm friend, at her head. "Now take it!"

Trish was terrified, her eyes wide and unblinking. Bruce took the revolver from Leslie. He didn't look at the chamber, he knew it would be empty. He just listened as his blood pounded a dirge beat in his temples.

Leslie backed slowly away towards the stairs. Above them, they heard floorboards creak, and then Mort called out for Leslie.

His brother paused, agitated at the interruption. He raised the pistol to point at Bruce, but reconsidered and lowered it slightly. "What?" he called out, not taking his eyes off Bruce.

Above them, there seemed to be scuffling. Leslie knitted his brows, trying to understand. He raised the pistol at Bruce, but then lowered it again. From the doorway above, very clear now, Mort called, "Leslie, come here!" This was followed by a thump and more scuffling.

"What!" Leslie called, but there was only silence from above.

Muttering nasty curses, Leslie walked backwards up the stairs, keeping the tip of his gun pointed at Bruce. He called for his brother again, and then he disappeared, as if he'd jumped up and away on powerful, spring-loaded feet. This was accompanied by more scuffling sounds and one last thump.

Bruce looked at Trish. Her eyes were wide with wonder. A foot appeared on the top stair, and Trish gripped his arm again, so hard he winced. But, whereas Leslie wore sneakers, this shoe was black leather. Suit pants followed, and when the man's head finally appeared, Bruce recognized the trim beard. "Bert!"

Walker's lackey held a pistol of his own, and after glancing briefly around the basement, shoved it into a shoulder holster under his suit jacket. Then he sat down on the stairs and studied them.

"Leslie, and Mort . . ." Bruce inquired after a moment.

Bert flipped his thumb up towards the top of the stairs. "Those two? Don't worry about them."

He just continued to look at them as though this was a pre-arranged meeting, and he was waiting for the rest of the attendees to arrive.

After the heart-stopping tension of being a finger-squeeze away from death by Leslie's Glock, Bruce was ready to burst, or to bounce around the basement like Pooh's friend Tigger. "So," he said, just to say something, "I guess it was Mike that they got . . . er, not you."

"It wasn't me they killed," Bert agreed, completely deadpan.

"Yeah, sorry."

"I'm not sorry it wasn't me," he said without even a hint of smile.

"No, I mean sorry about your . . . uh, colleague."

Bert didn't respond, but got to his feet and instructed, "Let's go," then disappeared back up the stairs.

"Isn't that the guy who killed Donald?" Trish whispered.

"Yeah, but it was an accident."

"He pulled the trigger of his gun and shot Donald, and that's an accident?"

Bruce didn't have a chance to respond, as Bert called from above for them to move it.

"Should we go?" Trish asked.

"We don't have much choice. Leslie wants to kill us, and Bert has a gun."

"That killed Donald," she added ruefully.

"Yeah," he agreed. He wasn't going to convince her.

Bruce led the way up the stairs, but stopped short when he came through the doorway at the top. Trish bumped into him, forcing him to step clumsily over Leslie's prone body. Mort lay a few feet away. Bruce saw blood on the back of the thick neck and beefy shoulder.

"Holy shit!" Trish exclaimed, staring. "Are they . . . dead?" She looked at Bert, who stood waiting in the next room.

"I didn't check," he replied. "Come on, hustle." He turned and walked through the living room and out the front door.

Bruce didn't need any more prompting.

Trish was right behind him as they headed for the front door. "Bruce, he wasn't breathing," she whispered.

"Who?"

"Mort—I think he's dead."

Bruce took a deep breath, calming the desire to sprint out the door and up the sidewalk to his dad's house, where he could crawl under his old bed and hide.

Outside, Bert held the back door of Walker's black Chrysler open for them, keeping an eye up and down the empty street. The setting sun cast long shadows across the lawn, reminding Bruce of late autumn, even though it was still August.

"Where are we going?" Bruce asked when they reached the car.

"Away from here."

"That's avoiding the question," Trish challenged. She seemed more angry than fearful.

Bert sized her up before once again glancing around at their surroundings. "To a safe place," he added.

"Why should we trust you?" she asked.

He glanced at her again. "You trusted Ariel."

Bruce said "Yes," and Trish said, "No," but, after exchanging looks with Bruce, she changed her answer to "Maybe."

"Well," Bert said, "she and I were actually working together."

"Really?" Bruce responded, astonished.

Bert nodded. "We're both in the oversight department."

For the dozenth time that day, Bruce's head spun to match a new orientation of his world. "She never told us that."

His face showed mild surprise, but then he shrugged. "Well, that's our business, isn't it? Keeping secrets?"

"You still haven't told us where you're taking us," Trish pressed. She obviously didn't trust him.

"Look," he replied evenly. "You're in a lot of trouble. I can help you."

"We're in trouble because of you and your . . . little drone thing," she persisted.

Bruce decided not to remind her that Ariel, and now apparently Bert, were simply overseeing the department that had actually developed the drones. Like Ariel, Bert seemed to wince at the very word "drone."

He sighed and shook his head a little. "I can leave you here, but it seems to me that the whole town thinks you're some kind of terrorists." He glanced at her. "They're not going to be very happy about those two guys in there," he warned, nodding his head towards Cab's house.

"You did that!" she exclaimed.

He shrugged. "You can try to explain that to them. Seriously, your only hope is to let the government take care of you, and believe me, we can." He turned his gaze to Bruce. "What do you say?"

Bruce looked to Trish, whose mouth was set firm. She shook her head slowly. She didn't like it. "I don't know what else to do," he confessed.

She looked at him darkly, then at Bert, and then at her shoes. "Okay. But I'm going under protest."

That was the ticket Bert had been waiting for, and he ushered them into the backseat and ran around to the driver's side. Seconds later, the Chrysler's powerful engine hammered the tires into a squeal as he sped away down the street.

Bruce felt relief to be escaping the town that had turned against him.

He just wished it didn't feel so much like guilty flight.

Chapter 20

"So, now do we get to know where you're taking us?" Trish asked as Bert raced north out of town, in the opposite direction of the highways.

He glanced briefly at her in the rearview mirror. "Like I said, to a safe place."

"It looks like you're taking us back to the falls."

The sun flashing through gaps between houses and trees created a strobe effect on Bert's face. "We have to make one stop on the way," he replied.

"You're going because of the last drone," Bruce guessed.

Now Bert looked at him in the mirror. "I have to see about it, yes. The safety of the town's at stake."

"But you also want to get it back," Bruce said.

If Ariel had, he would as well.

Bert watched the road a moment. "If that's possible, sure." Then he smiled at him in the mirror. "Good work, by the way, keeping quiet about it at that town inquisition."

Bruce felt a little uneasy, being placed solidly in the government camp. "So, you were listening," he noted.

Bert chuckled, "Like I said, that's the sort of thing we secret agents do, eh?"

This was a different man from the terse, no-nonsense staff assistant who had met Bruce and Ariel when they first pulled up at Cab's house, the one who had, accidentally, shot Donald.

He glanced in the mirror at Bruce again. "Boy, that Walker was something—a real old-school cowboy—the end justifies the means. I think he missed the old clandestine cloak-and-dagger days."

He certainly shared Ariel's opinions, Bruce thought. Almost the same words.

Trish rolled her eyes. She still didn't trust the guy.

"These drones are real bad-asses," Bert suggested, shaking his head demonstrably. "Real buggers if you don't have the background working with them."

"Yeah, I guess," Bruce agreed. It seemed strange to be talking about them so openly when the very subject had always been completely taboo.

Bert gave him a mirror glance. "You and Ariel de-activated one of them, didn't you?"

"That's right, just one. The first one we . . . well, we whacked it."

"Good job!" Bert commended. "So, you used the abort code on the second one."

"Right," Bruce replied. He didn't offer more, even though Bert was Ariel's colleague. Maybe it was her continuous harping about keeping quiet.

He also noticed that Trish was giving him a hard look. She didn't think it was a good idea to be talking so freely either.

"The first part of the abort code is the word 'Montana,' " Bert noted.

That was true. "Yeah," Bruce replied.

"The second part is visual," Bert continued.

"Uh, huh," Bruce agreed.

He saw that Trish seemed to be trying burn holes through his head with her eyes.

"It's a double cross," Bert elaborated.

Bruce didn't reply. It didn't feel right. An agent wouldn't discuss a highly secret code with him, or anybody.

"Isn't it?" Bert pressed.

"Well, that's what--" Bruce started, but felt a sharp kick from Trish. Her look was even more alarmed now. He realized why. "Look, Bert," Bruce said, "yeah, Ariel showed me the code— actually, we figured it out together. But I'm not . . . oh hell, I'm just not comfortable telling you any more."

Bert watched him in the mirror for a few seconds, and then shrugged and smiled. "Fair enough. I understand. You still don't trust me, but that's okay."

Bruce suddenly realized that he indeed did not trust Bert. It also occurred to him that he really didn't want to tell the agent that the third drone was choosing to ignore the abort code anyway.

The code was suddenly their main ticket—the only ticket, in fact—that bestowed worth in Bert's eyes. That this ticket had been rendered worthless had to be kept as their own secret at all costs.

They came to the parking area above the falls, and Bert pulled in and stopped the engine. He turned to Bruce. "Just one more thing," he said conversationally. "Do you think anybody else— those bumpkins that came down to arrest you—do you think they understood what they saw?"

"No," Bruce answered immediately. It was true, but he also had a reflexive need to protect his town, no matter how misguided some of them might be.

Bert looked at him a second, peering into his head for the truth. Then he smiled. "Good enough. Let's go get us a drone," he urged and got out of the car.

Bruce stared into the space where Bert's head had been. He realized that he'd just admitted that he and Trish were the only ones left with the dangerous knowledge.

ж ж ж

The sun had set behind the western ridge, and only the top of the east ridge still glowed with the final light of day. Even that faded and disappeared as Bruce watched. It would be dark in an hour, sooner down in the bowels of the falls.

Bert checked his gun, and then put it back in its holster. Bruce wondered whether the agent shared Ariel's philosophy that bullets were ineffective against the drones. He didn't want to think about any larger targets Bert might be considering.

The three of them stood in the grass at the mouth of the path. "Trish," Bruce instructed, "if anybody comes around, don't let them go down. I guess that goes without saying."

Both Bert and Trish threw him surprised looks. "I'm coming down," she stated.

Damn! He was afraid of this. He tried to communicate mind-to-mind. *We don't have an abort code that will work.* Her shields were at full strength, though, and she stood with her fists planted on her hips, ready to set off.

"Sounds good," Bert agreed. Bruce thought he sensed relief from him.

They started, Bert first, then Bruce, with Trish bringing up the rear. Bruce figured that the rear position could be nearly as vulnerable as the lead, but when he suggested that Trish trade places with him, she scoffed, asking whether he thought she was some kind of sissy.

The old-growth forest formed a tunnel over the topmost stretch of path, blocking what light was left in the sky. Bruce felt relief when they emerged into open air at the top of the first falls, looking out over the vista to the Susquehanna River, barely distinguishable in the evening mist. He reminded himself that the drones had never come up this far—in fact, they'd never seen them above the second falls.

Without a word, they started down past the cave overhang to the bottom of the first falls, and along the creek towards the second. Halfway, Bert let Bruce take the lead, as there were spots where he wasn't sure of the path.

"Do they have night vision?" Bruce asked over his shoulder.

"What?" Bert said.

"The drones. Do they have, you know, infrared imaging?"

"I have no idea," the agent replied with a shrug of irritation.

Bruce wondered if Ariel would have known.

They came to the tangled flood debris crowding along the second falls like a matted fur collar, and Bruce hesitated.

"What's the problem?" Bert asked.

"It's getting dark. We'll have to be careful through this rough stuff."

"Fine. We'll be careful," Bert said.

Bruce was actually thinking that on the other side of this natural barrier was the last place they'd seen the third drone, Gamma. It might be there right now, a hundred feet away, ready for them to come through.

"What are you waiting for?" Bert asked.

"My nerve."

"Give me the abort code if you're afraid," Bert suggested. His offer seemed genuine, like he was truly sympathetic.

Bruce looked at the agent. He could indeed show him the visual part of the abort code that he and Ariel had figured out. He wouldn't be lying—it really was the true abort code. But he'd be sending the man to an almost certain death.

He realized that he couldn't do it. It would essentially be committing cold-blooded murder.

Bruce plunged into the thick web of dead branches. Inside, it was nearly dark, but not as difficult to navigate as he'd feared. Passage through the debris jungle required each traveler to choose essentially the same precise steps, and the path through had become better defined with each use.

The literal light at the end of the tunnel was the pale blue of the dusk sky over the misty river, and here Bruce paused. Thankfully, Bert didn't pressure him. Instead he asked quietly, "Do you hear it?"

Bruce concentrated. He could imagine a warbling buzzing if he tried hard enough, but he knew that it was just his mind synthesizing it from the complex noise of the gurgling water.

"No. It's not here. At least not close by. Not yet."

"Let's go, then," Bert urged, back to pressuring mode.

The creek made a gentle turn to the right before plunging down the third falls, the water chute, the last place they'd seen Ariel, and each step forward opened up another slice of view—another opportunity to glimpse a silhouetted blur of lethal motion, like a stealthy bat in the falling light. By the time they arrived at the third falls, Bruce's armpits were wet, despite the chill air of the evening on his still-bare legs.

Bruce remembered vividly the attack of the first drone. He could pick out the very spot where he and Ariel had stood pressed together as he knocked the little machine out of the air. And then Ariel had . . .

"We hid the first drone near here," he said.

"The Alpha," Bert confirmed. "Can you find it?"

"I don't know—maybe. Should I try?"

"No, we'll just leave it for some kids to find—of course!"

Bruce ignored the sarcasm. Personal slights have less impact when your life is in jeopardy. He did note, though, that Bert was familiar with the labeling of the drones. Apparently he did know even more about them than Ariel.

He located the leaning tree, and started towards it. "I wondered if it was just a coincidence that it was the Alpha one that attacked us first," Bruce commented. He knew that he was jabbering a bit, a sign of his nervousness. "You know, we only assumed that the second one was the Beta. We never actually looked," he added as he plunged into the trees.

And that information was carried away down the creek along with Ariel's body.

"Well," Bert replied from the creek-side, "it's just the Omega we have to worry about now."

Bruce smiled. "That's odd," he said, a little louder since Bert was now out of view. "Ariel made the same mistake. The third one would actually be Gamma."

His rolled-up jeans were easy to spot, even in the deeper dusk under the trees. Ariel didn't have much time. It looked like she'd started to break off a leafy branch from a maple tree to use for camouflage, but then just laid the bundle on the ground and ran right back. He scrutinized it before picking it up, looking closely to make sure there were no damp spots, places were the poison might have leaked through.

Holding the jury-rigged package in his hands brought back memories of Ariel just hours before. She had a real mouth. She had spared nothing in her critical assessment of Walker, much as Bert had voiced as well. They shared the same low view of the old crony. In fact, they seemed to share even the same adjectives. Uncannily the same.

Bruce started back to the creek, but stopped. Uncannily the same. What were the chances that Bert would make the exact same mistake about Omega versus Gamma, unless . . .

Bert had been listening to her. He'd heard her say "Omega," and that had stuck. Ariel had been wired.

He heard a grunt and curse. It was Trish's voice. He ran the last dozen steps out of the trees and stopped short again. Bert had his arm around Trish's neck, and was holding his pistol to her head.

"You're the cronies' watchdog," Bruce declared.

"Very good, Sherlock," he growled.

It was exactly what Ariel would have said.

Chapter 21

"Okay, let's have the abort code," Bert demanded, waggling the pistol to emphasize his threat.

Bruce wasn't terribly surprised by the revelation of Bert's true identity. He'd never seemed an ally, not like Ariel. "I don't know about that," Bruce said, "it seems like I have even more reason to wait. You're obviously going to kill us both once you have it."

Bruce looked into Trish's eyes, eyes filled with terror at yet again having a gun to her head. Everybody seemed to view her as the perfect hostage, the person he most care about losing. *Maybe they were right.*

Bert gave one little nod, placing the tip of the barrel against her temple. "How about I kill Trish right now, sort of an incentive, get things kicked off."

Bruce knew the man wasn't bluffing—the bastard hadn't even checked to see if he'd killed both Mort and Leslie. His mind raced. He had to give the killer something. He figured that the actual code was as good as anything else. A lie closest to the truth carries the least risk. "When you say 'Montana,' you do this," Bruce explained, showing him the crossed fingers held out on each hand. "The double-cross."

He could see from Bert's face that the man believed him. Bert would have heard everything that he and Ariel had said as they deduced the true visual code. He would have known if Bruce had tried to make up some random gesture.

Bert nodded in satisfaction. He looked sideways at Trish. Bruce could almost hear the man's thoughts: should I shoot her first, or the other stooge? "Wait," Bruce started, but Bert was obviously not listening.

And then Bruce heard it.

"Bert!" he cried.

Bert caught that the alarm was genuine and looked at him.

"Don't you hear it?"

Bruce had to restrain himself from running to the tunnel of tangled branches along the second falls, the only place that might be safe from the drone.

Suddenly, the buzzing was very close. Bruce gasped when he discerned that it was hovering just ten feet in front of Bert and Trish. It was nearly impossible to see against the darkening sky.

Bert yelled and shot at it, a reflex response, since his goal was to capture it intact. The tiny winged machine easily avoided the bullet, and circled around, studying the situation. It had already seen configurations of people standing together, seemingly containing two heads, so Bruce guessed that it wasn't going to wait very long before attacking.

That urge to run and find cover was overwhelming, but it gave him an idea. He ran back into the trees, where it was almost too dark to see now. He found the limb that Ariel had started to pull down, and with one powerful yank, dislodged it. Seconds later, he dragged it out into the open.

Bert was standing behind Trish with his pistol to the back of her head, and she was facing the drone, calling the code word and forming the double cross with her hands. Bruce could swear the drone's jangling buzz was angry at the attempted seduction.

"Hey! Over here!" he called, dragging the limb along across the rocks and sand.

The drone rose a couple of feet and turned towards the interloper. An instant later, it rushed him, and Bruce heaved the heavy limb up, sweeping it forward to meet the attacker. When his view cleared, he saw that the drone had backed off and rose higher into the air. He didn't wait to see what it would do next, but raced on, calling for Trish to squat down. She did, despite Bert's frantic warnings that he was going to shoot. The agent must have understood the situation and what Bruce was attempting, for at the last moment, he too squatted down, wrapping his arms around Trish so that the thick covering of leaves and twigs enveloped them both.

And this left Bruce clear and in the open—the one obvious target.

He had vaguely imagined that he'd be able to provide cover for both Trish and him, but it hadn't worked out that way. He wasn't sure what they could have done once the drone took care of Bert, anyway.

But now he was the little mammal caught out in the open with a Tyrannosaurus Rex, except that the dinosaur was three inches long. He ran for the trees, but knew by the rushing swell of buzz that the drone was about to jab him in the back of the neck. He threw himself headfirst to the ground as the hyper-burring wings whirred past, but then stopped just a few feet away. He dug his hands into the sand, rolled over, and tossed a handful into the air. He heard the drone zip away, but almost immediately it returned, poised somewhere nearby. Bruce grabbed another handful and tossed it again towards the sound. And again, the drone retreated, and again immediately returned.

It had learned. It had analyzed the previous encounter with people and had deduced that thrown sand fell quickly. Moving out of the way for just a second was enough.

He grabbed two handfuls of sand, and yelled "Shit!" in desperation as he ran for the trees, throwing one and then the other handful over his head.

And then in the deepening dusk, he misjudged the height of a rock and tripped.

He fell hard. He didn't hit his head, but he jammed his knee on a rock, so that pain overtook conscious thought for a moment. The pain shrieked so loudly, he wasn't sure he would even feel the piercing needle. It might have already struck. The pain subsided, allowing awareness that he was still alive. The previous drone victims had succumbed in seconds. He could still hear the madly whirring wings nearby.

What the hell? Was it teasing him like a cat with a mouse?

Dreading the outcome, he rolled over on his back. He could see the black spot above him against a dark sky that held just a hint of blue. But then something light and fairy-like drifted by in the still air. Another slid into view, and the drone quickly rose a foot to avoid it. The fairies were little balls, puffs of fine cotton embracing a tiny dot in the middle. One of them touched his nose, and he caught it in his hand. It was a milkweed seed, suspended in the tiny hairs that gave it transport in the air.

He must have fallen on a seed pod. When he was a kid, they would tear them apart, releasing a shower of cold fireworks to sail off into the wind, an amazing quantity packed tightly in each pod.

He turned and felt beneath him. He'd fallen squarely on the plant, and he pulled off one of the pods, tearing the dry, crackly walls apart. His fingers remembered the childhood routine, and he deftly pulled away layer after layer of packed cotton and tossed the released fairy balls into the air, providing lift with puffs of breath from his pursed lips.

The drone had risen even farther, darting higher and higher each time a ball happened to float near. This phenomena was new. It would remember that the sand had almost brought it down when first encountered, and it wasn't taking chances. At least until it understood the details of this strange beast that flew so slowly but in such large herds.

Bruce knew that his reprieve was limited. It was only a matter of time before the drone deduced that these airy spheres were harmless, practically without substance.

Grabbing three more pods, he slowly sat up, tearing apart another ammunition cartridge. Then, launching a protective squadron ahead of him, he stood up. Where to go? To the debris tunnel. No, that would leave Trish as the next victim. He had to take her with him. The drone would probably eventually attempt to penetrate their hiding place in the debris tunnel, but it would at least buy them time to think of a next move.

Dispatching the cottony balls ahead of him like a fairy godmother tossing magic dust, he made his way back to where Bert and Trish cowered under their leaves.

"What's going on?" Bert asked nervously from under the blanket of maple leaves.

"I've found a temporary defense. We're going to retreat."

"What about the abort? Use that!"

"It's not working. I guess this one decided to ignore it."

"That's not possible!"

"Then I guess you don't know the drones very well. Lift the limb slowly—no, scratch that—throw it off quickly, then I'll step up and cover us all in these milkweed puffs."

"That's your defense?" Bert asked, incredulous.

"Shut up—if it hears you, the jig's up."

He'd meant to fight the fear tearing at his heart with a bit of humor, but he wondered if the damn little devil might indeed understand human speech.

"This is stupid!" Bert objected, but Trish jumped up, tossing the limb ahead of her. It was heavier than she expected, and instead of flying away, it flopped over towards Bruce, and he caught it, but then had to let it drop so that he could use both hands to keep the volley of cotton balls flowing.

Bert stood up cautiously as well. "It's really afraid of those things?" he asked, peering around at the cloud surrounding them.

"I don't think it can be afraid, but logic tells it to stay away from them—for now."

"Then we can use them to capture it," Bert concluded.

"You're crazy," Trish declared. "We have to get away."

"No, I think he's right," Bruce agreed, but probably not for the same reason. "Even if we hold it off with these, it's eventually going to figure things out. There's nowhere to really get away from it. Wherever we go, it will eventually get to us."

"Fine," she said. "How?"

"Maybe we can use . . . a shirt or something."

"Good idea," Bert said. "Take yours off."

"Why me?" Bruce asked.

"Here's why," Bert replied, and lifted his pistol and shattered the dusky silence with a shot that echoed on and on through the cavern.

No time to argue and nothing to argue with. Bruce handed the two remaining pods to Trish to keep the defensive shield up, and pulled his T-shirt off over his head. *Now what?* No time to even think it through. Just act. "Stop throwing them," he instructed as he pulled off a branch from the maple limb at his feet.

"Stop?" Trish said.

"Yeah."

"But if I stop, it'll be able to get closer . . . Oh, right."

Bruce pulled off a second small branch and stripped away the leaves. He now had two sticks about three feet long.

They waited, and sure enough, a slight upstream breath of air slowly pulled their defensive cloud away. As it dissipated, the drone moved closer and closer.

"I'm not so sure about this," Bert said nervously.

"Then try shooting it. Otherwise shut up and leave us alone."

To Bert's credit, he shut up.

Bruce laid the two stripped branches a foot apart, and then placed his shirt across one end. He lifted the other ends so that he was holding his shirt flat in front of him, parallel with the ground. Carefully so that he didn't drop his trap, he moved between Trish and the slowly advancing drone.

"Okay, Trish," he said. "Here we go. I want you to pull a bunch of balls only partway out of each pod. When I tell you, I want you to throw them high over my head. Got it?"

She hesitated, obviously wondering what the hell he was up to, but simply replied, "Got it." Then, "Okay, ready."

The drone suddenly zipped closer so quickly, Bruce flinched. But it stopped a few feet in front of him. The milkweed balls had all blown away, but it was being careful, making sure.

Now that it was here, hovering in front of him so close, he could once again feel the waft of breeze from its wings against his hair and he wasn't at all confident in his plan. Now it seemed incredibly stupid, a fantasy, the sort of impossible thing that only worked in comic books.

There was no turning back now, though. He held the shirt out as far as he could reach. "Go!" he called, and a moment later, two pods went whizzing over his head, and a blizzard of puff balls showered the dark sky, sinking slowly like gently falling snow.

The drone swayed nervously back and forth, reconnoitering the situation, seeking an exit, but the cotton balls formed a continuous cloud all around.

Bruce raised the shirt provocatively higher. As the balls settled, the shirt formed a protective cover. He was betting on the little silicon brain being supremely smart at ballistics and maneuvering, but dirt dumb at gauging human intentions. His gamble paid off when it moved beneath the shirt. In fact, it rose up as close to the bottom as possible to avoid the nearly weightless cotton fibers that were falling around on all sides.

He had an idea. "Sand," he said.

"You want me to throw sand over your shirt?"

"Yeah. That'll force it to stay underneath."

He intended to lower the shirt to the ground, trapping the drone beneath it.

"But won't that . . . okay, here goes," she said.

As soon as Trish tossed the first handful, Bruce realized his mistake—what she had probably already suspected. His T-shirt overhung the supporting sticks by just a couple of inches on each side. Most of the weight was already in the middle, and the small amount of sand that happened to land there was enough to cause it to sag inward. His plan was to lower the canopy slowly so as not to alarm the drone and give away the trap, but now he was forced to hasten the descent before the entire T-shirt structure collapsed. The sudden motion startled the drone, and it moved as though to escape, but Trish was ready, and pelted a blast of sand at it. Panicked, Bruce just let go of the sticks, letting everything fall.

The dreaded whine of buzzing wings ceased. The T-shirt jerked and twitched at a spot just a finger length from the edge.

"You got it?" Bert asked.

"Yeah," Bruce replied with wonder as he bent down closer in the half-light to peer at the ineffectual flicking attempts to escape.

"Good."

Bruce had never heard that word spoken so ominously before. He looked up to find the pistol pointed at his head.

Chapter 22

"Oh, come on!" Bruce objected as Bert waved his gun to herd Trish and him closer together. "We just risked our lives to catch your precious drone for you!"

The reality was that they'd caught the drone in order to save their own lives, but it sounded good.

Bert nodded appreciatively. "And I'm grateful for that."

"Grateful enough to let us go? We promise not say anything."

Bruce had heard that promise made so many times in gangster movies, he didn't really expect it to work. And based on Bert's response, which was to ignore what he'd said and instead peer at the weakly flailing secret assassin weapon, his suspicion was correct.

"You can't just shoot us here in cold blood," Bruce warned.

"I think he can," Trish corrected quietly.

"He'll never get away with it!"

"Who's going to catch him? The FBI?"

"Well . . . sure!"

It sounded dumb even as he said it. It certainly didn't seem to intimidate Bert, who, as far as Bruce knew, might sit in on weekly meetings with the FBI director, letting him know what cases to back away from.

Satisfied that the drone wasn't going anywhere soon, Bert turned his attention back to the two who knew too much. He glanced around, then waved his gun for them to move towards the trees.

"Is that a better place to murder us?" Bruce asked in sarcastic despair. He was talking in order to stall, saying anything to delay the inevitable.

Bert shrugged, agreeing that the rocks were as good as the trees, and raised his pistol. It was pointed at Bruce. Kill the man first. It was probably part of his training.

Somebody cursed.

None of them had opened their mouths, and this gave Bert pause. He glanced around, but only the sound of crickets rose above the gurgle of flowing water.

Another curse, this time accompanied by a stick breaking and a small thump.

It was upstream, in the debris tangle. More sounds of scrabbling and muttered curses drifted out, and then suddenly Leslie broke free, swinging his pistol in annoyance across his face, brushing away a spider web.

The volatile little redneck stopped short when he saw them standing there fifty yards away. He stood, staring. It was dark enough that he probably couldn't make out who was who.

Bert kept his gun aimed at Bruce and Trish as he moved quietly off to the side, behind a thin veil of brush.

"Who's that?" Leslie called.

"Me, Trish," Bruce called back. He glanced at the agent gazing through the brush. "And Bert, here."

The agent threw him a warning look, but turned back to the interloper.

"He's the one who killed Mort?" Leslie asked.

Bruce exchanged a glance with Trish, and then said, "Yes!"

Bert's gun exploded the quiet, and Leslie fell, but he continued cursing. A moment later, his own gun sent a returning blast, and Bruce heard the bullet thump into a nearby tree trunk.

Stealthily, Bert moved sideways, farther into the cover of brush. Bruce heard rustling, and then the crunch of feet breaking twigs. He was tempted to call a warning to the wounded Leslie, but held his tongue, fearing a silencing bullet from the agent.

Leslie let go a few more random shots that whizzed past their heads, and they both dove to the ground.

"This is our chance!" Trish whispered. "Let's make a run for it!"

There were only three directions: upstream where Leslie lay spraying bullets haphazardly into the air, into the trees, where Bert was maneuvering, or . . . "Downstream," he said. "Ready?"

Trish placed her palms on the ground under her, ready to launch herself up and away, but Bruce held out his hand. "Wait!"

In front of them, just a couple of feet away, his shirt twitched. Trish saw him looking at it. "No!"

It was stupid, he knew that. The thing was supremely dangerous. Just a mere touch could kill. They had invested so much trying to catch them, though. He wasn't sure why he chose to take it—because of that, or some intuition that was beyond logic.

He tried to glean where the lethal needle lay under the cloth. He was able to guess the basic orientation of the wings, and thus the axis of the drone's body. It was fifty-fifty which end death lay. They wouldn't have much time, so he just made a random selection. He brought two fingers down on what he assumed to be the middle of the body, and was rewarded with the feel of a solid cylinder. The cloth on each side jerked and tugged at a frantic pace now, as though the little robot were actually a live insect, desperate to avoid capture.

"Roll it up," he instructed.

Trish knew exactly what he meant, and began rolling the edge of the T-shirt, uncovering the pebbles and sand below.

"Careful!" he warned as she drew near his fingers, but was relieved when the blunt tail of the drone appeared, not the assassin needle.

"Okay," he said. "Back away."

With his other hand, he quickly probed under the rolled-up cloth, following the top of the drone's body, working his clamping fingers forward. He stopped when he felt the body curve down again at the front, towards the needle. He could feel the layered wings working, frantic to be free.

This was it. Either he could do this, or they'd soon be dead. He pressed down and simultaneously pulled away the shirt, and disaster struck. The needle caught in the T-shirt, yanking the drone along with it. His fingers were suddenly filled with the rattling chaos of beating wings. Without seeing or knowing what was happening, he slapped his hand down on the little storm of violent motion. He felt the smooth, thin metal of the needle along his forefinger, and he held perfectly still. The distracting rattle of the wings had ceased, buried under his hand, and he leaned in closely in the dim light. His breath caught. The needle's tip lay pressed against his finger.

Carefully, carefully, he reached over with his left hand and placed it firmly down onto the base of the needle, and then twisted his right hand and grasped the bundle of wings in his fist. They felt like stiff cellophane as they filled the spaces between his fingers.

He sat up, holding the assassin drone in his clenched hand, the kiss of death protruding, ready to deliver oblivion at the slightest scratch. Trish took his left hand and helped him to his feet.

The shots had ceased. The crickets started up again. This wasn't good.

"Let's go," he urged, setting off down the path at a trot. In the gathering darkness the stones were difficult to see, and after a few steps he stumbled, barely catching himself before he tumbled headlong. He stopped, and Trish nearly knocked him over anyway.

"What's the matter?" she whispered urgently.

"Oh, man. I have to be careful."

She looked at his fist with the wings sticking out at odd angles. "Yeah. Maybe I should go first. Stay close behind."

"But then if I trip, you might get jabbed."

"Then don't trip."

When they came out at the bottom of the third falls, they stopped and listened. "I don't hear anything," Trish whispered.

"I'm not sure we would with this guy," Bruce replied.

"What are you going to do with that?" she asked, pointing at his fist.

"I don't know, but I couldn't leave it behind."

"If you had, he might have left us alone."

"Maybe, but I don't think so. Besides, Ariel gave her life trying to capture them."

"And that makes it valuable? Worth risking our lives?"

He shrugged. "I guess."

"It's not like she was sacrificing herself for some noble cause. She was part of the government, part of the monster that created it in the first place."

"Yeah, maybe. But at least she was the part that was trying to keep the rest honest."

"Well, now it's all water under the . . ."

She gave him a quick, concerned look. The metaphor was too close to the last image they'd had of the woman.

"Come on," he said, "we'd better go before Bert catches us."

They hadn't gone more than a dozen steps when Trish stopped dead, and Bruce very nearly did jab her in the back.

"What's wrong?" he whispered.

"Holy Christ!" she hissed. "There's a body."

Bruce located their position in his mind. "That's Walker," he said, coming up next to her so that he could see. In the near darkness the large man looked like a baby beached whale. "Let's go. No time for eulogies."

Five minutes later they came to another body below the fourth falls. "This must be Dick," Trish guessed, squatting down to peer at the small portion of exposed face. "What happened to the farmer that got it—the one that came down with Leslie?"

"Dunno. We must have missed him."

He didn't want to think about the alternative. But what animal in Pennsylvania could drag away a full-grown man's body? A black bear could. And he'd heard that coyotes were returning to the area.

"Yeah," Trish agreed. "We probably missed him."

She wanted to believe it as much as he did.

They stood for just a moment before setting out again, and it was probably because of this that Bruce heard it, the fall of a stone somewhere up the creek. It was difficult to judge the distance, but Bruce guessed that Bert must be no more than fifty yards behind them, making his way down along the fourth falls.

Bruce suddenly felt bad for Trish. She'd been drug into this whole mess and had done nothing to deserve it. Not that he had, either. But she was a woman. Not that this should really make a difference. But he liked her. He liked her a lot.

"Listen," he said, "you can hide in the bushes here. No sense him going after both of us."

"You have the drone, you should be the one hiding while I keep going."

"I'm not gonna hide."

"Then why should I?" She seemed to consider this. "Okay," she said, "but be quiet!"

She stepped quietly away from the creek. Bruce waited just a moment until she disappeared into the dark growth, and then headed off.

The distance between the fourth and fifth—the final—falls was relatively short, and he arrived at the bridge buttress just a few minutes later. Here, large granite outcroppings framed both sides at the top of the roaring sixty-foot drop, forming a natural foundation for the two sides of the trestle span. He had been hearing the grumble and thrash of the tumbling water for a while now, but when he stepped up onto the massive rock shoulder, the full roar of the mightiest of the five falls expanded, like opening a door to a rock concert. So when he heard Trish crashing through the trees, he knew that she was making a hell of a racket.

That little weasel, he thought. He could hardly believe that she would dare this. He understood now why she'd so readily agreed to hide—because she never intended to hide. She was purposely trying to lead Bert away.

And that's when he saw the dim form a hundred feet back along the path. He wasn't sure at first, but then it moved, and he was certain that Bert had been close behind them indeed. The shape morphed a bit, and Bruce tried to make out what it was doing. A moment later a gunshot rang out, and the bullet zipped by his ear so closely, he thought he felt the heat.

Bert was running towards him. He wasn't taking Trish's bait.

Bruce looked around frantically, but he knew he had no choice. He'd spent enough time exploring as a kid. Before him was a sheer sixty-foot drop onto rocks washed by the spray from the base of the falls. He could head off into the trees, but the canyon narrowed here at the last falls, and the steep slope of the canyon wall was close. Bert would have him cornered within a hundred yards.

No, there was no other option—he'd have to cross the skeleton of the old cogwheel railroad bridge: two beams four feet apart, each just six inches wide, riddled along the entire surface with an obstacle course of rivet heads. He and his friends used to cross with hands outstretched and hearts thumping. A sixty-foot fall onto rocks was essentially death waiting with open arms—the ultimate challenge for a boy. But now it was nearly dark. And there was a man shooting at him.

He stepped out onto the right-hand beam, and immediately found that the rounded rivet heads were a problem. With just six inches within which to find each foothold, he needed a solid, flat surface, but instead his shoes wobbled around on what seemed like giant marbles. They had been barefoot as kids, and their small feet fit easily between the rivet rows.

He took a next step and then another, each time gasping as his foot seemed on the verge of twisting to throw him off balance. Far below, the rocks waited patiently.

He'd nearly reached the halfway point when Bert yelled to him. Immediately below him rushing water fell endlessly away, disappearing into the darkness, throwing back a mighty roar to announce the violence of its destination. He froze. Falling off the beam seemed imminent, almost inevitable. Next to the fear of this fall, Bert's gun seemed almost secondary. He waited. It was all he could do.

"Bring it back!" Bert yelled above the roar.

For one split second, Bruce didn't know what he was talking about until he realized that he meant the drone. "I . . . I can't!"

It was literally true. His brain was not capable of willing his feet to go backwards.

The blast of a warning gunshot nearly knocked him off his precarious perch. Bert thought that he was referring to some abstract moral principal. "No!" he screamed. "I mean I really can't come back! I'll fall!"

Behind him, Bert cursed. Bruce felt the slightest vibration in the metal beneath his shoes. The agent was coming to get it.

Now Bruce was truly terrified—not that Bert was going to shoot him, but much more primal—the visceral fear of danger approaching while he was trapped in such a vulnerable position.

He had to turn around to face the danger. He just had to. He inched the toes of his feet a bit around to the left. The left toe was stopped against a rivet, and he swayed before regaining his balance. He turned a bit more until he was facing upstream, the roar of tumbling water crawling up his back. Bert was ten feet away, his gun pointed at Bruce's belly. "Hand it over!" Bert called.

The drone was in Bruce's right hand. He'd have to transfer it to his left and then hold it out for Bert to take. But . . . "You'll shoot me as soon as you have it!"

Bert looked at him and then shook his head. "I promise!"

The agent's promise was meaningless. Without trust, a promise is just a word, and all Bert had done was lie and shoot at them.

His pursuer guessed at his reasoning, for he took another step forward, gun poised. Even if he fell, or was shot, Bert still had a chance to recover the drone—slim, but any chance might convince the man to take the gamble.

Suddenly, a woman's voice called out, "Bruce, let it go!"

It was—it was Ariel's voice!

Both he and Bert froze. Her voice echoed among the rocks. It was impossible to tell where it had come from.

"Let it go, Bruce!" she called again. "It will be okay!"

"Ariel?" he yelled, astounded. A small part of him wondered if her spirit had lingered.

"Yes! Bruce, let go of the drone!"

"Give it to Bert?"

"No! God, no! Just—let it go free!"

Bert shouted, "Don't!"

Let it go free? he thought. After all they'd gone through to capture it? What had Ariel done to earn his trust? She'd lied as well. But that was different. Why? Because she was a beautiful woman? Of course not. Because—because of everything she'd done. A million years of evolution had rendered humans adept at the game of deceit and trust. It was subliminal, what we call gut instinct.

"Bruce," she shouted. "It's okay—it won't go after the delivery agent."

He reached out his right fist and slowly opened his fingers.

"No!" Bert screamed.

Bruce wasn't sure what Ariel intended, but clearly she was counting on some programming it contained.

The drone had no hesitation. It was a machine. The wings beat a harmless patter against his palm, and rose into the air. It wobbled and tilted, and turned in two small circles. He had bent one of its wings with his rough handling. But the silicon brain was a master at control, and within seconds, it learned to compensate.

Ariel's voice called out into the evening, "Fontana di Tivoli!" She repeated it, louder, so that her voice cracked at the strain.

Bruce looked at Bert, and he saw the awakening of understanding. The agent's eyes went wide with fear. "No!" he yelled, watching the drone as it moved closer. "I'm not the target! God damn it! I'm not even a woman! Look!" he shouted, pointing at his beard, the beard trimmed so neatly that it looked like a hijab veil hiding his face.

For one second, one second of timeless eternity, when the night air was filled with just the forever rumble of the falls, the drone hovered, processing several million instructions of assassin logic, and then it was a blur, a flash of motion whose terminal point was Bert's neck.

The scream from the man was that of mortal anguish. He raised his pistol and fired into the air. He fired again, and then lowered his arm, as though the gun had suddenly become too heavy to hold. He dropped it, and it fell away, tumbling end over end into the darkness. Bert swayed, caught his balance. He looked at Bruce, and the terror in his eyes relaxed. He seemed suddenly calm.

And then he toppled forward, falling, falling, following after his pistol down.

Chapter 23

Bruce stood on the beam over the Powderhole falls and stared down into the darkness. A moment later, he saw the dim image of something floating in the water. It moved along slowly, carried away downstream towards the Susquehanna.

Then he heard it, over the sound of the falls. The drone!

For a moment, he'd forgotten the little killer. It hovered, right there before him, as though waiting for another task to be assigned. Ariel had promised that it wouldn't go after the delivery agent—him.

Ariel!

Holy shit!

"Ariel!" he called, but there was no answer. He called again.

Had it all been my imagination? he wondered, *or was it really her ghost that came to save me?*

He had to get off the bridge before he followed Bert to his death. He'd only taken a few careful steps when the sound of someone calling his name made him jerk and almost fall. It was Trish. "Hey!" he called, "I'm over here! On the bridge!"

"Bruce," he heard her say out of the near-darkness, "what happened to Bert—Ariel!"

"Do you see her?"

"Yeah—oh, Bruce, she's hurt. Bad."

Of course, she's hurt, he thought. She was shot.

He stepped off the beam onto the blessed solidity of granite, and saw the vague form of Trish squatting twenty feet away. He ran over, and his first impression was the same: Ariel was a horrible mess. There was a T-shirt tied around her waist, and Bruce could only assume that the garment had originally been white, for it was now completely soaked in blood. In the last faint light of the departing day, he saw a dark smear leading down the slope of the rock, the trail she had left when she apparently dragged herself up here. She lay there, conscious, but only barely, clutching what Bruce took to be a pillow, but then saw that it was foam packing— clearly the other half from the titanium case.

"Hello, Bruce," she said, managing a weak smile. "Hello, Trish. Is he gone?"

"You mean Bert?" Bruce said, squatting next to her, wondering what in God's name he could possibly to do help. "Yeah. He's . . . dead."

"Good," she said. "How about the drone?"

The drone!

"Ah! Shit! Where the hell is it?" he cried, scanning the dark sky. He heard the buzz, irregular now with the bent wing, but couldn't see it.

"It's okay," she assured. "We've got it now."

"Actually," he corrected, "we, uh, don't."

She shook her head once and held up the foam packing.

Bruce saw the indentations that they had predicted. Even in the darkness, he could make out the symbols: alpha, beta, and gamma. They were painted with luminescent ink so that they glowed as though on fire.

"Hold it up," she instructed.

Bruce took it from her and did as she instructed.

"Montana!" she cried weakly. "Home!"

Bruce flinched as the drone buzzed his ear, and settled onto its indentation. The wings folded, and it slipped into its bed. The bent wing didn't fold properly, and it lay crooked, but seemingly content.

"It's mission was accomplished," he guessed, a little in awe.

She grinned thinly and raised a weak finger to her lips. "At least it thinks so."

"Bert?" he asked amazed. "He was the assassination target?"

She laughed, but it caused her to cough, and it was a few painful seconds before she replied. "Unwittingly. He was the patsy."

"You mean, the drone just thought that Bert was the actual target?"

She smiled in answer.

"Bruce!" Trish hissed, pulling him away. "She needs help— badly. She's obviously lost a lot of blood."

"Right," he agreed. "What do we do?"

What the hell could they do?

Trish glanced around, as though looking for an answer among the granite. "Shit," she hissed. "We'll never get her out of here." She was whispering, not wanting Ariel to hear the devastating news. Her face contorted at the thought of the inevitable outcome. "Not alive, anyway."

Bruce caught a fleeting flash of light out of the corner of his eye. He had thought that the rhythmic thud-thud he'd been hearing was some sort of oscillation effect of the waterfall, or maybe the blood pounding in his ears, but now he realized that the sound was coming from a distance. He saw the light again. Far up the canyon, it sped down along the creek, a precise circle of blinding daylight. The intense white illumination surged this way and that, back and forth, sometimes climbing the trees on each side.

A spotlight! It was one hell of a powerful spotlight.

"It's a helicopter!" Trish shouted at the same instant that Bruce understood.

They both jumped up, waving their arms wildly and shouting, even though they couldn't be heard over the roar of the falls. Bruce tried to direct the spotlight by sheer willpower. It took its time, though, carefully searching each section of the creek. Finally it reached them, sliding over their rock, instantly blinding Bruce and then moving away, but returning within seconds to hold them transfixed under the radiant glare of god-like brilliance. The screaming growl of the powerful engine and the whirring thud of the rotating blades increased in volume until together they overwhelmed the roar of the waterfall. Amid this storm of audible chaos, a voice filtered down from above, the figure impossible to see in the glare.

"Larry?" Bruce called, astonished.

"Yeah!" his invisible friend replied, his voice nearly lost in the noise.

This was completely surreal, like traveling to Beijing and finding your brother at the hotel counter checking you in.

"Where the hell did you come from?" Bruce yelled, his voice raw.

"I'll explain later! We need to get Ariel out of there!"

The lowering basket nearly knocked Bruce over.

They were going to get Ariel out of there. Bruce wanted to jump for joy. Those were the best words he'd heard in—hell, ever.

Something grabbed his ankle. It was Ariel. He bent down and put his ear right up to her mouth so that he could hear. "The drone," she said.

He nodded understanding.

"Hide it," she gasped.

He nodded agreement. "You can count on me," he said.

Her weary eyes closed.

A hand gripped his shoulder firmly and moved him out of the way.

They were going to get her out of there.

ж ж ж

Bruce and Trish lay in the grass in the parking area above the Powderhole falls, waiting for Larry and Ariel. From their positions next to each other, they watched the slow procession of the September day's few cumulus clouds. He was holding her hand, and he didn't think he could be any happier.

"You really weren't disappointed when you found out Ariel was married?" Trish asked.

"Actually, yes."

She yanked her hand free and smacked him across the chest.

"Ow!" he cried, feigning pain.

"She is beautiful," she observed.

"She is," he agreed. "But I was never really attracted to her—not like you."

Trish probably knew he was lying, but it was sort of a mutual deception—they both benefited from the pretense.

He had a thought. "If she's married, you didn't have to give that hundred dollars to Larry."

She shrugged. "Well, the bet was just that he couldn't get her to have coffee with him, and he did that—every day for three weeks. There was nothing in the bet about her actually being available. I probably owe him, like, twenty-one times a hundred dollars."

"Funny," Bruce observed. "He kept going back to see her at the hospital, even after he knew she was already married. Most of the time her husband was there with him."

Trish looked sideways at him. "Bruce, you are a male chauvinist."

"Because you think that I think that the only thing a man is interested in is sex."

"You do."

"I am deeply offended," he replied with affected sincerity. "Guys like Larry are also interested in marriage, although in a way that's sort of the same thing."

She scoffed. "And not you?"

"I'm not the one under the spotlight," he objected. "But yes."

He let that one hang there, hoping the embarrassing moment would slide away with the puffy clouds.

"In any case," he finally said, moving away from the whole marriage thing, "it should be Ariel who pays him the hundred. Heck, she owes him her life."

"You don't understand—I welcome the opportunity to help Larry."

"Ha! I remember when you thought he was a jerk."

"Not true. I said he was a troublemaker. And he is, but he's also sort of a hero."

Bruce had thought it out of character when Larry had run off into the woods at this very spot where Leslie had them at gunpoint. He didn't know at the time that Ariel had talked with his friend earlier about contingency plans. She'd recognized a character strength in the guy that most people missed. She had told him that if at any point he saw that she had lost control of the situation, he should go and fetch a note from her car—the note with the number to call—and climb the ridge to see if he could get cell service from more distant towers. If he could get a connection, he was to call that number and explain everything. That number had called in the cavalry, and they'd brought Larry along, since he knew the terrain.

The other minor hero was Dagger. After giving up the titanium case, he'd suspected shenanigans and didn't really want to get involved, but had hung around anyway. It was Dagger who had pulled Ariel from the creek before she went over the last falls. He wrapped up the wound in her side with his shirt—not a terribly serious wound if she'd gotten help immediately, but enough to bleed her to death eventually. The aging man had retrieved the other half of the foam padding for her, and then had run eight miles and flagged down a car to call for help. By that time, whole layers of government had been alerted and focused on the isolated Powderhole, and the connection had been made—thus the helicopter crew included EMTs to help the wounded woman.

Bruce and Trish had sought out Dagger, to thank him and maybe see if they could get some official recognition for him, but he was horrified at the idea. He just wanted to be left alone, and was glad the whole bother was over.

He did invite them to come back for a beer any time, though. Bruce planned to do just that. It would be good to talk to someone who knew his dad when he was young. There was a lot he could learn from Dagger.

Bruce and Trish sat up when they heard a car. It was another rental, and Ariel was driving. That was good news. They waited while she parked. Larry got out and trotted around to the driver's side to help Ariel. She moved slowly and carefully. Her wound was healing, but still painful. She was well enough to fly, however.

Bruce guessed that this little clandestine meeting was about recovering the gamma drone. Although a whole parade of suits had sequestered themselves away with her in her hospital room behind closed doors—just as each of them had been grilled multiple times—she hadn't discussed anything about the events with the three of them.

Larry had brought along a lawn chair, which he set up in the shade for her, and the three of them then sat in a semi-circle around her. "You've probably been wondering why I haven't talked to you," she began.

"Because your room was bugged," Bruce suggested.

"I guess that would have been obvious," she agreed. "I'm flying out later this afternoon, so this is our only chance to get caught up. Most important though, we still have a little matter of government property to take care of."

Bruce had already retrieved the gamma drone from where he'd hidden it that night.

"But first, you probably have some questions. Once we process the property, we'll have to skedaddle," she added.

"You're really going to tell us?" Bruce asked.

"What I know."

He was skeptical. They'd been willing to kill people to keep it a secret.

"I have just one favor to ask, though," she explained. "Please keep this to yourselves. I'm not happy about how our government has handled this, but there's a bigger picture than you—or I—probably see. Do I have your word?"

They all nodded.

"Okay, then," she continued, "Bruce, you've got to be wondering why I told you to release the drone—how I knew that it would go after Bert."

"Somehow it was fooled into thinking that he was its target," Bruce said. This much was obvious. "And somehow, you knew that it wouldn't assume that I was the target."

"That was easy," she replied. "You were practically naked, and the drone knew for an absolute fact that the target would not even show bare legs."

The pieces were coming together for Bruce, but she spoke before he had a chance to guess.

"Have you heard of Fareeha Anwar Gandapur?" she asked.

After a moment, Trish said, "Isn't she the wife of the Pakistani president?"

"The former prime minister."

"But isn't he supposed to be reinstated?"

"Maybe."

"What about her?" Bruce asked. But he saw it, all in a flash. "Holy shit! It was her? I mean, it was supposed to be her?"

Ariel smiled at her star pupil. "We've known for some time that she has strong allegiance to certain Afghanistan tribal leaders."

"Let me guess," he interrupted. "Taliban."

She shrugged agreement.

"That was Pakistani that you called to the alpha drone!"

She nodded. "Urdu."

"The veil!"

She nodded again, "The hijab veil."

"Angie's scarf!" he exclaimed. "The towel around Dick's mouth! You pulled your shirt over your mouth to attract Alpha! Wait a second . . . Bert's beard?"

She shrugged again. "It was close enough for the drone."

"What are you talking about?" Trish asked, a little annoyed.

"The drone was programmed to identify her by her veil," he explained.

"Not just her veil," Ariel was quick to point out, "but that was obviously a key component—as we found out."

"And that's why it would never attack me with bare legs and chest," he concluded.

"Because a devout Muslim woman would never appear like that in public," Trish offered, glad to be in the game. "Wait. You're telling us that the drones are that smart?"

"It's not a matter of smart," Ariel corrected. "More like specific programming."

"But what about that Italian name you called out?" Bruce asked. That had clearly been important.

"Fontana di Tivoli?"

"Yeah."

"The Fountains of Tivoli," Larry said.

They all looked at him.

"What? You guys never watch Globe Trekkers? The Italian fountains are famous. There's this big waterfall right in the middle, and it's in a big garden, all lush and green . . . uh, just like the fifth falls."

Gears whirred in Bruce's head. "You were waiting at the lower falls," he said.

Ariel nodded. "I'd about given up hope. I figured that the drones would stay nearby—that was the closest thing to what they'd been expecting when deployed. The Prime Minister and his wife are visiting Italy as we sit here. Then you showed up carrying the damn thing."

"Except I was being followed by an evil man with a gun."

"And a beard that looked vaguely like a veil covering," Trish said. She sounded like she wasn't sure she was buying all this.

"It was dark," Bruce reminded.

"And the drone's brain is about this big," Larry added, holding his thumb and finger a sliver apart.

"And speaking of drones and little brains," Ariel said, "I guess we should get on with the disposition."

Bruce sighed and got to his feet. He wasn't going to miss the little assassin, but it had saved his life. No, he corrected himself, Ariel had saved his life. And the drone's brothers had killed innocent people.

He went into the trees, found the marker log, brushed away the leaves he had strewn, and returned carrying the foam packing. He placed it in Ariel's lap. Gamma drone lay in its indentation bed, slightly crooked, just as it had been that evening weeks ago.

"Larry," Ariel instructed. "Bring me a flat rock if you can find one. Bruce, see if you can find another round one about the size of your foot. Trish, could you get the towel on the back seat of my car?"

Bruce found a rock and handed it to her, but she asked him to hold it for now. Larry came back with a flat slab of shale, and Ariel handed Trish the foam, and patted her lap for Larry to place his stone. She lay the towel on the rock, took back the foam packing, turned it over, and gently shook the little assassin drone onto the terry cloth. Its one bent wing stuck out like a tongue. She folded the towel over the miniaturized miracle, took the round rock from Bruce, lifted it with both hands, and brought it down squarely on the invaluable secret government property. The crunch sounded like walnuts being cracked.

The gasp was mutually shared by all three friends.

Ariel tossed away her makeshift hammer, carefully pulled away the towel, and studied the shards of inscrutable electronics. She slowly handed the flat rock to Larry. "Take this down and throw it in the creek. Be careful you don't spill any of it on you. The poison will dilute in the water and be harmless before it reaches the river."

Larry walked away down the path holding his burden like he might a delicate baby.

Bruce shook his head. "I don't get it. Isn't that going to set development back a whole year?"

"Hopefully more like two," she replied.

He looked at her.

"Hey," she said defensively, "I'm not a traitor or anything. I'm just taking back what I saved. I could have let you fall and the result would be the same."

He shook his head again. "You're supposed to be working for the government."

"Not anymore."

Bruce and Trish exchanged glances. "They . . . fired you?" he asked.

That would be so shitty, after all she'd sacrificed for them.

"No. I quit. They don't know it yet. Otherwise we probably wouldn't be here alone together."

"What . . . why . . . ?"

She looked at him like he was missing something. "How many people have died?"

"Er, let's see, including Angie . . . and Ted, I guess that makes, uh—"

"I think I've made my point."

He nodded. He'd somehow forgotten that people worked for the government by choice. "What'll you do?"

"Go back to law. Having lawyers as colleagues will be like the ministry by comparison."

Larry came trotting back. "Hey! Is there going to be, like, a whole bunch of dead fish floating down to the river?"

She sighed and slowly stood up. "Some problems just go away if you ignore them. We'd better be going."

She turned to Bruce and Trish, and held out her hand. They shook it in turn. "I have no way to properly thank you," she said, taking in Larry with a glance as well, "other than to promise that you have a friend for life."

Bruce grinned. "A friend who's a lawyer. That could be handy—and you may be sorry."

She gave him a big grin back. "Try me."

She waved for Larry, and they walked toward the car. She gave Bruce and Trish one last wave and climbed painfully in. A moment later, the rental car bounced off down the country road.

"I guess we should head home," Trish suggested.

Home. Home to an empty house full of memories of a life that should remain just that—fond memories—not be relived every day. Powderhole would always be a place that he loved, but now it should to be a place that he loved to visit.

"You know what?" he said, as they walked to her car.

"What?"

"Those Indian sites you were studying—the Delawares—"

"The Lenape, of the Delware group of tribes."

"Yeah, those. You, uh, ever get an itch to go back there and pick up where you left off?"

She looked at him, trying to understand what he was getting at. Then she grinned. "I don't know. Maybe. If I had an assistant."

"An assistant."

"Yeah."

"Not, like, a colleague?"

"With a degree in—what—electronics? What kind of colleague is that for archeology?"

"There must be electronic equipment used in archeology. This is the twenty-first century."

"Sure, but that doesn't constitute a colleague. That's assistance with equipment—something an *assistant* does.

"An assistant who would have to lug your guns around."

"Of course. Dozens of them."

She smiled at him as they got into her car.

"Because after all that happened, you still love guns."

"That's silly. Guns are inanimate objects, useful tools. Besides, I'll bet you wish you had one standing there on the bridge."

"I would have ended up shooting myself. Or you!"

"That's your fault, not the gun's."

They drove back toward Powderhole, still arguing.

Blaine C. Readler

About the Author

Blaine C. Readler is an electronics engineer, inventor of the FakeTV, and surprisingly, a writer. He lives in San Diego, where the weather allows him to walk around outside year-round thinking about stories.

He encourages you to visit him:
http://www.readler.com/

www.ingramcontent.com/pod-product-compliance
Lightning Source LLC
Chambersburg PA
CBHW060325260626
47160CB00007B/2681